A haunting narrative of clim[...]
the fierceness and vulnerability of motherhood, *Dark River* is
a compelling, devastating first novel. Rym Kechacha writes of
cycles within cycles and how they echo across millennia, and
reminds us that none of us are immune to the unstoppable
forces of the times in which we are living.
Lynda E. Rucker, award-winning author of *The Moon Will Look
Strange*

Dark River is a deeply affecting tale of two women struggling to
ensure the survival of their families. The ambitious scope of the
dual narratives is often startling, but the focus never strays from
these two mothers separated by 8,000 years, each grappling with
a changing natural world. Rym Kechacha's precise depiction
of families striving against the odds makes for a gripping,
haunting read.
Tim Major, author of *Snakeskins* and *Hope Island*

Dark River is a haunting parable for our times, weaving past and
future together into an intricate tapestry of love, loss and the
human desire for safety. A chilling but utterly essential read.
Helen Marshall, award-winning author of *The Migration* and
Gifts for the the One Who Comes After

A work of narrative magic. It conjures its mirrored strands of
families searching for survival with a rare and enviable skill.
The love and determination of Shante and Shaye will stay in the
mind for a long time.
Neil Williamson, author of *The Memoirist* and *The Moon King*

With writing as sinuous and powerful as the water itself, Rym
Kechacha provides a stark and beautiful testament to what we
hold close on the hardest of days. *Dark River* is a story of love
and determination mirrored across a gulf of time and dares us
to consider what we owe the Earth and what the Earth owes us.
Peter Haynes, author of *The Willow By Your Side*

Also available from Unsung Stories

DARK RIVER

RYM KECHACHA

UNSUNG
STORIES

Published by Unsung Stories

3 Rosslyn Road, London E17 9EU,
United Kingdom

www.unsungstories.co.uk

First edition published in 2019
First impression

Paperback ISBN: 978-1-912658-05-3
ePub ISBN: 978-1-912658-06-0

Edited by Dan Coxon
Proofreading by Robin Triggs

Cover Artwork © Vince Haig 2019

Cover design by Vince Haig
Text design by Cox Design Limited
Typesetting by George Sandison

Printed in the UK by TJ International

FOR THE FIGLET

It is a day when the river smells like the ocean. The musk of the deeper silt drifts to the surface where it pools and eddies along with the tides, mixing with the tang of salty air from downstream. It smells like promise, like moving on, like things growing elsewhere. It makes Shaye's feet itch to follow the river to its mouth, to see the place where the blues of sea and sky meet.

The water is high again, higher than Shaye has ever seen it. The swollen river laps at the trunk of a willow, making a skirt around its roots. The water is flowing quickly upstream, faster than she could run. Since she's been sitting here, the sun has moved behind her and the water has crept further towards her feet. It's coming from the ocean. It's been coming from the ocean for days now.

A scatter of stones makes her turn. She sees her son gather a fistful of poplar down and splay his fingers to let it drift back to the ground.

Look Ma! It's like the snow! he yells at her, and she smiles back at him, makes a sound as though she is impressed. He crouches to gather the down again, and rolls it into balls of fluff between the pads of his fingers. Then he presses it, watching it give under pressure. He is becoming fascinated with what his hands can do. He spends hours placing both his hands solemnly into the mud the way he used to place them on her ribs when he suckled. Then he turns his palms to face him, peering at what he finds there. He picks at the grains of sand, makes patterns in the dust, pushes the earth towards the creases. He likes it best when the dirt is wet. Then he can drag one forefinger across the other palm and see through to the pink skin beneath.

She watches him. He ignores her, absorbed in the white fluff. His hair falls forward into his eyes and he blows it out of his way. She wants to reach towards him and let her fingers find the soft parts of his face, to run the back of her fingernail across his cheek to make sure he is still warm, still alive. She wants to feel his small hand clutching at hers, the grit of whatever he has been playing with smeared between their palms.

The air is humid. There is a thin coating of sweat on her back like the water has stuck to her from the air rather than bubbling up from beneath her skin. Midges dance in a shaft of light between two hawthorns and Shaye watches them. They are they only creatures she's seen who don't seem to be infected by the heaviness of despair for the river. There are no water birds, not anymore. They have deserted this place. There is a hollow in her ears where the splashes of divers and herons should be.

She tips a pile of hazel kernels from her pouch into her hand and whistles gently. Ludi looks up from his crouching position, his eyes wide. She shows him the nuts and he abandons his exploration of the poplar down and trots towards her, wiping his palms on his thighs. He sits down on the riverbank beside her, cupping his hands around the nuts she gives him. He eats slowly, one nut at a time, smacking his tongue against his teeth. Shaye eats too, peeling a hazelnut then tossing the shell into the river to be carried away upstream, to wherever the water is in such a hurry to go.

Is it true, Ma? Ludi chomps noisily, enjoying the crack the nuts make in his mouth.

Is what true?

Are we going to the oak grove soon?

Shaye turns to look at her son. Who told you we were going to the oak grove?

Reo did. He said his Ma told him we'd be walking soon.

Maybe. Shaye sniffs. We usually go later, not until the first frosts, but maybe Reo's Ma knows something else.

Ludi balances a nut between his front teeth and tries to crack it.

What do you do at the oak grove, Ma?

Well, you dance. And sing.

What else though?

Shaye hesitates. You give thanks for the springtime and the rains, and for the water. You ask for the land to come back to life again.

Ludi thinks for a moment. You must have said good thank-yous last time you went, Ma.

Why do you say that?

He cracks the last nut between his teeth, then gestures towards the heaving river. Because look. There's loads of water now.

Shaye looks back to the river. There is loads of water now. No one can talk of anything else. First thing every morning, they all scramble down here to see where the river has risen to, and then the elders will get a deep ridge in between their eyebrows when they see that it has risen still further than the previous day. Then they mutter something about moving away from the river, further into the forest. The women stare at the muddy ripples, waterskins hitched on their hips, and they think of the way this river used to run, clear and cold, each pebble on the waterbed sharply visible. There used to be tides here, the water eddying around the sharpest rocks when it turned. Now the river only flows in one direction. The wrong one.

Come on. Shaye gets to her feet and adjusts her pouch over her shoulder so the honey mushrooms she picked this morning don't tumble out. Ludi jumps up too, bringing the last of his nuts to his mouth and filling his cheeks. Gai Gai caught some hares this morning.

The boy goes ahead of her, up the riverbank. She follows him. She reaches out to catch him when his foot slips from a mossy rock, but he recovers his balance. He doesn't see her hands.

The clearing is quiet for the gloaming time. There is only old Cherl sitting on a fallen branch, his silvery head bowed deeply towards his hands as he sharpens a flint. He grunts without looking up as they pass him and Ludi pauses for a moment to watch the sparks flying from the stone as the man strikes it. Then the smell of roasting meat hitches on the wind and Ludi's attention snaps towards the breeze. He breaks away from her side, running towards the clearing place between the elms where the fire pits are. It's a new thing, the way she follows him. Before, it was her who directed their movements, hauling him around, moving him from earth to sling to water. Now he leads and she follows, always a few steps behind where he doesn't notice her until he needs something.

Gai Gai is kneeling next to a fire pit, prodding at one of the hanging hares with her sharpened stick. Their skins lay drying next to her, neatly laid out across a fallen branch. She can't reach far over the mass of her belly so each of her pokes just makes the meat swing. As she comes closer, Shaye hears her soft curses.

Ludi comes to kneel behind the woman and props his chin on her shoulder. Gai Gai reaches her hand up to his head and strokes it.

I'm hungry, Gai Gai, Ludi says, and he places both hands on his belly, puffing it out in imitation of hers. Both women laugh, and Shaye plucks the long stick from Gai Gai's fingers. She kneels beside the fire pit and gently unhooks the hares from the stakes, placing them on a boulder. Ludi shuffles to sit down beside Gai Gai, reaching his hand across her for the meat.

How is the water? Gai Gai asks her as Ludi twists a thighbone from the animal with a crack.

Shaye puffs her cheeks out. Still high. Higher.

She takes some mushrooms from her pouch and pierces them with a stick. She waits until Ludi has finished with his meat, then she passes the stick to him to place into the fire. He tosses the thighbone into the ashes and takes the mushrooms greedily. He leans forward, his face turning pink from the heat, his tongue pushed out from between his teeth from the effort of holding his stick still. Gai Gai pulls him by his wrap to sit back on his haunches.

A guest came, one who wears the shells. Gai Gai tears a strip of flesh from the hare and waves her hand in the direction of the larger fire pits. He's with Sala.

Shaye places some more mushrooms on a stick and shuffles forward to hold it in the fire. She watches Ludi, his trunk swaying as he tries to hold the mushrooms still. Gai Gai holds his wrap with one hand and a hare bone with the other.

Do you think we're going to the oak grove early?

Gai Gai sniffs. Maybe. Or if not the oak grove somewhere else. If it carries on like this the river will drown us all.

Shaye takes a mushroom from her stick and balances it between her front teeth to let it cool. The flesh of it melts as she chews, and she pulls more mushrooms from her pouch and rolls them between her palms to remove the dirt.

How are you feeling? she asks Gai Gai. Do your legs still hurt? She throws a bone, stripped of its marrow, into the fire.

Gai Gai shakes her head. Just my back, now. She places one mushroom between her teeth to cool too, and Shaye reaches out to the flat, hard plane at the bottom of Gai Gai's back and rubs it as if she is making fire. She remembers the last moon of carrying Ludi, the dragging weight of him making it hard to think.

When they have finished eating, the mushrooms all devoured and the hare meat stripped from the carcasses, Shaye helps Gai Gai to her feet and tries to take Ludi by the hand. He skips out of her reach, but follows her as she goes towards the big fire, where everyone else is beginning to gather. Usually when there is a meeting, Sala sends a child around with a message to tell them to come to the big fire, but news of the guest draped in shells has spread quickly and everyone knows to present themselves as darkness begins to draw closer to hear what he has to say.

Shaye helps Gai Gai sit down first, then turns to find Ludi. She catches his elbow as he runs past her and pulls him to sit down next to her. He protests at first, but when he sees that his friend Reo has been caught in a similar way, pulled to sit down and shushed, he relents. There are gaps around the fire pit, even with the children sitting next to the fully grown. They are few at the moment, and mainly women. The hunting party never returned in the springtime and so only the very young boys and some elders remain.

Sala stands up, and raises her arms to the sky for quiet. She is almost as old as Cherl, but her hair has not become silver yet. It is the reddish gold of a dying leaf, like Shaye's, and if she stands with her back to the sun during ceremonies it looks as though the light is setting her head aflame.

Sala begins to sing. Her voice mingles with the crackle of the fire, singing a song of welcome for the one who wears the shells. Shaye joins in, and then she hears Ludi begin to mumble the words too, faltering as the melody becomes faster and faster. Shaye closes her eyes and listens to Gai Gai singing, next to her. Their mother used to love to sing. She taught them both all the old songs, even the ones that were hardly spoken anymore. She said there was magic in the old songs, and hummed them over and over again as she walked, or wove, or swam in the river.

Sala raises her arms again, and everyone lets their voices tumble into silence.

That will keep the wild creatures away, says Sala, and she bows deeply to the man sitting beside her. Welcome, Sala says, her voice lowering so as not to disturb the night spirits, to this guest come from our kin by the ocean.

She gestures to the man, and he rises from his seat and comes to stand next to Sala. His face is now illuminated by the firelight, and Shaye sees the twin swirls of the skin-painting on his cheeks. He wears a wrap around his waist, but his chest is bare. Shaye lets her eyes drop to the shapes painted across his skin, following the pattern of the snake across his ribcage. She has always imagined what it would be like to experience the pain of those skin drawings, the sharp flint slicing the flesh, the indigo dye trickling through the rivulet, mixing with the blood. Perhaps that is why the ones who wear the shells from the oak grove hardly ever smile, she thinks. They are reliving the agony of their initiation each day.

There is a heavy silence for a moment as everyone stares at the guest's painted skin, broken by the stuttering cry of a cricket. There are moths skittering above the flames of the fire, moving just out of the light so that they seem like tiny black shadows. The guest opens his palms to the fire and takes a breath.

Your elders tell me your river is high. They tell me the water tastes sick. They tell me the river birds are gone.

He pauses, looks around the fire. Shaye looks away from him, looks back to the flames. The sight of his painted skin is making her palms sweat.

And I am come to tell you that you are not alone in this suffering. I have been walking, and everywhere I have seen people like you struggling to stay in their usual plenty-time camps. Some have moved to higher ground already, where they can.

He pauses. He knows that here their plenty-time place is flat, and all they can do is move further away from a river that might still crawl upon them as they sleep, with no levee or sloping bank to protect them.

Everywhere, the waters are high. I tell you all, there is a sickness in this land. The guest slaps the flesh of his thigh and the sound echoes around the clearing.

So I ask you all to leave this place and come to the oak grove early. This is a terrible time for all of us, we cannot wait until the lowest sun as usual. We need to do the healing as soon as we can, and it is planned for the night of the ancestors.

And you come as a representative of the people at the oak grove? someone asks.

Something flickers across the guest's face. Shaye can't see him properly now, there is a fire shadow across his body. I come as a representative of all people everywhere. And I come as a representative of the spirits.

Sala closes her eyes. Shaye watches her shiver. Everyone is silent, only the fire hisses and spits.

Old Cherl stands and clears his throat. Why don't you think the river will go down? he challenges. Why should we leave before we have to? It's seasonal swelling, nothing more, I've seen it over and over again. He folds his arms across his body, holding each elbow. It is the rains from the thunder moon, it happens each and every plenty time. It needs to happen, it's natural. It's what the spirits say is right.

Sala shakes her head. You know it didn't rain as much as it should have in the last moon, Cherl. But the river kept rising.

Then it rained somewhere else! Cherl's voice is harsh, and his voice bounces off the trees.

The guest shakes his head slowly. You are an elder. You have a duty to tell the younger ones how it was. He waves his hand around the fire. Tell them. Tell them how the river was when you were a boy, tell them what it looked like after the spring melt when you came back from the hunt, tell them what a real plenty-time river looks like. Tell them that this is not the same, that this is something new, something you have never seen before, not in all the frosts and plenty times you've seen.

Cherl says nothing, but he does not sit down. He stares at the guest, his eyes narrowed, the firelight glinting on his silver hair. For a moment, Shaye sees him as he used to be, as she remembers him when she was a girl. Tall, proud, distrustful of everyone.

The river is high, there's no doubt about it, says Cherl quietly, and everyone around the fire has to lean towards him to hear what he is saying. But I trust in the spirits. Their wisdom guides me, not the arrogance of this man from the oak grove who thinks he can trick them into providing what is not ours to have.

I do not think I can trick the spirits, elder, the guest says calmly. But I think they are asking something of us. We would be foolish not to give it.

Cherl stares at the man in the shells for a moment longer, then he turns and walks away from the fire, out of the gathering. Nobody goes after him, but now there is a sour taste in Shaye's mouth. Cherl has never walked away from a gathering before. He frequently argues and shouts, tells people that they are wrong and stupid, but he never leaves a gathering. There is a tension around the fire in his absence. Sala's mouth tightens, but Shaye cannot tell if it is with anger or sadness.

Shaye turns away from the guest, towards the fire. She is worried about the water, they all are, but it is easier to imagine that the river will turn soon and they can stay until the first frosts, when they usually go walking. It is difficult to imagine that the river is sick. People get sick. Not rivers.

You know, your own sons are there, the guest says, breaking the uneasy quiet. They came to us at the oak grove.

Shaye does not take her eyes from the flames, but her ears sharpen. She feels Ludi wriggle beside her, but she does not move her hand to his back to attend to him, to tell him to stay still while the elders are talking.

Who? Which ones? Sala asks.

Your hunting party, from the last snowmelt. Someone coughs, and Shaye tries to turn her ears away from the sound to listen harder to the guest. They had to go further and further to find the game, and they came within a day of the oak grove. They stayed with us there. There is plenty to eat at the oak grove although the waters are no longer low.

And you saw them, with your own eyes? someone asks. Shaye turns to the voice but cannot see who asked in the gloom.

The guest lowers his chin slowly, then raises it again. They are at the oak grove, along with many others, and more are arriving each moon. They have come to honour the sprits. The guest blinks. I am walking to tell anyone I can find to gather there.

Will there be a ceremony? Sala asks.

The guest nods again, slowly. Yes, there will be a ceremony. The spirits demand it.

He waves his hand away from the sinking sun, towards where the bloated river gushes.

Sala looks around at the gathering, sees the lowered eyes. She looks back at the guest, and sighs.

I've heard enough. Sala stands and reaches out her hand towards the guest. He takes it, placing his forehead on her palm to honour her. The land is sick, we can all see that. I will leave here tomorrow and I will lead a group of whoever wishes to come to the oak grove, where we will dance for the spirits.

Sala looks around the fire. It is fully dark now, and the lightning bugs glitter above their heads. Shadows flicker on worried faces that watch Sala as she turns to each adult. Shaye waits to be asked. She would have given her consent to move on even before the guest came, she always agrees to move on. Shaye is one who likes to walk, to seek the veins of the earth with her feet and follow them. She sees the same hunger in Ludi. But now she knows where Marl is, now the guest has told them all where the hunting party is, she cannot stay any longer. Even though none of the cloth on the looms is finished, even though they haven't finished drying the skins and hides for the frosts, even though there will be so much to carry. She doesn't care, she wants to leave.

Everything in her body is buzzing. She wants to jump up from her seat, grab Ludi's hand and run along the river path, taking her chances with beasts made bold by the darkness of night and not stop until she can fling herself down between the sacred stones at the oak grove.

But she doesn't move. Her heart thumps in her chest and she places both her hands to her throat to calm herself. She had thought she would never see him again, had dreamt each night of his dark head lying close to some other woman's in some other plenty-time place, but now this guest wearing the shells has set her free. She sees Gai Gai turn to her, feels her eyes searching for a hint of what she is thinking, but Shaye doesn't return her gaze. She is afraid that she will look too happy, and Gai Gai will guess that she thinks and dreams and longs for Marl, still. She turns to Ludi instead and reaches for the back of his wrap. She teases the fabric between her fingers, lets her hands pass to the places on his spine where his bones stick out, picks off a piece of dirt. She imagines them together, Ludi and Marl, their two dark heads huddled together as Marl shows the boy the wrapping of a spear, or the intricacies of a deer trap, or whatever else it is that the men do on the hunt.

Sala moves around the fire, pausing in front of each adult for them to speak their agreement.

First she asks the other elders, Brig and Yael, for their opinion. Brig heaves a long sigh, then nods briefly. She has never shown any warmth to any initiate from the oak grove, but not even she could say the river rising is their fault. Yael has tears in his eyes, Shaye can see them flicker in the firelight, making him look as though the spirits are dancing inside his head. He bows to Sala and then looks to the initiate. I believe we have no choice, he says, shaking his head.

Then Sala asks the woman sitting on the other side of the initiate, the woman who predicted this and told her son Reo: Ayla. She is a serious woman, with thick shoulders and haunches, who sometimes accompanies the men when they go off to hunt. She does not say a word, only dips her head to signal yes. Sala asks Ayla's daughter Rilk for her assent too, even though the girl has not yet had her first moonblood. She blushes to be asked what she thinks, like one already grown, and squares her shoulders like her mother. Yes, Sala, she says clearly, without looking for guidance. I say we should take the path to the oak grove.

Vesti sits next to Rilk, one hand resting absently on the soft curve of her belly, the other twisting a strand of hair that has escaped from her braids. Her baby is due to be born during the wolf moon, when the frosts are at their most vicious, so Shaye knows she will say yes to leaving. Better to be safe in the warm caves at the oak grove to grow a baby, not watching the river rise here.

Now it is Gai Gai's turn, and she murmurs yes, without hesitation but not without sadness. Shaye looks up to see Sala standing before her, and she swallows carefully. She does not trust her voice to be mournful enough, her joy at leaving will betray her. Sala's face is shrouded in shadow, but Shaye knows that Sala can see her. She nods, once, then twice. Then she opens her mouth and says, Yes, I will come to the oak grove, and Sala moves to stand in front of the initiate to say, We have all decided. We will join our kindred at our sacred place.

Everyone but Cherl has spoken their agreement, and there is nothing left to say that is not too mournful so the gathering breaks up. Shaye helps Gai Gai to her feet and takes Ludi's dirt-encrusted hand. Only in darkness does he fumble and let her guide him, back to the sleeping clearing along with everyone else.

Ludi never takes long to fall asleep these days. He crawls over her mat and curls up next to where Gai Gai is already lying down, her breathing hard. Her mat rustles as she shifts and fidgets. She finds it difficult to get comfortable enough to sleep soundly, so close to her birthing time.

Shaye lies next to Ludi, arranging her hair around her head. She listens to Ludi snuffling and turning over. Leaves and twigs crackle beneath his body until his breathing slows and his body grows heavily still. She listens to the sounds of the darkness, of distant owls calling to each other, to the scuffles of mice and foxes. The forest never sleeps, there is always something alive in it, even one of those things that lives for just a day deep in the soil bed.

She cannot shut her eyes, she cannot sleep. She watches the sky as the stars appear, one by one, weaving with the weft of the dark patches of canopy to make a twinkling sky cloth. There have been no clouds for a few days now. There has been no rain for almost a moon.

They are going walking, at last. Shaye has been feeling the call of the winding paths that follow the river for days now, almost as if her feet knew the guest was coming to tell them to move on. She rolls onto her side, away from Ludi's soft snores. She tucks her knees up to her chest. She is always warmer that way.

And she will be walking towards Marl, taking Ludi to him. Each step will be sweet with the knowledge that soon she will get to drink in the sight of him. She wonders if the guest has seen Marl, perhaps spoken to him. She wonders if she can go to him when the sun rises, give a description and ask if there is any news of him, any at all. Perhaps Marl spoke a message for her, or a kind word for Ludi.

She remembers watching him leave for his first hunt with her family, moons and moons ago. He stood before her with his eyes closed as she anointed him with the crimson blood of the snake. She got to look at him greedily, as he could not see her. His hair tightly shaved, looking like he had smeared ashes all over his scalp; his skin just a fraction darker than hers, the colour of a hazelnut shell; a wet leaf stuck to the hollow at the top of his ribs from his immersion in the river; his head, bowed towards her so that she could reach his face.

She dragged her thumb across his forehead, then down between his eyes to the tip of his nose. She had pressed his lips, gently, leaving a smear of blood there that would dry to the same colour as the earth beneath them, and when he had felt the pad of her thumb against his mouth he had opened his lips and her finger slipped between his teeth to find his warm, quivering tongue. His eyes blinked open to see her staring at him. She smiled, and as she took her hand away from his mouth she felt like a dense grey cloud sparking with lightning. The centre of her began to ooze.

The hunt came back a moon later when everything was in bud, dragging the stiffened bodies of does behind them. His eyes darted around the shouting, whooping welcomers, and she followed his gaze, watching to see if it would settle when it landed on her. He found her face and a slow smile spread across his lips. She smiled back, and did not take her eyes off him as he paraded the catch along with the other men. There was something harder about his jaw, he stood straighter, his shoulders had widened. He had become more of a man. There was no trace of the fear she had felt beneath her fingertips before.

He came to her at the fire that night as she knew he would, presenting the insides of his wrists and bowing his head. His hands had been shaking. She placed her palms in his and followed him into the thicker woods.

She remembers how she transformed into a writhing snake beneath his weight, her skin melting into his and into the earth, her flesh soft like a berry under his touch. She remembers how she seemed to swell, her body rising to meet him and then the piercing thrust that broke everything into little shining pieces like stars, how the wetness of them mixed and spread underneath them, sinking into the grateful earth. His grunts and her cries echoed around the canopy, and after he shuddered to a halt and her burning hunger had been sated, they laughed and let the slick of sweat between their bellies dry.

He came to her again and again that spring, and into the plenty time too, wrists exposed and a heaving chest that betrayed his excitement. She remembers how she went to him too, to place her palms around his neck and pull his ear towards her lips to whisper the invitation. They bathed together in the river during the languid days – it had been clear and fresh then – and gorged on the stone fruit when the trees ripened. Shaye missed her bleedings and watched her belly swell like the berries coming into blush. She felt as if she were holding her heart outside of herself, like she had swapped some vital piece of her with Marl and held something of him inside her too.

She still feels this way, even though Marl has not shown her his wrists for many moons now. She still lies awake at night and thinks of his weight on top of her, of anointing him in preparation for the hunt, of his hard, hot mouth on hers. And now they are all going walking, and they will be walking towards him. Shaye turns over onto her back to watch the stars again. He's there, at the oak grove. Is he looking at these same stars? Is he thinking of her, of Ludi, of this plenty-time place where they had come together, and lived, and loved each other so brightly?

It is a day when the river smells like petrol. Sharp in the back of her throat, like she's just been sick. It smells like rubbish too, walking along it is like walking behind the bin lorry on collection days, trying not to breathe until she can overtake it on the pavement. It doesn't always smell like this, she knows. Sometimes it smells like trees and the other tangled green things growing along its banks. At other times it smells damp, the pavement releasing tiny water droplets into the air after rain. And occasionally it smells like the sea, heaving in the east, lurking there at the borders of the city.

She can see the petrol too, if she leans out over the railings and peers into the water. It's a slick dirty rainbow splayed in this eddy, dammed in by scratched bottles and a torn sock. There's other abandoned junk in the river, gently bumping against the concrete bank with every pulse of the tide. Bottle caps, in every primary colour. A blue plastic bag. A cotton bud, its puffy ends black with whatever stains the bank.

The water is almost completely still and stagnant in this concreted inlet, but out in the river the tide is high, the flood tide flowing westwards towards the white-columned houses of centuries gone by. The river is still and black here, but where it is flowing it is grey, its particles of silt lying just below the skin of the water, visible in clouds where there are shafts of light from the busboats.

The air is heavy. She sticks out her bottom lip and blows upwards, to release some air onto her damp forehead. It's been a hot summer; the tannoys issuing heat warnings, water shortages at peak times, fires in apartment blocks from electrical surges. The heat has to break soon. The newscasters have been saying so all summer, but now it's September and the children are all back at school and everyone's waiting for the storms to begin. They've been talking about atmospheric pressure over the Continent, warm fronts travelling from the western ocean, unseasonable tides, but still there's this blue sky and the feeling of it pressing down on her shoulders, weighting her to the ground.

She likes to walk by the river. She likes to listen to the pumps as they work, rhythmically sucking and hissing as they draw the water out of the river and away to the water plant. She remembers when they built these pumps. She was eight, and her class came to a visitor's centre on a school trip. They had seen the pistons in action and drawn pictures of them on their tablets. There had been a man who had explained that the best engineers of the territory had been employed to design a drainage system to keep them all safe from the sea. He had pointed downstream, towards the east, and she had imagined the sea as a kind of blue-grey monster, hoping to devour them in their sleep.

She passes an abandoned patch of scrub with green leaves spurting wildly from the dirt. If Locke were with her, he'd want to know what the green leaves were called. She'd invent some names for the plants, putting together the strangest collection of sounds she could think of with a perfectly straight face until he'd say, Mum! You're being silly. And he would turn away from her to examine the green leaves again, and he would not be sure if she really knew the names of the plants or not.

But Locke is at home, probably asleep by now. Grainne is looking after him tonight, giving him the dinner of pasta and tomato sauce she left out, bathing him, reading his favourite story about the robot lost on the moon, and drawing the sheet over him as his eyelids flutter with tiredness.

Her tab beeps softly for data, muffled by the cardigan in her handbag. She ignores it, she's got another few hours before it'll start to beep with admonishments. She'll watch the newscast later, ring Zeb, check her account. She has to pay the rent next Thursday, and if she needs to ask Zeb for money she'll have to steel herself for the conversation. I hate paying money for that hole that's just going to fall into the river one of these days, he says. Ring the emigration office again and ask them about the visas. She'll murmur that she will, and he'll send as much money as he can, but she never rings the emigration helpline. She's heard they slow or stop applications when people harass them.

There is no one on the path but her. Her lute bumps on her back as she walks, the strings protesting softly with each step, jangling as if to remind her that what she carries is precious. She passes an abandoned brewery, a faint smell of yeast still seeping from its bricks, and turns away from the river to head towards her home.

A street light blinks on above her. The houses on this road were vacated long ago; this is Flood Zone One, which has been submerged at least once a year for the past hundred years. The old owners of these houses have long ago claimed compensation and moved. Back in the days when the authorities were still giving compensation, back before the Clearances, back before the city borders shut. There are still sandbags blocking the doors here, but they're ancient and spilling onto the street. The paint on the door frames is chipped, there are snakes of black mould climbing the walls and broken windows and the pavement is still slimy with silt from when the river breached its banks last April.

Zeb left back in January, when the last of the underground lines flooded after a winter storm. They'd watched the newscast together, seen the footage of the firemen wading into the tunnels and bringing out the bloated corpses, and he had left the room and shut himself in the bathroom rather than let her see the tears glistening in his eyes.

He was lucky. With his passport from the north, he was let through the city gates without a single question, and the very next day he'd submitted the forms to bring her, Locke, Grainne and her father up to the city with him. They'd been waiting for months now, all through the spring and the summer, for the visas to be approved. Every day, a message from him when she wakes up: Morning sweetheart, crossing my fingers it will be today, give the little man a kiss from me. And every evening, a message from him when she goes to sleep. Goodnight, sleep tight, dreaming of you. See you soon.

Most of the people who can leave already have. The city has emptied like an upturned sack of spuds, its citizens rolling away in all directions, leaving mainly the poor, the stubborn and the careless behind. Everyone still here has a plan to leave, sometimes several at a time. Rumours of cities still taking asylum applications fizz like sea foam.

This western city has closed its borders for good, this northern one is only accepting applications from people with healthcare skills, if you can get through the edgelands to the coast then there are boats that go to the Continent and there they're not so strict.

Today at the party, any talk Shante had overheard had been on this topic. It was supposed to be a wedding, but the guests had tight faces and stiff necks, and talked of nothing but how many points they had, the applications they had rejected. Shante listened furtively, with a stone in her stomach, thinking of her own visa that should be arriving any day now. A hundred and forty-seven, she kept thinking, the number echoing in her head. A hundred and forty-seven, my magic number. The total number of immigration points for her family; for being a spouse and a child of a resident, for Grainne's coding qualifications, for their healthy bodies, for her father's electrical engineering career. A hundred and forty-seven. That's what me and mine are worth to the city at the highest altitude in this territory.

When she went to the toilet, she came upon one guest crying to another. I'd rather take my chances in the edgelands than stay here, the girl had wailed, and the other had hushed her, looking over her shoulder to see if anyone had been listening. Shante stared straight at her reflection as she washed her hands, giving no sign that she had heard. You didn't want to say, or hear, anything about the edgelands. You didn't know where that information might end up.

She rarely does weddings, these days. She rarely works at all, to tell the truth; few people want to spend money on blowout parties now, and the few events she does play at have a desperate, frantic edge to them. The people there talk too loudly, dance too sloppily, drink until they weep, certain it might be their last chance to do so, wondering if the flood that will end it all is rising in the estuary even as they sip imported whisky. Watching them as she stroked her strings today had given her the same uneasy feeling that she gets when she watches the city lights blink off during a night-time blackout. Of something nasty slithering on its belly through the city.

Zeb would say that she should stop being melodramatic, that she can't afford to turn down work just because she'd rather be playing for happy people, but Zeb is not walking beside her along these deserted streets tonight and she can think exactly what she likes.

There's no other work now. The clubs are shut, the only music left is the computer-generated jingle you get when you ring the council and the revellers have either left the city or are waiting out the end of the world at the illegal raves in the old underground stations. Shante's been taking whatever she can get, but the number in her bank account is getting lower each time she checks it. Counting down, like a rocket poised to launch. She wonders what happens when she gets to zero. Grainne moved in to help look after Locke and save on rent, and Zeb sends money when he can, but she knows he sometimes skips meals to send her money when she asks for it.

She wonders what he is thinking about now, right at this moment, as she is walking through this dirty old city towards the home she used to share with him. She used to look at him in profile like an old coin, when he was busy staring at something else, and wonder where his mind was.

His eyebrows drawn together in a frown of concentration, his black hair curling slightly as it grows longer, hiding the essence of himself from her. What are you thinking about? she'd ask, cringing, hating the need to know, trying to make light of it. Nothing in particular, he'd reply, and brush his thumb lightly against her shoulder. And she'd turn away, embarrassed to be caught being dazzled at the sight of him, determined never to ask him the question again.

She crosses the old motorway, pausing to let a couple of bikes pass her, then a couple of cars going the other way. She arrives at the top of her road. She can hear a drumbeat coming from one of the houses over the road, and the hum of a generator. It's peaceful, this area, at dusk. Most people have left. This motorway used to be one of the arteries of the city, its traffic flowing westwards into the green edgelands, but now the concrete is cracking and the white lines marking out the lanes are faded. The drains constantly bubble with water, being so close to the river. To the west the road soars, balancing above the ground on long concrete stilts to make a flyover. There used to be a roundabout beneath it. Now it's a dumping ground for the things nobody wants anymore; rusted washing machines and chairs with three legs and mattresses heaving with maggots.

She turns to walk up her road and sees the tall shapes of the trees in the park ahead, silhouetted against the murky sky. She had chosen this flat when Locke was born precisely because it was close to the park, somewhere peaceful and protected to take him on walks. He used to walk down this road towards the grass, unsteady on his feet, veering from side to side on fat legs. She smiles as she pictures him, waddling on this pavement between the wheelie bins and the cars, bouncing off the electric charge points and plopping down onto his padded backside. It was only a couple of years ago that he was that heavy, compact bundle of soft flesh burrowing into her for comfort. Now he is a person all of his own, with a control of his arms and legs that astonishes her. He's become competent at so many things without her even noticing. He only started school a few weeks ago and they tell her he can already read. Could she read at five? She can barely remember what the world was like then. Will he just keep changing and changing behind my back, she wonders, until I turn around one day and don't even recognise him?

She pulls her lute case out of the way of a bike chained up to a lamppost and opens the gate, which swings with a whine of its hinges that reminds her of all the times she's stayed up late and listened for it, meaning that Zeb was home at last. She can hear the thunk and whir of the upstairs neighbour's generator and sighs. Why he needs extra appliances on at this time of night is beyond her, when the rest of them do fine with the solar panels and the battery. But he owns his flat, and nobody else in the building does, so he gets to do what he wants, and keep everyone else awake with the humming of a motor that only he profits from.

Grainne opens the front door to her flat before she can put her key in the lock. Shoddy windows, Shante thinks. Not soundproofed at all, you can hear everything from the street.

You're home! Grainne tugs at her arm, pulls her inside and shuts the door behind her. She's holding both her hands behind her back, the way their father used to when he brought them a present. I rang you, sent you messages. Don't you check your tab?

I'm not late, am I? Shante's right hand flies to her left wrist, where she wears her watch, but she doesn't look at it. She knows she isn't late. She left the wedding exactly on time.

Look! Grainne whips out her hands from behind her back and shows her four black booklets, all embossed with the crest of Zeb's home city. Our visas came!

Relief drains through Shante's body from her head downwards and makes her feel shaky in its wake. She takes Grainne's wrists and holds them up to the light to see them better. She takes one, opens it to the middle and sees Locke, six months younger, his hair freshly cut for this photo, his lips pale in an attempt not to smile.

They arrived today?

Grainne nods. A courier brought them at about five. Look, I've been packing. She gestures to the living room, where two suitcases lie on the floor with clothes exploding from them.

I've rung Dad, told him to pack too, and I've checked the train times. We can get on one tomorrow morning at ten past eight. She pauses. I didn't tell Locke. He's asleep now. I thought it would be a nice surprise for him in the morning.

Did you ring Zeb? Shante asks. She feels unsteady on her feet, and suddenly hungry.

Grainne beams. Not yet. I thought he'd rather hear the good news from you.

Shante takes off her lute and leans it against the wall. She steps past Grainne and moves towards what she calls the kitchen. It's only a few shelves with packets of food and stacked plates, a sink, a fridge and an oven, but she likes to pretend it's a real room all of its own.

She opens the fridge, staring into the light as though it contains an epiphany, but she can't remember why she opened it, or what she thought would be in there. She feels naked suddenly, as though she's wearing one of those backless hospital things with everything exposed. This is it, she thinks. I'm not coming back here ever again.

She unwraps a compacted fruit bar. She sits on the sofa and watches Grainne drag clothes out of the wardrobe, then fold and refold them. She moves quickly, but Shante notices that she doesn't seem to be achieving much. She is thrumming with impatience and nerves.

She has imagined this moment every day since Zeb left and they filed the papers. Every hour she's spent waiting in lines for health checks, interviews, data processing she has sweetened by imagining those dark booklets in her hands, sitting on a train speeding north, Locke throwing himself into Zeb's arms at the other end. She knows exactly how long it takes to get to the train station. She knows the weekday and weekend train timetable. She has an email drafted to send to Locke's school, and another to her friend Jordi to come and take whatever he wants from this flat. She has a mental list of everything she will put into a suitcase when the time comes. She has held every item she owns and assessed it for its worth in her new life with the questions, do I need it, is it valuable, will I miss it if I don't have it, and found in most cases that the answers are no, no and no. Leaving here will be a fresh start, a time to break free of all this stuff and streamline her life. Like a bird, flying across continents with nothing but the feathers on its back and its instincts threaded through its cells, telling it where it can best survive.

Now the moment has come without premonitions or omens, and it has taken her by surprise. There is a churning feeling in her stomach. To think that this time tomorrow she will see Zeb and feel his hard body against hers and smell that cream he uses in his hair makes her itch inside. That she'll spend the winter in a place where the river doesn't burst its banks, where there's always electricity, where the stink of uncollected rubbish doesn't permeate laundry hanging out to dry when the wind is still.

She takes her tab from her pocket and runs her thumb over it. She needs to tell Zeb they're coming, but Grainne is right here, moving her clothes in circles around her, pretending not to listen.

I'll be back in minute, she tells her sister, crumpling the fruit bar packet in her hand and throwing it into the bin. Just going to ring Zeb.

She leaves the front door ajar and stands in the hallway, kicking at the exposed plastic weft of the threadbare carpet tickling the skirting board. She presses Zeb's name, watches the dial ring and ring, waiting for his face to appear on her screen. She hopes he doesn't pick up, and guiltily, when the call drops, she writes a message. Great news! The visas arrived, we're coming tomorrow. Will let you know what time train in the morning. Goodnight love, hope you're ready for us all!

She lets the message send, then turns its volume markers to silent. She doesn't want to talk to Zeb tonight, but she doesn't want to think about why. I need to concentrate on packing, she tells herself. I don't need to spend the whole night on the tab. I want to be here, the last night I'll spend in my home. I've got the rest of my life to talk to him.

She shuts the front door and locks it behind her. Grainne still hasn't managed to get much into her suitcase, she's sitting in the same place on the floor, a pair of shoes in each hand.

Shan, tell me about the weather up there, she says. Do you think I need to take these boots, or should I just bring my wellies and some thick socks? Does it rain a lot? Can you maybe ring Zeb and ask him?

He didn't answer, Shante replies, coming to sit on the floor next to Grainne and pulling one of the suitcases towards her. I left him a message. Pack the boots, leave the wellies. Zeb said it gets cold.

She puts everything that was on her mental list into the suitcase; changes of clothes for Locke and her, spare strings for the lute, the solar charger for her tab. The photo album she made for this occasion, a whole bound book filled with photos of herself, Grainne, Locke. Even her parents, her grandparents, a whole family history told in random images of birthdays, school uniforms and never-to-be-forgotten moments. She flips the pages, lands on a picture of her mother and sister in a park. Grainne, about seven, is sitting in their mother's lap, her head cocked coquettishly, her hands wrapped around a secret object only she knows about. Her mother is tying Grainne's long hair back, her face half hidden. A precious, ordinary slice of time that no one would have thought worthy of capturing in an image; but for some reason, someone, probably her father, did. And now the photo sits beside hundreds of others like it, commemorating nothing more than the delicate fragments of human lives, transforming them from there to here over and over again with only a single glance.

She gazes at her sister the girl in the photo, ignoring her sister the woman beside her. Did Grainne know she was staring into the future as she looked down the barrel of the camera? Shante wonders what her parents knew then, as they were living in the moments before, during and after this one. Had the winter floods already started? Were the cities already building their walls and closing their borders? Shante wonders what secrets her own eyes would tell Locke twenty years hence, if she were to take a picture of herself right now. Unknown, unknowable. She's just casting a line out into a roaring sea, hoping it'll catch. Just like everyone else.

She shuts the book and puts it on top of the clothes. I will not touch that book until I get to Zeb, and it becomes a happy thing again, she thinks.

She's only filled the suitcase halfway, she's been too conservative in her planning of what to take. She tries to remember if there were other things on her list, but there is a blank space where her thoughts should be and all she can think of is how much she had been looking forward to Locke's parents evening next Monday. His teacher told her he was doing really well in school and she could have a look at the paintings he's been doing. She won't get to go now. Locke won't get to say goodbye to the boys he runs around the playground with, and when he asks her why, she'll only be able to mumble about going to live with Dad, at last, and if he asks her when they'll be coming back, she won't manage any words at all.

She looks around the room, searching for anything she's missed, but she sees nothing she cares about enough to choose over something else. What's the point, she thinks.

One day, all this is all going to be destroyed. Perhaps not this winter, but maybe next. She's seen the videos on the news of other cities flooding out, their rivers tumbling over their banks until people are wading waist deep in water, dead dogs floating past them. They're close to the river here. She imagines the silty water seething with bacteria rising to the level of her flat and ruining all these things that keep her shackled to the world. The books on the shelves they bought at the market and painted themselves, the tall purple lamp from her mother's house. The water filtration system Zeb worked overtime to save up for when the mayor made the statement about the taps. The clock hanging above the door, the radio on top of the fridge, the pots and pans and knives and forks she uses every day. She needs none of it now, it can all be left behind to be sucked into the river.

She opens a drawer in the wardrobe and takes out the folder with their passports, Locke's birth certificate and all the other scraps of paper that tell the story of her personhood in the modern world, pieces of fiction that others believe in too, sometimes above the evidence of her physical being. She takes the black booklets and places them inside the folder, wraps it in three plastic bags and then zips it safely in her handbag. That folder is the most important thing she owns, next to the lute. She feels guilty for putting the papers and the instrument in the same category like that, but it's the truest thing she knows about her life at this moment. Zeb would say, Come on Shan, you cannot be serious. But she is. She will wrap up the lute in a similar way to the papers, inside a waterproof casing and then inside the padded bag that bumps on her back. She will not let it out of her sight until they're safe in the north.

Grainne, I'm going to bed. She pulls her tab out of her pocket and presses her thumb to the clock icon. What time shall I set the alarm for?

Maybe half five? she says. She's filled a suitcase now, full of bright scraps of clothes, but she's still holding each possession up to the light and considering them one by one before discarding them to a pile on the floor. We have to pick Dad up, and if we have to walk it'll take about an hour.

Shante nods. They both know exactly how long it will take to walk to the station. They've timed it, walking at Locke's slower pace, they've discussed it and argued about it and told each other they won't talk about the logistics of leaving anymore while they hear nothing about their visas because it could all be for nothing, they might have to stay and deal with the winter's floods, and then talked about it all over again.

She opens the door to the bedroom carefully and waits to see if Locke stirs before she shuts it again. She crosses the room to the cot bed where her son sleeps. He is lying on his back, his T-shirt rucked up around his chest and his sheet kicked onto the floor in the heat. The thin curtains are lit with the orange light of the streetlamp just outside and it gives his dark skin the glow of hot coals.

She kneels beside his bed and listens to his breathing. For a moment, she can't hear anything. She feels suspended in the seconds between his breaths, paralysed with awe at the separateness of him, his breaths so totally unconnected to hers, his body so independent of her own.

Then he inhales, and she catches her own breath too, and now they are breathing in unison, mother and son, sharing the same stuffy air, in the same cramped room they have shared since he was born.

Shante fiddles with the curtain, trying to close the gap between the two sides of it and leaving it exactly as it was before. She goes to her own bed and takes off her clothes. She isn't sure where to put them, holding them in a bundle in her arms. The laundry basket is already full of clothes, hers, Grainne's and Locke's; she had been planning to take them to the public washing machines tomorrow after she dropped Locke off at school. She puts today's clothes on top of them. They'll never be washed now, probably never worn again. She wonders how long it will take these two rooms to become truly empty of the three of them. A week? A month? The housing association will probably realise this place is empty and requisition it before the winter floods. She pictures a housing inspector taking a picture of her laundry basket, filled with worn underwear and T-shirts pickled with sweat under the arms, and she wants to laugh. It should be a shameful thing, to think of yourself so exposed like that, intimate particles of yourself left for a nameless bureaucrat to pick over, but she can't help but see the funny side. It's not as if she has another choice.

She sits on the edge of the bed and pulls out her tab. She tilts the screen away from Locke so the blue light doesn't wake him up and inputs her data points; her temperature, what she's eaten, her mood and geopointers. She presses the options mechanically, not bothering to check any of her picks. Grainne says that accuracy is never the point with tab data, that it just needs something of you to program into the algorithm and then it'll do the rest. She flicks away the pushes to view newscasts, music videos or ads. She doesn't want to see them now.

She lies down in the bed and pulls a sheet over her. She lies on her back, feeling the pull of the mattress where it sags in the middle. Zeb used to call it the black hole, that sunken patch, because no matter where they started off in the bed, by the morning they would have rolled into it and would be clutching at each other, her face pressed against his chest and his fingers tangled in her hair. But the same thing doesn't happen with Grainne now she sleeps beside Shante in this bed each night, and Shante makes a note to tell Zeb that. It wasn't the black hole that made us wake up in each other's arms, she'll tell him, it was because our bodies couldn't bear to be apart. And then he'll laugh and pull her towards him and say something like, And now we'll never have to be apart again.

When the sun rises, and everyone is awake, Sala leads them all to the riverbank. Shaye walks with a waterskin hitched onto her hip, and her pouch slung over her shoulder. Ludi scrambles along in front of her, competing with his skinny friend Reo. Shaye wants to call to him to come back to her, to tell him to stay close as they approach the water, but she bites her lip. He doesn't seem to think of her now, his mind lives in the sweet stretch of his limbs as he loops and weaves around his friend.

They reach the riverbank in silence and stare into the water. It is not a thoughtful silence, not the quiet of people wondering what they will say next; it is akin to the grief of a burial rite. For the river is higher still than yesterday, now it laps at the top of the bank. It is not just the people who are quiet, there are no birds to fill the air with sound either. No calling of jay, no soft wing quiver of crane, no splash of coot. Nobody knows where the water birds have gone, and it is this silence that saddens the most.

Shaye pulls her skirt over the mouth of her waterskin and drags it through the river. She does not have to step down the bank anymore, her toes gripping the damp silt on the slope, she only has to crouch and then she can reach into the water. It is sick water, they all know it when they drink. The women pass it through their skirts to leave behind the worst of the silt, then they let their waterskins stand in the shade for a while to let the silt settle at the bottom. Finally they pour the clearer water away into another waterskin before they drink it, and even still there is a memory of something rotten within it, something that the tongue curls up to touch.

Ayla and Rilk come to join Shaye with their own waterskins and collect their water in the same way. They turn towards Sala for her judgement. The guest stands next to her, looking into the murky water, his fingers worrying at the shells that hang to his navel. He has the same ridge between his eyebrows as the elders every morning.

Shaye looks more closely at the inked patterns on his chest. There is barely a finger's width of bare skin to see, every part of him is tattooed. She realises he is older than she thought yesterday, looking at the lines at the corners of his eyes, and the detail of his skin-painting. She knows that the initiates of the oak grove receive more patterns every springtime. This man must be one of the elders there.

Fix yourselves to leave at sunrise tomorrow, Sala calls, and although her voice is strong her mouth wears the same twist of mourning as everyone else's. We can't wait any longer. The guest does not look at her, but he closes his eyes briefly, as if the sight of the muddy river hurts him, then turns his back on the water to return to the clearing.

Shaye leaves Ludi to run around the forest with Reo as she prepares to leave. She touches her thumb to each of her flints to see which are the sharpest, and buries the old ones at the foot of an alder. She tucks a spindle and a combing paddle away in her pouch along with the best bone needles. She takes all the nettle cloth she has woven down from the branch it hangs on, and tips their nut store from the woven birch bark baskets into it, wrapping it up safely in her pouch. She makes a loop for her waterskin, tying it around her neck over and over again until it is comfortable to carry. It makes her glad to be readying herself to leave. This plenty-time place is her favourite place to be settled, but there is no joy like the joy of moving across the land, one foot after the other, and to be walking towards Marl is the greatest joy of all.

She wants to run and scream like the little boys, chasing each other and tumbling down into the leaf drifts when they are caught; she wants to stamp out her joy through her feet and shout it out through her lips, just to let the buzzing in her fingertips dissipate. But in the clearing the other women are weaving frantically, trying to tie off the cloth that is not yet made on their looms. There is little nettle at the oak grove, and so what they have gathered, dried and spun here must not be wasted.

Shaye kneels next to Gai Gai in front of an empty loom and picks up the threads hanging from the weft. It is a type of trance, to weave. The whole world shrinks to the movement of a thick strand of nettle undulating between its sister strands and the fingers that make it move so, dancing across the loom and back again. Weaving can be a time for chatter and stories, or songs and laughter, when all the women join their voices together and secrets and the giggles are woven into the cloth. Birds love weaving too, and often robins will come to sit on the branches above the women's heads to observe, singing helpfully when someone's threads become tangled.

But weaving can also be a time for silence and contemplation, and on this day there is a heaviness to the

gathering. Nobody sings and nobody tells any stories. Rilk
weaves quickly, her tongue stuck out in concentration, and
Vesti cuts and ties off the pieces which have been hastily
finished. No one wants to leave, but they cannot bear to
stay either.

When all the threads have been knotted securely and
the dangling threads cut with a piece of sharp flint, Ayla
dismantles the looms and lets the taut wood sink back onto
the ground. Then each of them gathers up the rounded
pebbles from the old river that hang from the warp as loom
weights and bury them too. No need to carry them to the
oak grove. There is a whole beach there filled with smooth
round pebbles to use for future cloth.

Shaye glances at Gai Gai, watches her wince as she shifts
on her log. Gai Gai will now have to birth on the road,
and the path to the coast is not always good for stopping
to rest after a birth, even before the waters rose. Shaye
turns her mind to the things she will need to help Gai Gai
when the baby comes, measuring how much cloth she has
for wrapping the baby, how many waterskins they carry
between them to fetch water, if there is any clean water to be
had. There is a spring between here and the coast by the oak
grove and she tries to call to mind exactly where it is. There
is a holloway of hawthorn and blackthorn, she remembers,
then a break in the undergrowth. She hears her mother's
voice reminding her, If you see a doe bounding away from
you or hear the scuffle of mice and hares disappearing at
your tread, then you will be close.

It is good to keep her mind busy with the path, the birth,
the preparations to leave. Then she will not imagine Marl's
knees gently nudging her thighs apart, nor see his head

ringed by the dappled light of the canopy.

The half-dried skins are a problem, and there is much discussion of what to do. All throughout the clearings of their plenty-time place the branches are draped with the hides of ponies, deer, hares waiting for the first frosts to come, when the women will take them down and sew them into warm tunics and leggings for the cold days, packing away the skirts, girdles and wraps for the next springtime.

Ayla favours leaving the clothes which are only half made behind for the frosts, and hunting again by the coast; but that seems wasteful to everyone else. Normally they wear the skins to make the journey to the oak grove, but normally they leave when the air is already chill and everybody needs a tunic to keep warm. Shaye doesn't want to wear the skins to carry them, it's too hot. Even her skirt and girdle stick to her skin unpleasantly. She has decided to carry the skins which are already dried, even if they are heavy in her pack.

No one cooks as dusk comes, all the fire pits are cool and still. Ludi comes to her, spitting seeds from the corner of his mouth the way Reo has taught him, a deep crimson crab apple clutched in each fist. He holds the fruits up to them proudly as Shaye and Gai Gai take apart the last loom, each crab apple sitting small in his palm. Gai Gai takes one and sniffs it.

What a fruit you have found, sweet one! She takes his cheek in one hand and pinches it gently. What a clever boy this one is, Shaye. She takes a bite of the fruit and makes a show of her pleasure. Ludi smiles to himself, his shoulder hunching slightly with shy pride.

Shaye crouches to her son, plucking his offering from his

hand. She presses her lips to his damp forehead and gathers him close towards her, feeling a swell in her chest at the way he wraps his arms around her back, squeezing as hard as his tired arms can manage. She lets him go, sweeps the hair back from his eyes and begins to eat her crab apple too.

Mmmmm! Shaye looks up at Gai Gai, and they make smacking noises with their tongues. Ludi smiles shyly again. You have done so well, my little star.

She doesn't try to take his hand to walk back to the place where their sleeping mats lie, but follows him as he meanders in and out of the fallen branches and finishes her fruit. He seems leaner now, as though that one act of giving has transformed him from a gurgling baby to a scrawny boy with freedom buzzing in his newly powerful limbs.

He throws himself down onto his mat with his arms and legs spread far apart from each other. When Gai Gai lies on one side of him he rolls over to place his hand on her belly, and they both giggle when he feels the baby kick.

Goodnight, baby, he whispers, and turns back over towards Shaye.

It is fully dark now, but Ludi is not sleepy. There has been a hum of excitement in the clearings today, a nervous kind of tension that is tinged with the thrill of what even the smallest child knows to be something of an emergency, and it has made the boys restless. Although they do not understand what is so bad about the high water, and neither can remember the oak grove at all, they know they are going walking, and they know there is a delight and a thrill hiding around every corner on the path, and this makes them wriggle inside their skin, flush with anticipatory pleasure.

Ma? Ludi whispers. Are you awake?

Shaye has not yet even shut her eyes. All over the clearing mats are rustling, voices dancing around each other as they fade. Ludi is not the only person keeping a restless night-time vigil.

Yes, sweet one, I'm awake. What is it?

Why is old Cherl upset?

Shaye is silent for a moment. She thinks of Cherl, striding away from the gathering with his shoulders hunched and angry. He's just worried about the river, but he doesn't want to leave this plenty-time place. He likes it a lot here.

Do you like it here? Ludi does not sound at all sleepy.

Yes my love, I do, but I know we can't stay. We're going to the oak grove where we'll be safe from the river.

Will we see the ocean tomorrow? Is that where we're going?

Shaye turns on her side to face him. She can't see his face but she can feel heat coming from his body. She reaches a blind hand out to his hair and winds a few strands around her finger. His hair is the colour of the hazelnuts when they ripen, not like hers. When he was a baby, this would calm him quicker than anything else. She used to examine each strand of hair closely, looking for any flame-coloured strands hiding among the dark.

We are going to the ocean, but we won't get there tomorrow. We have to walk and walk and walk before we get there, the path is long. She feels Ludi's breathing calm and he burrows further into his mat. Do you remember the ocean?

Ludi sniffs and smacks his mouth gently. Sort of. There's lots of water, isn't there? And we swam with Gai Gai and Sala and everyone, and it was cold but it was nice. Is that the ocean?

Shaye smiles. Yes, sweet one, that's the ocean. And it

smells like nothing else in the world, so fresh and clean. But you can't drink the water, you'll be sick if you try.

Shaye's own mother used to lie with her in the darkness too, describing the ocean. There was something that called to her about it, something salty in her blood that recognised the sea and begged to be reunited.

And it's blue, but not like the sky, darker than that. And you can't see the end of it either, there's so much there. It goes right until it meets the sky, as far as me or you could see.

She thinks Ludi has fallen asleep, but when he speaks again she realises he has only been quietly considering her descriptions, trying to conjure memories of the moon they spent by the coast at lowest sun.

What's at the bottom of it, Ma?

Shaye smiles wistfully into the dark. No one knows, sweet one. It's not like the river used to be, you can't touch the bottom. It's like how you can't touch the sky. The ocean's as deep as the sky is tall.

And that seems to satisfy him. He rolls away from her onto his back to settle into sleep. Shaye listens to his breathing for a while, waiting for him to be settled in sleep before she allows her own eyes to droop. The night sounds dim, and the last thing she hears before she falls asleep is the breath of the ocean rolling across the sand near to where the oak grove stands watching; never still, never silent.

The alarm goes off as the sky turns from black to indigo. Shante turns over, gropes for her tab on the floor and turns the shrill noise off. She connects it back to the network and waits for a second. The machine buzzes, and behind her Grainne gets out of bed and goes into the bathroom. A message from Zeb. !!!!!!!! YES! FINALLY! Make sure you have all paperwork ready at the border and don't worry if they ask weird q's, you've got nothing to hide. Can't wait to see you all.

Locke is stirring in his bed by the window. Shante pulls the curtains open and looks out at the dim sky. Across the road there is a pigeon sitting on the roof of a house she knows is empty, and she watches as it turns to face her. It is perfectly still for a second, and she has the fleeting impression that it is staring back at her as though it knows her. Then it flaps, tumbles off the other side of the roof and is gone, away to its secret hiding places, waiting for the humans to depart so it can be left alone with the abandoned treasures of the city.

She kneels down at Locke's side and nudges his shoulder.

Wake up, she whispers. Time to get up.

He turns onto his side and opens his eyes. It's early, Mum. I'm sleepy.

Sweetheart, it's a special day. She pulls the sheet off his

legs and retrieves Pup, the tattered bear he sleeps with, from the bottom of the bed. She puts it into his limp palm, and his fingers close around its leg. We're leaving soon, and guess who we're going to see?

His eyes are fully open now, but he's frowning. There is the beginning of grumpiness written on his mouth, and he pulls Pup up to his chin.

We're going to see Dad, she says, and there it is, finally, the excitement and the joy and the feeling of leaving the sadness behind.

We're going to see Dad? he asks, and sits up in bed. Really?

She nods, and holds out her hands. Come on, when Auntie Grainne gets out of the shower you can go in, and then we've got to get dressed and go to the train station.

Are we going to go on a train, Mum? Locke asks, in disbelief. Really?

She laughs. She forgot that would be an exciting thing for him.

Yes, we're going on a train, she says, pulling him out of his bed. She hears the hiss of the shower start in the bathroom. And at the other end of the train Dad's going to meet us and take us to live in a new house.

She takes him into the living room and lays out some clothes for him to wear. A damp, grey light peeks in through the living room window, and there is already a neglected feeling to the room, as though the walls have sensed the imminent journey and are retreating from her. The two suitcases are lying side-by-side in the middle of the room, Grainne's finally filled, and Locke stops when he sees them. Can I take Pup with me?

Of course. She hands him a blue T-shirt. Here, put this on.

He takes off his pyjama top and drops it on the floor. Shante wonders if she should pick it up and put it in the full laundry basket, or if it really matters.

Can Auntie Grainne come on the train? he asks. She laughs again.

Of course, she's coming with us. And Granda too.

Locke looks delighted. I've never been on a train before, Mum. He pulls his arms through the sleeves of the shirt.

I know. She gives him a pair of shorts to put on.

Have you ever been on a train before, Mum? he asks her.

Yes, sweetheart, I have. A long time ago. He looks interested.

What was it like?

You'll find out for yourself soon.

The bedroom door opens and Grainne emerges, dressed, her hair wrapped in a towel.

Auntie Grainne! Locke runs to her and wraps his arms around her waist. We're going on a train!

I know! she says, smoothing his hair back from his forehead. I'm excited too.

Shante showers quickly, and fills a small bag with things from the bathroom cabinet; toothbrushes, toothpaste, plasters and paracetamol. She shuts the cabinet door and rests her hands on the sink for a moment. She presses her forehead against the cool mirrored door and closes her eyes. She wants to remember this place, she realises, even though there's nothing special about the black mould around the bath, Locke's toys balanced on the rim and Grainne's lotions and potions lining the shelves by the sink. She remembers when Locke was tiny, when she would occasionally feel smothered by his need of her. She used to leave Zeb with him in their bedroom, come in here and lock the door to bathe not in water, but in solitude. She feels guilty about that now. She won't ever get that time with him again.

She straightens the sheets on both the beds out of habit, and locks the window.

Locke comes into the room.

Mum, can I take some toys with me?

She hesitates, thinking of those birds migrating to happier places with only their feathers and their instincts, and then she picks up his school bag. She unloads the books and the pencil case, and puts them in a neat pile on his bed. She feels a pang at the sight of the books that will never be returned to his school now.

You've got five minutes to fill this rucksack with your favourite toys, she says, and Locke snatches it from her to stuff Pup in there. Five minutes only. Then we need to go and get the train.

A pang of hunger reminds her to pack something for their breakfast. She takes a loaf of bread and a few pots of jam from the fridge and wraps them up in a nylon shopping bag, to get out on the train. She looks back at her kitchen.

Before she knows exactly what she's doing, she reaches out and takes the packet of crackers from the shelf. Unopened, the wrapper still sealed. She considers its weight for a moment. She can't remember buying these crackers, but they might be useful. Good to have snacks as well as breakfast, in case Locke gets hungry. She puts it in the suitcase next to the photo album and takes a box of the compacted fruit bars from the shelf too. She tells herself that she doesn't want to waste this food, that leaving it here to rot would be worse than leaving all her other possessions because there are so many in other territories who don't have enough to eat, but there is a whisper telling her that she should not leave this food behind, that the suitcase is half empty precisely because it was waiting for these things. So she clears her cupboards of everything vaguely edible and packs it all in the suitcase until it's bulging. Packets of rice, two cans of beans, two bags of salted peanuts, dehydrated banana slices, dried apples, biscuits, crisps, corn. Everything. After a moment's hesitation, she packs the water purification tablets she bought during the water crisis two years ago. They were expensive, she tells herself. No sense in wasting them.

She zips both the suitcases shut and stands them up, ready to be dragged out of the door. They look like characters from one of the cartoons Locke likes, faithful little trunks with both legs and wheels that bark and miaow and follow the two main characters wherever they go on their adventures to save the world.

Shante is hitching the lute case onto her back when Grainne opens the door to the bedroom, and pushes Locke into the living room. He's fully dressed, his bulging backpack fastened across his chest. She holds her hand out to him and he crosses the room to take it. As she leads him down the dark stairs, she hears Grainne locking the door behind them, her keys jingling as she puts them back into her bag. Habit, Shante knows that, but she stops on the stairs and lets her eyes shut for just a second, but long enough for Locke to tug at her hand.

Come on, Mum, he says. Dad'll be waiting for us.

Then Grainne's footsteps thud behind her and she has to move again, downstairs and out onto the street to begin her new life. As she lets the front door slam behind them, a fleeting sadness passes across her shoulders. I didn't say goodbye properly, she thinks. Perhaps that will always be her life now, as an exile. Never being able to remember the last time you saw something, never quite knowing which exact moment was your last.

> • <

The porch of their father's building is cool and quiet, the grey tiles on the walls repelling heat and deadening sound. At any other time of day it's alive with coming and going, children kicking a ball against the green tiles and a huddle of people waiting for the lift. Competing smells of cooking usually waft down the stairwell, and with them the echoes of distant music.

This morning it is deserted. The porch remains dark as the gathering light hasn't reached here yet. No cooking, no footsteps, no voices. The building is drowsy, the living beings still breathing slowly in sleep, their warmth huddled in their beds instead of pouring into the dead stones stacked on top of each other.

Grainne presses the buzzer that reads 'Charlie Alcorn, 278' in their father's handwriting. They wait as it rings, then their father's face appears over the videocom, smiling brightly.

Hello girls, lovely to see you both.

Shante feels a rush of relief at the sound of her father's voice, so normal, so welcoming. They might be popping over for dinner, or coming to watch an episode of the manga cartoons Locke likes to watch after school. The buzz of the door opening.

There you go, did you get it? Come right up.

The lift smells as it always does, of disinfectant and urine. Shante thinks of when he first moved here and she carried a bag of his clothes into this box, gagged theatrically and asked him what could be possibly be so wrong with a person that they would pee in the lift of their own home, but her father had given her a stern look and told her that hers was not to judge, but to understand, and that times were hard for being human in.

They are silent as the lift judders upwards. Grainne's bracelets jingle as she taps her thigh. Shante checks her watch; twenty past six. She wants this morning to go even slower, she wants everything in the world to freeze around her while she walks around and examines it one last time, to tighten her life here in her memory.

The lift doors peel open, and they walk down the hallway. Locke tugs at Shante's hand.

Can we stay to watch Diva and the Yeti? He pauses, senses that he needs a stronger argument. Granda likes it too, honestly he does.

We can't stay, sweetheart, we're just picking Granda up and then he's coming with us.

Locke brightens. He's coming with us to see Dad?

Shante nods.

Locke squeezes her hand. Thank you, Mum, and she feels that old wobble in her knees from when he was first learning to speak and said thank you to everything, as though she was some kind of deity dispensing good things from the sky.

Grainne pushes the never-locked door open.

Hi Dad, Shante calls out. We're here. You ready to go?

They turn the corner into his living room, which has a kitchen wall just like Shante's apartment and a bed in the corner. The walls are decorated with hundreds of paper postcards, images of all the parts of the world that he has never visited, all in the shape of a world map. When he picks Locke up from school they sit together on the floor, the old man telling the boy stories about all the different places. When Charlie doesn't know the facts about a picture Locke has pointed to, he makes them up, and those are Locke's favourite stories, the ones he tells her when she comes to pick him up, the ones she catches him re-enacting with the cheap plastic figurines he got last Christmas.

He's sitting on the floor now, his elbows around his knees, looking at his map. Locke goes to sit next to him but he doesn't point to a picture and ask for a story. Grainne walks to the middle of the room but Shante hangs back in the doorway. Her father hasn't packed. Everything is still in its same old place.

Come on Dad, Grainne says. We're trying to get on the ten past eight train north, and if we miss that one we might not be able to get out until later tonight. She looks around for his bags. Where's all your stuff?

Shante feels her mouth become dry and her heart hop. She knows what her father is going to tell them. She should have guessed it. He has always been so stubborn about this place, so fierce in his adoration of the buildings, the skyline, the sluggish river itself, taking them on long walks through different neighbourhoods and pouring the intricate history of the streets into their half-listening ears, so that even now as an adult she will go somewhere and inexplicably know what notable philosopher used to live in a house on this street, why it bears the name it does, and what the pub on the corner used to be called.

You all set to go then? He doesn't turn around from his map to face them.

Dad— Grainne begins, but he holds up a hand to stop her.

It was your mother who collected all these pictures, did you know that? She'd cut them out of magazines and things, kept them in folders labelled by continent and country. Then, when the borders shut and the cities changed their names, she spent hours online relabelling all her pictures so she could track what was what and where all the old monuments were.

He clears his throat. Locke is sitting very still, looking at his grandfather with a cocked head. Perhaps he thinks this is one of his stories, Shante thinks. Perhaps he doesn't understand yet what is going to happen. Perhaps Grainne doesn't either.

I made this wall for her as a surprise, the last time she came out of hospital. You both know that, you helped me set it up. We wheeled her in here, didn't we, and I had the bed turned so she could sit up and face it, and look at it all day long. Oh and we did! For hours, talking about all the places in the world. She'd seen more of them than me, of course.

Charlie sighed. I like to think I gave her a few more months with this wall. Something to live for, something to look forward to seeing every morning.

Dad, come on, Grainne says, a warning tone to her voice. This really isn't the time. Get your bag and let's go.

Well, sweetheart, I've been thinking. He pauses, lets his knees fall outwards so that he's sitting cross-legged, smoothing his hands over his jeans. He looks up at his window, towards the city skyline with its needle skyscrapers. He won't look at them.

I think it's best if I don't come with you girls, he says quietly and there is another short silence where Grainne takes a sharp breath. I think I'll stay here and see what happens, if it's all the same to you.

It's not all the same to me! Grainne grabs his limp hand and tugs at it as though he's a toddler refusing to eat the green sludge on his plate that everyone tells him will make him grow up big and strong. Come on, stop being stupid and let's go.

He pulls his hand away from Grainne's without looking at her. I'm not ready to leave yet.

Please Dad, come with us, Shante says. I know it's sudden, but we're lucky. You might not get another chance.

Grainne tuts, and Shante winces. He's going to dig his heels in now. Don't you dare tut at me, he's going to say. I'm your father, young lady, and I lived for forty years perfectly well before you came along to patronise me.

Charlie turns his head sharply towards Grainne and looks up at her. She bites her lip and shuffles back from him a fraction. She looks like a little girl, trapped in a battle of wills with her father that he will win by virtue of sheer patience.

I was born in this city, and your mother died here. In this very room. This is her final resting place. He waves his arm vaguely towards the window behind him, but Shante knows the picture in his head is not vague at all, he is imagining the pot of ashes that he tipped gently into the river, humming under his breath and sniffing helplessly. Later, Shante had asked him what he had been humming. He told her it was the song that had been playing in the bar when they first met.

I have lived here all my life, and I have been proud to. If this is the end of something, then let it be so. Everything has to end at some time. Everything has to have its winter. Even me.

Shante stares at her father, the delicate folds of skin falling over each other at the corners of his eyes, the wisps of white hair at his temples, the thinning patch directly on top of his head. This is the angel's door, the place where the soul enters, her mother used to say, pressing it gently with the tip of her finger when they were in the bath. This is your direct line to the heavens, girls. And then she would tip her head back and laugh, and Shante and Grainne would laugh too because it was so nice when their mother laughed, they felt as though the whole world broke out into sunlight and nothing could possibly be sad. But their mother never lived long enough to see the hair draw away from the angel's door on their father's head. Shante wonders what she would have said about it if she had, how she might have pressed her finger, or maybe her lips, to that place now.

From the corner of her eye she can see Grainne turn to plead with her, but she doesn't look back. Her vision blurs with tears, the light in the room dims. She steps forward and kneels by her father on the floor.

Listen, Dad. We've got you the visas and everything, all the paperwork's done properly, we promise. You have to come with us. There's not going to be anything left soon. You know that. I know you don't like watching the news, but they're saying the city's going to completely flood. Probably in the next few months when the tides turn.

She hears Locke shift on her father's other side, and she

hopes he doesn't hear everything she says. She shuts her eyes against the prickle of tears.

I know all about that, my love. He hasn't moved from his chair since they arrived in the room. But I'm not going. You girls should, though. Take the boy and go, see your husband, start a new life. Apply for a visitor's permit for me and I'll come and see you. But I can't leave. Not for good. Not now.

Nobody moves. The generator whirs in the cupboard behind the front door and a bike bell rings outside.

Go on, he says. You said yourselves you haven't got much time to catch your train.

Grainne opens and shuts her mouth, an expression of pain hardening her eyes. Then she turns towards the door, grabs the handle of her suitcase and walks out of the flat. Locke watches her go, and Shante watches him. How to explain to him what his Granda wants to do, how to tell him that he will likely never see the old man again?

She stands up and places a hand on her father's shoulder. It is softer than she expected, and it is troubling to her to be so much bigger than him, standing when he is sitting down. She can't remember if she has ever looked down upon him like this before. Whenever she thinks of her father she thinks of him looming over her; her small, clammy hand clasped in his big, dry one, running and skipping to catch up with him as he strides.

Locke leans against the old man's shoulder for a second, and Charlie ruffles his hair. Locke reaches a hand across his body and they share a silent high five, without the slap of palms. This is their greeting and their leave-taking, their private signal that each of them share with no one else in the world. The look of tenderness on her father's face is more than Shante can bear. She turns away and presses the hem of her T-shirt to her eyes.

Bye, Granda, Locke says. We're going to see Daddy, but we'll come back for a visit and we'll see you soon.

Goodbye, little man. You'll be good for your mum and your auntie, won't you?

Locke nods, then stands up and looks at the picture map. Shante presses her lips to the bald spot on top of her father's head, the angel's door, and she wants to whisper a prayer right into that space but there's no time and no words and nothing to do but leave.

Bye, Dad, she says. The words choke her. It doesn't seem right that she says this exact phrase when she picks Locke up from his flat after work, just before she puts down the tab, just before she went to bed as a child. There should be some bigger words for this, she thinks, I need more to say when I'm sure I will never see him again. But those bigger words do not come to her, only the echo of this thin, inadequate farewell, and so she takes her son by the hand and follows her sister out of her father's home, shutting the front door behind her. She finds Grainne outside the lift, her face in her hands, her shoulders heaving with sobs.

Locke breaks his hand from Shante's and runs to his aunt, wrapping his arms around her hips. Grainne lets one hand fall to his head and strokes his hair.

Don't worry, Auntie Grainne, he says. Granda will be alright.

Grainne sniffs, wipes her nose with the back of her hand.

And if he isn't alright, then at least he'll get to see Mimi again, Locke continues, still looking up at his aunt. I reckon he'd like that, don't you think?

Grainne stares down at the little boy. She glances at Shante, who is looking at her son with awe. Who are you to be so wise? she thinks. And then, that is my son, that is my boy, that is the child I carried inside me and fed from my own body and sang to each night. That is my son. She presses the button to call the lift and the three of them listen to it click click click as the carriage clunks up the shaft. She leans forward and presses her lips to her son's head, right at the angel's door, covered in soft black curls.

The lift doors open with a creak and they step inside. And as Shante smells that familiar mixture of disinfectant and urine, she looks around her, trying to brand the details of the lift on the inside of her eyelids the way she did with her bathroom. She's really an exile now. Even the people of her past will only exist in memories like this one.

Nobody wants to be the last to leave the clearing, to see it desolate and mournful, the trees whispering at them to come back; but nobody wants to be first to begin to walk the path either, for fear of what the high water might have brought.

Shaye rolls up the sleeping mats and threads them through the handle she made for the waterskin. She thinks about leaving the mats behind but they were newly woven that spring, and the bulrushes she made them from now lie a man's height under the river. Gai Gai slings another waterskin on her back, where it won't swing into her belly as she walks. Shaye arranges the nut store and the extra cloth and skins inside her pouch, adjusting it so it doesn't poke at her stomach or her breasts. Ludi hops from one foot to the other, watching nervously as everyone gathers up their sleeping mats and picks up the last of the things they'll take walking. She hears the path singing to him, as it is singing to her, but it makes her laugh to see him itchy inside his skin like this.

Keep still, she tells him with a smile. We've a long day of walking yet and you need your legs.

He stops moving, his feet splayed outwards, his thighs straining at his wrap. Gai Gai takes his hand and tips a palmful of nuts from her store into it. He brings his mouth to his palm to suck up the kernels, then sees Reo on the other side of the clearing. He turns to Shaye, his eyes hopeful.

Go and play, Shaye tells him. But stay where I can see you.

He bounds off, hopping over the items the grown ones have laid out for packing, and pulls on Reo's arm by way of greeting. She watches as the boys crouch by a fire pit, scratching at the rocks with thin twigs. When she was a child and they would leave a plenty-time place like this, she would take Gai Gai by the hand and lead her, walking in front of the grown and the elders, feeling important by pointing out everything she could see and making Gai Gai repeat each word.

Sala moves among them all, helping secure waterskins in their loops, advising on which pieces of flint are best to take and which are best to abandon to the river. She approaches Shaye with a smile. Her hair is beginning to glow with the strengthening morning light, and for a second Shaye sees her mother walking towards her instead. Sala gestures to Gai Gai, standing in the shade, swinging her weight from foot to foot with her hands clasped under her protruding belly, and the vision of the dead woman is gone.

It's near her time, isn't it?

Shaye nods. But she's strong, and she's had no troubles yet. She moves her toe into the dirt and drags it across the ground. She is restless, impatient with everyone who is not yet ready to start walking. She looks around the clearing to see who's still packing up. And I'll be with her, I know what to do.

Sala glances at the roving foot and smiles. I've always considered it a blessing, to be born on the path. You were. That's why neither you nor that boy there can keep still.

They both look to Ludi, now hanging off a tree with a mouth full of beechnuts.

Your ma had her first birthing pains as we were coming into a marshy valley. We had a different plenty-time place in those days, and we hoped you'd wait a bit to be born there, but you were too quick for us. There were still a few days of walking left when the birthing began, so the others went on ahead and we joined them later. It was the hottest day since lowest sun, your ma was sweating and panting, seemed like she was trying to get out of her own skin. Then you came, at about moonrise if I remember rightly. Your ma was up and walking by dawn, and that's why you've got the wanderlust woven through each bit of you.

Sala's eyes are clouded with remembering, a gentle smile making her lips dance.

Gai Gai was born when we were settled, though. Your ma didn't move for days while she suckled her, and you were a real treasure. I remember you brought her everything she needed, like you were the ma, and then you took her pouch to go gathering. You stopped playing with the others.

Shaye smiles. She has heard this story before. She remembers her pride at pulling her ma's sling around her and following Sala and the other grown ones to pick what they picked. She remembers shaking away her childish hurt when her ma wouldn't let her poke the berries she picked into the newborn Gai Gai's mouth, and smiles at the thought of Ludi trying such a thing.

Sala watches the packing in the clearing, alert, ready to attend to anyone who needs her help. Shaye follows her gaze, sees almost everyone who was at the meeting last night. Except one.

Sala, the guest – where is he?

Sala sniffs. He left. Began walking just before dawn. She looks at Shaye carefully but she turns away. She doesn't want Sala to know how much she thinks of Marl. She would only shrug and say that there are other men if she would have them.

He was not going back to the oak grove, Sala says. She pinches the space between her eyes, her face drooping with tiredness. Shaye knows she was awake long into the night talking with the guest, and from now until they reach the coast she will be called upon constantly to help, to judge, to mediate. And all that with the worry nagging at her mind: what about this water? Why is it rising? How long will it take to hurt my people, and what will I do when it does?

He is going to find more people, to tell them to gather early in the grove.

Did he say anything about the ceremony?

Sala shifts her gaze away from Shaye's abruptly. She looks back to the tree where the boys are playing. Reo has climbed to the highest branches and is stripping them of their nuts. No. He said nothing about that.

And then she shivers, as though she has been standing too long in the thick shade, and brushes the backs of her fingers against Shaye's arm to take her leave. We have to start moving, she says. Tell everyone that we need to get on the path as soon as we can.

An uneasy quiet falls upon the clearing. A wary look comes into Ayla's eyes, as though she has just happened upon a wounded boar, and Vesti places her waterskin on the ground guiltily, as if she has been caught sneaking berries from an unripe bush.

So you're all leaving, comes Cherl's voice, aggressive and loud. Sala steps towards him, her head cocked to one side. You're all abandoning your home, just like that, because a man with snakes painted on his skin tells you to.

Cherl, pack up a waterskin and your mat. We're leaving soon.

Sala reaches out to him, trying to place her hands on his shoulders, but he rears away from her as though her hands are burning.

Don't touch me! He waves his hands around the clearing, stumbles as he dashes away from her. His eyes are drooping, his wrap askew. He looks as if he hasn't slept at all. You're fooled by that man! You're fooled by the power they say lives in the oak grove. What about the power that lives here, eh? What about our spirits?

The spirits at the oak grove are our spirits too, Cherl, Sala says patiently, but there is a warning note to her voice. And the power that lives here will drown us if we stay.

Maybe we should drown! shouts Cherl, and Sala turns her face away from him. There is a soft intake of breath among the watchers. He puts his hand on the trunk of a withering ash and leans into it. He shuts his eyes, his mouth moves silently. Shaye looks at the two boys by the fruiting beech. Their faces are creased in pity. Cherl says little to them; but sometimes, if he comes across them playing when he is going about his gathering, he gives them the berries in his hands.

What do you want me to do, Cherl? You might want to stay, that's your choice, but I have to think of everyone else. Sala's voice is tight and she puts her hands on her hips, her fingers pressing into her waist. Stay here if you want, find yourself at the bottom of the river come sunrise if that's what you think fit, but don't make everyone else suffer for your own stupidity!

Cherl hawks and spits, but says nothing. Sala restrains a flinch and narrows her eyes.

We're leaving, Cherl. Sala's voice is hard now. Everyone gave their assent except you. If you stay, you'll be alone.

Cherl looks around the clearing wildly. Shaye! Gai Gai! he cries. You can't leave. This is your home, where your mother lived, where your son was born.

The note of panic in his voice makes Shaye's heart twist. She remembers him calling her name when she was small, no bigger than Ludi is now, shouting to her to come and eat as she splashed in the river. She remembers him swinging Gai Gai around and around, giggling, asking her if she had had enough yet, teasing her when she lurched with dizziness and begged for more.

Gai Gai gives a loud sob, and she steps towards him at the same time that Shaye drops her waterskin to the ground. The bulk of Gai Gai's belly slows her down, and Shaye gets to him first.

Ba, we have to leave. You know we have to leave. Come with us. Shaye takes his hand with hers and places the other under his arm. She feels him rest some of his weight onto her, and the sight of him so vulnerable stuns her. Gai Gai kneels in front of him, places her hand on the trunk of the ash too, her fingers stretching towards his.

Come with us, Ba, she whispers. Please.

He is hiding his face, turning it towards the old tree, but Shaye can see the dampness on his cheeks, the wet disappearing into the grey beard.

No, he mutters. I belong here.

We'll come back, Ba, says Shaye quietly, in the same tone she uses with Ludi when he falls and hurts himself. We're only going early, we're coming back, come with us.

He is trembling. Shaye can feel his skin quivering under her hand even though her touch is light. She feels as though something is slipping from her grasp, she wants to dig her fingernails into his skin and drag him with her but the thought makes her recoil. He has the right to refuse, he has not given his assent to move. But Shaye suspects there is something else, some kind of canker that is rotting inside him. He has been retreating from them all for moons now. As the water has crept up the bank, Cherl has become surlier and quicker to temper, given to spending all his time crouching by the bank, staring at the water. Shaye has watched him, wondering what he knows, or thinks he knows. Now she realises that he doesn't know anything at all. That all those long days, he was begging the water for an answer, slowly driven mad by the river's bloated, insolent silence.

Please, Ba, whispers Gai Gai.

And he shakes Shaye off, backs away from Gai Gai, and without looking either of them full in the face he walks away from the clearing. Away from everyone he loves and into the deep forest, following tracks nobody else knows.

Gai Gai sinks her haunches back onto her feet and covers her face with her palms. Shaye watches Cherl leave, her eyes itching. When she can no longer see his silvery head weaving between the branches, she turns to Gai Gai and helps her to her feet. Everyone is watching them, but Shaye looks only to Sala, who smiles tightly. No one speaks, but Gai Gai holds her hand over her mouth, trying to muffle her sobs. Shaye strokes her forearm with one finger, and bends down to pick up Gai Gai's sleeping mat to thread it through the loop she has made in her own waterskin.

Slowly, everyone returns to their preparations, picking up the things they had abandoned when the sight of Cherl made them falter. Now there is nothing left of the settlement they created in the springtime apart from the hollows in the ground ringed by blackened stones where the fire pits were, and flattened patches of leaf mulch where sleeping mats used to lie. By sunrise tomorrow, wildness will already be creeping back to the clearing.

When each person is ready, their possessions comfortably draped around themselves, they turn to Sala, who is leaning on one of the sleek whittled branches from the dismantled looms. Shaye holds Ludi's hand, which is fluttering with excitement, and watches Sala draw a sharpened flint from her pouch and hold it up towards the sky, finally dotted with clouds.

She brings the tip of it towards a finger, and presses until a prick of blood springs from beneath her skin. She squeezes the pad of her fingertip to draw the droplet out, then lets it fall to the ground. The others watch in silence. Brig and Yael move their lips gently, forming the names of the ancestors who might bless their journey, while Gai Gai and Vesti soundlessly say the name of the turbulent river spirit who is forcing them from their home. Some of them, like Shaye, are pleased to be moving on. They feel the path calling to them and are always eager to walk. Some, like Gai Gai, mourn for the settled life of plenty time, and look to this journey with a heart full of stone. But everyone knows this journey is different, that something is stirring in the land, something dark and powerful that they all know will not be sated with only one drop of blood, and that makes leaving all the more bitter.

Sala sucks the finger that the flint pricked, then says the same prayer that always begins a journey.

May the earth guide our feet and the wind our eyes. May the sun warm our hearts and the moon track our days. May there always be water, and always be fruit, may the path ever lead us forward.

And with those words, Sala turns and walks away from the clearing. One by one, her kin follow her, everything they own fastened to them, everything they have left behind buried in the earth for others to find if they choose.

They've had the tickets booked for weeks: four one-way, date-and-time-unspecified tickets north. Shaye went to the northern station and bought them the day after they handed in the paperwork to the woman at the emigration office. She wanted them in her hands, she wanted them as a magic talisman that could whisk her away from this place with a moment's notice.

She had put the tickets in the folder with all their other papers, and most nights after she'd put Locke to bed, she would spread it all out across the floor, making a fan of every document that would save her from the drowning city, running her fingers over all of it, assuring herself that it was still there, that the stamps were valid, that the information was all correct.

Now, as they approach the plaza in front of the station, Shante feels the urge to stop and rummage in her handbag for the precious folder to check the tickets are still there. Twice she almost grabs at Grainne's shoulder to tell her to wait, and both times she stops herself, makes do with checking the zip hasn't come undone and the folder hasn't slipped out onto the road.

An electric tram hisses to a stop outside the station plaza and a few people step off. It's too early for the real rush hour yet, but some people disappear inside the glass office buildings that line the street on both sides.

When the tram moves on again, some pigeons come to sit on the electric lines, all facing the same flickering billboard. This one switches between pixelated naked women and cans of sweating aluminium. The whole street is alive with these animated billboards, flashing with pictures of different things Shante doesn't need or can't afford, but she can't help but look at them anyway, her eyes drawn insistently to the flickering screens. She doesn't need an integrated water filter, a new fruit snack, handbags, shoes, shampoo or a purebred dog, but she'd like to be able to afford them. When we get to Zeb, she thinks, we'll be able to afford a bigger house, a better filter, some new clothes. Their lives have been on pause until yesterday, when the courier delivered those magic talismans to Grainne. When we get to Zeb, when we leave this place, when we're safe from the water again, everything will be alright, she thinks.

As they pass the armed soldiers at the entrance to the station, Shante squeezes Locke's hand. Another thing she's picked up from her mother, that aversion to the men with machine guns in public places. She has a dim memory of her mother crying and breathing hard into a paper bag, perhaps in a park. There are armed soldiers there, on the edge of her vision, and she remembers picking up a stray strand of her mother's hair and winding it around her finger like a kite string, as though that would pull her back to tranquillity. Later, when she was an adult, her father told her why her mother had hated to see those soldiers. Because of crossing the sea in that dinghy, her father said, perhaps thinking of that space on his wall map. She saw some awful things, back then, your mother. She hated to be reminded of it all.

Shante looks up at the high brick arches. It's cooler in here than outside. Their shoes clatter on the tiles and she can hear a distant train engine judder. The last time she was here, she was saying goodbye to Zeb. Locke was waving manically, his arm flagging every so often and then spurting up again when Zeb turned back to blow them a kiss. Grainne strides off towards the passenger desk. They're here. It's finally happening.

When they reach the desk, Grainne does what she usually does and hands over responsibility to Shante. Her face says, you're the oldest, you know what to do, off you go.

She smiles at the middle-aged woman on the other side of the glass partition, and the woman holds out her hand in response.

Tickets, please, the woman says.

Shante slides the tickets into the steel bowl under the partition and keeps her hand resting on the counter. She can't bear to be too far apart from them, they might lose their magic.

The woman pulls her spectacles from a chain around her neck and settles them on her nose.

Do you want to get the ten past eight or the eleven thirty train? the woman asks.

The ten past eight, please.

The woman looks back at the tickets. Shante wipes her palms on her jeans.

Passports and emigration documents please.

Shante slides more of the precious talismans under the partition one by one. Locke's visa, then Grainne's, then her own. Charlie's left in the folder, best not to mention that now.

The woman examines the papers. Shante watches the movement of her eyes across each document. She seems to be reading each line, even the generic bits. She's trying to catch them out. Shante's read about this, the way officials at stations will try to find fault in your documents somewhere so they can deny you entry and make you have to reapply.

The tannoy crackles. It announces the departure of a train to a city somewhere in the west. Shante doesn't want to look at her watch while she's standing right in front of this woman, but if she leans a little to her left she can see the reflection of the station clock in the glass. Seven forty-two. There's time. Don't panic.

The woman takes off her spectacles and lets them dangle by her collarbone.

It's all in order. She slides the tickets, the visas and the passports under the partition and Shante grabs at them. Enjoy your journey.

Grainne takes Locke's hand and they walk briskly towards the platform. Their ticket says they have to board the train at least half an hour before the departure time for a customs inspection, and she can't face the prospect of getting this close for nothing.

There's no queue at the platform, so their bags go through the scanner with no delay. The train is mostly freight, with only one empty passenger carriage. By seven fifty-eight, they are seated at a table seat, their bags stowed in the luggage rack and a loaf of bread on the table, its slices smeared with jam.

Shante sweeps her hand over the plastic surface to gather the crumbs under Locke, and brushes them onto the floor.

There's no one else in the carriage, and so they can be as messy as they like.

Grainne slumps in her seat, one knee tucked up and resting against the table. She puts a slice of bread in her mouth and shuts her eyes, and Shante can see the tension melt from her shoulders. Nothing's been easy for her these past few months. When her boss found out about the asylum application he sacked her, and she's been cobbling together freelance work ever since, trying to put something aside for the future. She wears her heart outside of herself, Shante's always thought, like their mother. Her feelings visible on her face with every turn of the conversation, her triumph and her hurt displayed with absolute candour, every time. Shante's more like their father, everyone's always said. Still and secretive, sometimes with her heart hidden even to herself.

The train moves off with a lurch and Locke presses his nose against the window to look out at the city. His leg is jiggling, his jammy fingers making tiny smears on the glass. Shante leans behind him as they move out from under the high iron arches of the station. She wants to do what Charlie might have done if he were here, pointing out all the landmarks and the oldest buildings, telling Locke when they were built and why, and by whom, but her eyes are blurring with tears. This is the last time she will see her city alive.

They pick up speed and the city becomes a blur of brown and grey. It is easier to see their reflections in the glass than to follow the buildings passing by the window, but Locke doesn't seem to care, and his eyes flicker as he tries to catch a glimpse of each and every building before it disappears.

She sits back in her seat and lets her head nestle into the headrest. Now she realises that she never expected this to happen, even as she was wishing for it and telling Grainne they'd have no trouble and the visas would arrive any day now. She thought she was never going to see Zeb again. When she woke up in the middle of the night to hear Grainne breathing softly behind her and Locke kicking his legs in his twisted sheets in the other bed, she used to wonder what Zeb would do if their applications were denied. Would he come back, try to get a better job and move them to one of the tower blocks with a pump in the basement and solar glass? Or would he abandon them to the sinking city, sending money when he could, telling her there was nothing he could do for them?

She doesn't have to think of that now. She has carried it all off. Charlie's absence is bitter, but she could have foreseen that her father would refuse to leave if she had admitted it to herself. It's her own fault for not discussing the possibility he would stay with Grainne the way they had discussed everything else. She watches the blur of grey terraced houses slip past the window. What would her mother say, if she could see them now? Her daughters leaving their home for a safer place the way she did? But it's not the same, she thinks. Mama got in a tiny boat knowing that most of the migrants who'd been making that journey for decades drowned. We filled in some forms and got on a bullet train. It's not the same thing at all.

The door to their carriage slams behind them and Grainne leans into the aisle to see who is approaching. Shante hears footsteps, but before she can turn around a train guard is standing by their table, wearing the same navy blue uniform as the woman back in the station.

Good morning, he says, smiling broadly. Shante smiles back at him. It makes her feel normal, as though she's taking part in any old transaction that can be undone at any time.

Can I see your tickets and papers, please?

Shante slides the pile out of the folder again. She's more relaxed about giving them away now.

How long is this journey? Shante already knows the answer, she's known since she bought the tickets, but she feels the need to make conversation with this man. Maybe she'll tell him she's going to see her husband, she's leaving this city for good, that her sister's a software programmer, and ask if he knows of any jobs going in the north. If he's nice, maybe she'll tell him about Charlie, ask him if people usually go to visit their friends and family in other cities.

Four and a bit hours, madam, he says, shuffling the pile of documents. He nods to Locke, still pressed against the window. You'll have to find another way to entertain the little one I'm afraid, we'll be going inside the tunnel in a few minutes.

A tunnel? Locke turns around quickly, his eyes wide with delight. A real one?

The train guard smiles. Oh yes. Not as interesting as you'd think though, young man, I promise you.

He places the documents on the table, and his casualness with her magic talismans makes Shante relax. The difficult bit is over now. Only four hours, that's it. By lunchtime she'll be there with Zeb.

I wish you a pleasant journey, and if there's anything you need at all, just press that button over there. He indicates the door. I'm just in the next carriage. Only us lot on this old clanger today, so it'd be no trouble at all.

Thank you, and Shante taps Locke's arm.

Thank you Mister Train, says Locke, and Grainne chuckles. The guard waves and turns back towards his carriage.

Shante unwraps a fruit bar and gives it to Locke just as the view outside the window goes black. Now all he can see is his own reflection and the occasional orange light.

He watches the blackness for a moment, then takes the fruit and sits back on his seat so that his legs swing, not touching the floor.

Why do we have to go through a tunnel?

Because it helps the train go faster. Shante crumples up the wrapper and pushes it into the waste disposal under the table. She knows Charlie has told him all the stories and urban legends about the edgelands, about how all the criminals live there, witches and robbers and child snatchers, the same stories he'd told her and Grainne when they'd been his age. She has no idea what is really out in the edgelands. She suspects it's only wind farms, factories and the occasional prison, but every city has to have its dark and scary places where everybody knows not to go. How will anyone care about the light, if they can see everything they need in the dark?

Grainne has pushed her earpieces in and shut her eyes. Locke is looking droopy too, and she lets him lean against her, pulling his shoulder into the space under her armpit and nestling his head against her breast. There's not much time left of him wanting to snuggle against her like this, she wants to savour it while she can.

She munches a cracker from the packet and shuts her eyes too. She won't be able to sleep, not even with the rocking of the train, but it feels good to rest her gritty eyes and think about Zeb and the new life to come.

She met him when she was playing at a wedding. His cousin's, she remembers. She had been settled in the corner of the dining room, under the window on the other side of the room from the table of food, and it had taken her a while to notice him standing a bit too close to her, staring at her fingers dancing on the strings. What kind of instrument is that? A lute. He frowned. I've never heard one of those before. She smiled. He was handsome, skin a shade darker than her mother's, his hair twisted into thin locks to his shoulders. It sounds like you've time-travelled from another century. She ducked her head to hide her pleasure, and began another piece. At the end of the night, he asked for her number, and she had saved it on his tab with little hope of romance, but perhaps some more work.

She won't send him a message now, she'll wait a bit until they're closer. She doesn't want him hanging around the station at the other end. She drifts into the floating space between wakefulness and sleep, rocked by the gently bouncing train.

He never liked her city. He'd come there a year before he'd met her, to work in a shipping insurance company. From the beginning he told her how wonderful his city was, how there were bike lanes in every street, how every building was panelled with solar glass and the parks filled with cultivated orchards with real, fresh fruit growing on the trees. His parents got visitors' visas and came to see them when Locke was born, and their manners were so impeccable that Shante knew they had never had to shove into a queue for food, or rewire a failing generator when the authority electrician didn't turn up, or dip endless water-testing kits into the sink every time you ran the tap.

Everything will be better there. Locke will go to a better school and Grainne will earn more. She'll get to know other musicians in the city, maybe she could record, join a band, even teach a little. Possibilities, a future, a whole life swells in her chest. She'll apply for a visitor's visa for Charlie as soon as they get there. Maybe when he sees how much better it is, he won't want to leave and they can reapply for him to get residence.

The train is slowing. Shante checks her watch, twenty past ten. She thought this was a direct train, but perhaps it has to stop to unload some cargo. It stops with a screeching hiss that wakes Locke up and he reaches to her, bleary-eyed.

Are we there already?

I don't think so, she says, peering behind her into the aisle to see if the train guard is coming back. We've just stopped for a bit. We'll be going again soon.

She leans past him to look out of the window and sees that they've pulled into an abandoned station, one of the ancient ones from the old slow trains, maybe even from the diesel engines before that. There's a sign on the wall with a place name Shante's never heard before, and torn posters for long ago plays featuring long dead actors. The walls of the station are the same reinforced grey concrete of all train stations everywhere, but this one has little squares of light beaming from high windows. It looks grimy, as though centuries of soot and dust are coating the concrete.

Grainne takes her earpieces out. What's happening? I thought this was a direct train.

Maybe it's a cargo stop.

Locke tugs at her arm. Can we get off and look around?

No. She listens for the train guard's step behind her, but it doesn't come. Stay here. It's going to get going any moment now.

They wait. The music from Grainne's earpieces tinkles faintly until she presses a button on her tablet and it stops. Locke has his nose pressed against the window again, looking at every detail of the old station. The minutes tick by. Shante checks her watch. It's ten thirty-four. Nothing is moving. There are no noises of unloading, no people or machines on the platform.

I'm going to ask that guard what's going on, Shante says. She gets up and presses the red button by the doors to the carriage. She hears the intercom connecting with a crackle, but no one answers. She waits, listening for a voice, but none comes. The intercom disconnects and she sits back down next to Locke. Grainne is sitting tense and upright now, her hands gripping the seat.

No answer. Shante drums her fingers on the table, collecting some stray breadcrumbs on her fingertips. Perhaps I should go into the next carriage and see if everything's alright.

She doesn't move, and neither does Grainne. She waits, listening for movement. The silence is like a smothering blanket, there aren't even any mechanical sounds of hunks of greased metal clanking together or the rasp of plastic sheets of wrapping over the cargo sliding over each other.

I'm just going to have a look in the next carriage. Shante

stands up and brushes her fingertips lightly to get rid of the crumbs. Perhaps that intercom is broken.

Grainne doesn't offer to go instead. She nods, and looks out the window to the abandoned station.

It seems strange that she can get into the guard's carriage by pressing just one button, but the doors slide open for her and she steps into the rubber concertina part between carriages and then presses another for the next set of doors. This carriage isn't like the passenger seating, it has one set of four seats around a table, like in their carriage, and then shelves and shelves of neatly labelled boxes, all held behind glass doors clasped shut. She's looking at the boxes and reading their labels when she sees a shoe sticking out from behind a seat.

The shoe is completely still. There is an emptiness to the carriage, the unmistakable feeling that she is alone and unobserved that reminds her of waiting in the room for her father to come home, after her mother had died. She hadn't been scared then, waiting on her own with a dead body lying in the bed; just lonely.

She leans behind the seat. The guard's neck is twisted at an improbable angle, his face pressed against the wall. She wonders at the force it must take to wrench someone's neck like that, so hard that their spinal cord is snapped and their life over. She walks closer to his body and steps over his back so she can see his face. She crouches to look into his eyes, wide and unseeing. She wants to close them so he can rest easier in his death, but she knows she shouldn't touch him. She holds her hand above his cheek, hovering just over his skin to see if it is still giving off any warmth. None.

She presses the two buttons to let her back into the passenger carriage, and Grainne stands to meet her. Locke pokes his head sideways into the aisle.

Are we going again yet?

Not yet, Shante says, struggling to keep her voice calm. She wants to scream, to punch these carpeted seats and see a satisfying cloud of dust puff from them, souvenirs from all the lucky bastards who have made this journey safely. I need you to do a job for me, are you ready?

He nods.

I'm going to show Auntie something and I need you to stay here and have a good look at this station for me. If you see anyone moving, or anyone comes into this carriage, I want you to scream as loud as you possibly can. Do you think you can do that, sweetie?

He nods. Shall I have a practice scream, just so you know what to listen for?

No, don't do that. Just have a good look out that window.

She turns back towards the guard's carriage and Grainne follows her. Her step falters for a moment, she wonders if she is doing the right thing by leaving Locke there alone, if she should go back and get him, and the document folder too, perhaps the lute, maybe all of their stuff, just to be sure; but she doesn't want him to see the corpse. Her head feels foggy. She stops just before she presses the first button. She doesn't know what to do. This wasn't supposed to happen.

What's going on, Shan? Grainne prods her in the back. Where's that train guard?

Shante presses the button and moves quickly between the carriages. Grainne stops when she sees the foot, lets out a soft groan. She kneels beside him and leans in close to study his neck. She had a summer job in a care home when she was at university. Dead bodies don't bother her.

Do you think he had an accident? Shante asks, knowing that he didn't, knowing that the last thing this man saw was someone who was desperate enough to kill him.

No. Grainne bites her lip and it turns white under the pressure of her teeth. This wasn't an accident.

What happened, then?

Grainne shakes her head. Probably illegal stowaways. Maybe they wanted him to help them get into a city, and when he said no they did this and stopped the train here. They probably didn't know we were here too.

Those pictures she's seen on the news from the aerial cameras, the streams of people moving along the old motorways between cities, their homes under metres of dirty water, their governments fled, their fields and factories flooded. Camped out on city borders, hoping they'll be allowed inside to start their lives again.

That's going to be them now. Stranded in the dead zone between cities, this dead man the only person who could help them. What are we going to do?

Grainne shrugs. I think we're going to have to walk there.

Come on! Shante pushes her fingers through her hair, but her clammy hands feel sticky on the strands. Her head is buzzing with panic, everything is slipping from her grasp. Her stomach is swooping at the thought of how close they came to lying in the carriage with their own necks twisted like this. She remembers that she's left Locke on his own with desperate, dangerous people prowling and dashes back to the gap between the two carriages. Locke is still sitting at their table, his nose pressed against the window.

We're in the middle of the edgelands, Shante says, we have no idea where we are or where we're going, we're illegals ourselves if we get off this train. You can't be serious, Grainne.

Do you want to stay here, wait for someone to come, and explain that it wasn't us who killed this man?

It wasn't us! Shante turns away from the body on the floor. It feels strange to be talking about him while his skin suit is right there. He was a nice man, why would we kill him? We're properly shafted now without him.

And you think that's good enough for the immigration police, do you, who are gagging for arrests to make up their quotas?

Shante takes a deep breath. Grainne keeps up with the news even more than she does, she knows about the refugees and the edgelands patrols and the border shootouts. You're right. We have to leave.

Oh fuck. She covers her face with her hands. She is so stupid. Not two hours ago she congratulated herself on how close she was to being safe, to Locke meeting his other grandparents, to breathing without a weight on her chest again. She told herself she would be kissing Zeb by lunchtime. Fucking stupid.

She shakes her head, balls her fists. Pull yourself together, she tells herself. You have the visas, you have authorised passports. You just need to get there.

Right. Grainne is looking at the train guard's corpse sorrowfully, and Shante puts a hand on her shoulder, pulls her attention away from the wasted life. So we're going to have to walk. Does your tab work out here?

It should do.

Okay. You need to figure out where we are, which direction we need to go in and how long it's going to take us. I'm going to try to get some things together we might need.

What about Zeb?

What about him?

Are you going to tell him what's happened?

Shante pauses. Zeb's no good in a crisis, she's teased him about it often enough. Skin as thin as a butterfly's, she used to tell him when he was in a flap about something or other.

I'll tell him we were delayed, or something. No use in stressing him out.

Grainne nods.

Can you go and sit with Locke? Don't tell him too much. Shante flaps her hand back at the carriage where the little boy sits. Tell him we're having an extra adventure, or something like that.

Grainne turns and leaves. Shante has an urge to cry out and tell her to stay in the carriage with the train guard's body, but she clenches her jaw. She needs her to be with Locke.

She starts to flick the clasps on the stacked boxes, pulling them out and rummaging through the contents. Shit. Should she be touching all these things with her bare hands? When the patrol get here they'll track her fingerprints. Too late now.

She couldn't explain to anyone else what she's looking for, but when she sees something she thinks will be useful in any way, she pulls it out of the box and dumps it in a pile on the floor. A box of matches, a steel container, a ball of string. She doesn't stop to consider why all this is in here or who officially owns it, just adds it to her pile. Then, the holy grail, in one of the larger boxes there's water, bottle after bottle stacked on their sides. She pulls it all out, not thinking about how they're going to be able to carry it. Maybe she'll have to dump some of the clothes, maybe Locke can carry some of it. Never mind. Don't think of that now. Think of the lucky thought you had yesterday. She remembers the way her arm reached out that morning towards the packet of crackers on the shelf at home. She's heard of this, the times when an angel protects you and yours from certain calamity in the future with a strange action in the past. Her mother used to talk about angels, she was old-fashioned like that. She would have fallen to her knees in that embarrassing, passionate way and cried her thanks to the sky, which is where she thought angels lived. But Shante doesn't believe there were any angels hovering in her flat making her fill her suitcase with food. Only good sense, mistrust of the authorities who have been getting so much wrong for so long now, and any mother's desire to protect her child.

She carries it all through into the passenger carriage in several trips, dumping it all on the table.

No one came, Mum, Locke tells her as she rolls the first of the water bottles out of her arms. I looked really hard. It's dead quiet out there.

Good boy. She touches her fingertips to his warm face, needing to feel the life throbbing within him. Can you do me another job now? She drags their suitcases out of the luggage rack, lays them down on the floor and unzips them. Put all this stuff in here. Auntie Grainne will help you make room if it doesn't fit.

Are we going to have an adventure in the edgelands, Mum? He's sitting on his hands and swinging his feet as though they've planned it all for his amusement.

She hesitates. She needs to make it a game, he mustn't be scared. Something like that, although it's not the real edgelands, just a place a bit like it.

She goes back to the guard's carriage to do one last sweep for anything she might have missed. She finds two packets of biscuits and a box of salted nuts. Before she presses the button to go back to the passenger carriage, she turns to look at the body of the train guard.

Thank you Mister Train, she whispers. I'm so sorry.

Grainne has everything packed and their suitcases zipped up again as she comes back down the aisle of the carriage.

Shante gives Locke a bright, false smile and takes his backpack down from the luggage rack. Come on, put your backpack on. We've got to get walking.

She turns to Grainne and lowers her voice as Locke fusses with the straps. Did you work out how long it's going to take us?

Grainne grimaces. I can't get on the network. Shante shuts her eyes, briefly. Of course. She should have figured that out.

I've tried everything I know, even the dark net, but nothing's working. Grainne's face is pale. Maybe there's a blackout, maybe it'll come back on soon. She holds her tab in her hand, the clever lump of silicone now dangling off the web of connections and more useless than anything else they own.

Right. Well, maybe we'll get the network back at some point. Shante is just talking to have something to say. She takes her lute bag from the shelf above their heads and tucks the extra food into it, hoping the packets don't scratch the wood.

Let's go.

She passes the long strap of her handbag across her body then shrugs the lute onto her back. It's useless for the journey, or worse than useless as it's weight she doesn't need to carry, not like the water bottles. But she doesn't even consider leaving it behind.

Ready everyone? She places her hand on the handle of her suitcase and Locke nods solemnly. Grainne puts her tab into her pocket and takes the handle of her suitcase too.

Shante turns around and presses the button on the outside door in the side of the carriage. For a moment it doesn't move, and she pumps at the button, panicking, feeling that the metal is throbbing around her and trying to trap her inside. Then one of the doors slides open leaving a crooked exit, and she steps off the train, hauling her suitcase after her.

The platform has a musty smell of damp concrete and decay. The air is cool and still, it hasn't passed through a pair of living lungs in a long time. There's a yellow line painted along the platform's edge, and Shante steps over it towards an exit sign to her left. Locke trots to catch up and the wheels of Grainne's suitcase roll behind her.

The exit sign points to an alcove with stairs extending up in a square spiral. It's not dark, the very stop of the staircase is open to the sky, the same bright blue as the city this morning. There is fresh, sweet air coming from up there, and Shante takes a deep breath of it. She wants to get to that light, she wants to be out from under the dark ceiling of this cavernous ruin where everything's gone wrong.

She pushes Locke in front of her. You go first. Hold onto the rail and take your time.

They climb the stairs slowly, moving towards the light. Shante's thighs start to cramp, protesting at dragging her weight against the earth, and her hand burns with the friction of the railing. She swaps hands and tries to breathe deeply. Sweat drips down her spine into the crack of her buttocks and her lungs become tight. But they are coming closer and closer to the light with every heavy step and when they reach the top of the stairs, they round a corner and are greeted with a dappled green light.

She squints, cupping her hands over her eyes. So this is the edgelands. It's trees. Gangs of dark trunks and a green canopy of the kind she's only heard about in Charlie's stories. The back of her head prickles and she thinks she feels something move behind her. She spins around; there is nothing there. Only a leaf falling from a branch and drifting lazily to the concrete in the breezeless air.

These trees aren't the type she recognises. These ones are growing haphazardly everywhere, not like in the neat avenues of the city where their trunks sit in the pavement with concrete skirts and their roots submerged beneath the roads. These trees are growing wherever they can find a space. The concrete path they are standing on has cracked with a root growing under it, as though boasting of its power. There have been no human feet stepping on this path for many, many years.

They walk away from the exit to the staircase, along the path. First Shante, then Locke, then Grainne at the back. They don't talk. The silence is heavy, as though there are sounds happening elsewhere but the trees are muffling them. This is what Charlie would call a forest in his stories, a collection of trees so large that you look into them and you cannot see the buildings on the other side, trees gathered together and standing still, as if they had been dancing only a second before they appeared. Perhaps Charlie told her a story like that once, she can't remember now.

She feels as though the trees are watching her walking among them, the knots of their wood like eyes that might blink open to see right to the core of her. They're all one being, staring at the invaders like strangers at a party. A mob, connected with invisible thought threads, breathing as one. A shiver tickles her shoulder blades.

Now there are noises; she was stupid, the trees are not silent at all. The rolling of the suitcase wheels, their footsteps on the grey path. And the sounds of the trees, the murmur of their uppermost leaves rustling in the wind, a bird singing somewhere. The shade of the trees is cool on her face and neck. They smell damp, as if there's just been a heavy rain. She is surprised by how pleasant the smell is, how she almost wants to drink it in. There's a quick whisk of something moving through the layer of half-rotting, brown old leaves on the ground. Shante's eyes flicker to it but she is too slow to see it. A squirrel? A fox perhaps.

She walks along the path because she has nowhere else to go, and because if she stops walking she will fall to her knees and begin to sob, and she cannot do that in front of her son. She dreads the look of confusion on Locke's face when he sees that she doesn't know what to do. Keep going. Keep moving forward. Perhaps it will be the end of the trees soon.

This is the wrong thing to do. She doesn't belong here. She should take them back to the station and wait for a patrol, take their chances with the police. She fumbles in her handbag for her tab, pure habit. She's used to doing this a hundred times a day at home, running her thumb across the screen to see if Zeb's messaged her, if Charlie's sent her a picture of something he's found interesting, if there's an update from Locke's school. She touches her tab like Locke touches Pup, unconsciously, greedily, the feeling of the smooth screen under her fingertips calming her. She swipes her thumb across the screen, and it lights up but doesn't offer her any pings. Disconnected from the network.

She feels it twist her guts much more than when Grainne told her that her own tab wasn't working. She's bereft now, sliding the silent tab back into her handbag, alone. Zeb won't know what's happened to them. She told him they were coming today and now they're out in the edgelands, untraceable, unmoored from everything in the world, moving through these stubborn trees. Something in her feels untethered, an anxious hum of loneliness settles in her stomach.

The concrete path is beginning to slope upwards, making a kind of bridge. She notices the strange forms in the middle of the trees below them. Buildings, some of them two or three storeys high, grown over with trailing plants and vines and flowers drooping from in between the bricks.

Now the path is bordered by rusted railings on either side of them, some of the poles missing to make large gaps. She imagines Locke stumbling and falling through one of them and turns back to him. He is gazing at the trees in wonder, each thumb hooked through the straps on his backpack. He turns to her and smiles shyly.

Hold onto the railing, she tells him. I don't want you to fall.

She's glad to be going upwards. The trees are oppressive, crowding her. She wants to see a horizon, maybe they can get high enough to see where this forest ends. She quickens her pace, bends her thighs into each trudging step. She's already tired. Walk all the way to the north? She can barely cope with this gentle slope.

The path turns left at a right angle, it seems to have been designed geometrically. She's at eye level with the shorter trees now, gaining in height on the taller ones with each step. The path turns left again, perhaps it's going in a circle. She turns back but she's already lost sight of where it was in the trees. Looking back is worse than looking forward, the terror on Grainne's face, Locke's determined frown. She can't see any trace of the path or the old station behind her at all. It's like the forest is creeping behind them and brushing away their footprints so they can't go back.

A right turn, then a section of the path with no trees on either side of it at all. Just the concrete and the railings, suspended in mid-air. Shante blinks. Perhaps this is all a horrible dream she's having on the train, one of those that wakes you with the feeling you have something urgent to do, something that you discover was only a fragment of your imagination tricking your senses.

She walks forward and hears Locke's steps behind her. The trees are at her eye height now. With a shaking hand, she reaches for the railing. She leans out to see what's below this floating pathway and is shocked to see a road.

Its grey surface is cracked with weeds, the white lines faded to almost nothing. There's a rusted partition in the middle between the two directions, a vigorous weed with a purple brush at the top of each thick stem. It's tumbledown and tatterdemalion, but it's recognisably a road. Her heart jumps to see something made by humans, evidence that they are not the only ones with heartbeats who have ever set foot here.

The metal is warm from the sun, giving off that singed welding smell like cars in the midday heat. Locke rests his chin onto the railing beside her, and she sees Grainne take out her tab. She waves it around, swipes a few times.

Anything?

Grainne shakes her head and puts the tab back in her pocket. No. Still not connected. I have no idea where we are.

They look out at the road, a lazy breeze puffing at a few twigs on the concrete. Shante imagines cars speeding up and down this very track, three lanes of traffic on each side shooting under this bridge at all times of the day and night. Those long ago people couldn't know that one day their road would be taken over by weeds and choked by trees on each side, last year's leaves scattered where their wheels used to turn.

Do you think it follows the railway line? Shante asks.

Grainne moves her head from side to side. It could do. Dad told me something like that, I'm trying to remember. Something about always building roads and railways on top of old routes. She stares along the track, as far as she can until it curves to the left. We should follow it.

Shante nods. It's their best option. It's a bit too open; if any of the deranged criminals who are said to roam the edgelands come across them, they will have nowhere to hide. But the alternative is to walk through the trees, trying to stay in a straight line, wondering where on earth they are wandering.

So which way then? she asks. Grainne turns to look behind them, where the road extends in just the same way, curving to the left again and out of sight.

It's a fifty-fifty chance, a binary problem. Grainne looks both ways, then up to the sky.

What's the time?

Shante looks at her watch. Quarter past eleven. Grainne nods and squints up at the sky again.

We should go that way. She points behind them. I think that's north.

Are you sure?

No. Grainne looks helpless for a moment, like a little girl who has lost the adults she belongs to. She shrugs and looks back to the sky. She points to their right. I think that's east because it looks like the sun rose over there. She turns to face the other side of the old bridge. So that must be north.

Shante nods slowly. We need to get down there then.

Grainne takes the handle of her suitcase and continues across the bridge. Locke follows her. They cross over the old road and find themselves on a path sloping downwards again. They descend once more to the tree level, and Shante starts noticing the movement of the forest. The whispering of the leaves as they move, a flurry of wings as a bird takes off from a branch at their approach, as though the trees are welcoming them. The path turns sharply to their left and keeps sloping, and Shante tries to keep an awareness of which way they decided to walk along the path. She's no good with directions, Zeb used to tease her about it. Couldn't find your way out of a plastic bag unless your sister's with you, he told her once when she was an hour late for a party. Now she thinks the path is behind her, and she holds onto the thought, chanting it silently.

Grainne stops and peers over the edge of the railing. I think we can get down here.

She swings one leg and then another until she's sitting on the metal bar, and then she jumps off. There's a thud and a scraping of leaves, and then Grainne's head appears again by their feet. Locke claps his hands and grabs onto the bar too, trying to swing his leg high enough to get it over the railings, but Shante pulls him back by his T-shirt.

No you don't, she says, her hand resting on the back of his neck. Wait for me to help you.

Chuck the suitcases down here, Shan, she calls. It's really soft, nothing will break.

She lifts Grainne's suitcase onto the railing and balances it there. Do you still know which way to go on the old road?

Grainne laughs, and for a moment everything feels normal again, and Grainne is just teasing her about something everyone knows she can't do very well, and Shante is being too bossy and worrying about things that don't matter at all.

Come on, Shan. I know which way we're going. Get the suitcases down.

Shante pushes the suitcase over the railing and it lands with the same splash of leaves. There's something liberating in it, something careless that touches hysteria. Nothing is the same here, out in the edgelands, the same rules don't seem to apply.

Shante pushes her own suitcase over the bar, but she keeps the lute on her back. She takes Locke by the hand to a spot a bit higher up where there are vertical bars missing. Grainne follows them and holds out her hands. Locke sits down on the path with his legs swinging over it; Shante holds him under his arms.

Auntie's going to catch you, alright? She knows she's making a bigger fuss than there needs to be, he probably does more dangerous things than this when he goes to the playground with Charlie after school. But Grainne's arms only reach to his dangling feet, and scenarios of him hitting the ground and hurting his legs, or falling and smacking his head on a gnarled root flash through her mind. Grainne calls, Ready! and she loosens her grip on him. Her heart rises to her mouth.

She lets him go, and sinks to her knees to watch him fall. Grainne catches him with a loud puff and she staggers backwards. Locke whoops as he scrambles to his feet.

Come on Mum, jump! he calls up at her. It's so much fun!

She jumps from the same place Locke did, and feels the strings of the lute jangle in protest as she lands on the crisp layer of leaves. Grainne has already begun walking, dragging the suitcase with both hands over the ground.

It isn't far to the road, Shante can see the place where the trees thin from where she landed, and she follows her sister under the concrete path, around the mossy pillars that support it right to its edge. Grainne has stopped, waiting for Shante to catch up.

It's this way. Grainne points in one direction on the road, and Shante has no idea if it's the same way she said earlier, Locke jumping has wiped her determination to hold the direction in her mind, but she has no better ideas so she joins Grainne on the road. The surface feels unexpectedly hard under her feet after only a few minutes of walking on the soft covering of soil in between the trees, but now there is the familiar smell of hot concrete and this comforts her. It isn't a nice smell, not compared to the fresh smell of the leaves in amongst the forest, but it's one that she knows. It tells her that the wild has not yet taken over.

Shante steps out onto the road in the direction that Grainne pointed. One step, another, the wheels of the suitcase tumbling behind her. She veers out into the middle, towards the steel bar separating the two sections, out of the shade the trees cast. She has the same feeling she gets when she is about to start playing a new, difficult piece. Opening the sheet music in front of her, propping it up on the stand, glancing through its first few bars to see what kind of thing she's up against. A journey of a thousand miles starts with a single step. That's what Charlie used to say when they complained that something was hard, they couldn't do it, there wasn't any point in starting if they knew they couldn't finish. Just take the step, she hears him say in her head. Then another. Good girl. There you go, now you're walking.

Sala leads them through the forest, following a wide track bordered by beeches, until they reach higher ground and can walk along a ridge of elms which follows the course of the river. They walk against the unnatural current, still flowing in from the sea and higher again than the day before. It smells so ripe and salty Shaye can almost taste it.

Nobody knows how the path that leads to the ocean was made. Shaye has heard stories of giant people who lived long ago and walked the forests just as they do. Some of the stories tell that these giants commanded so much respect from the trees that the trunks would jump out of the way when they passed, and that is how the path was made. Sala tells this story, but on the night of the full ancestor moon she also talks of all the people who came before who walked those paths and wore a muddy groove into the forest with the weight of their feet. Shaye has always wondered why the path should pass exactly this way and not another way, but no one has ever been able to tell her. It is so, Sala said once when she was a girl. Why is the leaf green and the fox sly?

As she walks, she glances at the river from time to time. She can see it between the trees, the light glinting from its muddy surface. She remembers when she fell from a spruce when she was young and hurt her ankle. It grew fat and purple, and her mother fussed at it with poultices of yarrow and comfrey. She knew it hurt, and she knew that she should not test it with her weight, but as the moon passed she became impatient. She would stand and try to walk a few steps, just in case a miracle had occurred and she was completely healed, but each time she groaned in pain and ended up sitting down with a thud. She is looking at the river like that. As if she hopes it will be healed by magic in between her glances.

For Ludi and Reo, there is an atmosphere of celebration. They loop around the grown ones like starlings in the sky, running and shouting at their secret games that their mothers do not ask about. Occasionally Rilk succumbs to the temptations of childhood and runs with them, laughing and shouting as though she is not almost a woman already. The little boys are not sure why everyone is sad, but the freedom of the path has infected them and they feel like dancing.

But soon the boys grow tired of running and jumping and skipping, and their steps become heavier. They slow to an ordinary walking pace, gazing at their mothers every so often with a faint longing to climb into the slings they left behind some frosts ago. They strip blackberries from bramble bushes as they pass them, and jump to catch a spray of rowan berries the colour of flames whenever they come across a low tree in fruit. They talk about the river, about the stones they find, about who can throw this slightly curved stick the furthest. Shaye and Ayla only attend to the boys with half an eye, looking to check what they pick from afar. They have withdrawn their attention from the children towards their worry.

Vesti and Gai Gai are spinning as they walk. They have pulled out their spindles and tucked the bottom of their combing paddles into their girdles, their fingers dipping in and out of their waterskins to moisten the thirsty nettle fibre. It comforts Shaye, to see thread whirling into being, creating something strong and ordered from the mess of fibre on the paddle. Perhaps she'll spin too, tomorrow or tomorrow tomorrow. She finds it hard to be unhappy when she's spinning. Her thoughts begin like the lumpy green tangle, and as she begins to tease the fibres into one long line of yarn her muddled feelings straighten out, placidly coiling at ease just like her thread.

Shaye walks at the back of the group, mostly alone. Sala turns around every now and then to seek her eyes, to ask if all is still well. Shaye returns her concerned looks with a smile and a slow nod of her head. It is an honour to walk last, but it is a burden too. She has to watch for anyone becoming too slow, make sure the children don't wander off, and pick up anything that's dropped. She has to listen for the padding of a lynx, or the scuffles of a boar, and raise the alarm. If their group of walkers were a beast, Sala would be its whiskers, twitching in the air as it creeps forward; and Shaye would be its tail, delicately undulating to keep the balance of the whole being just right.

The clouds have been getting darker since sunrise, and now they drop their burden. Droplets of rain begin to pitter-patter noisily through the canopy. The water sparkles as it drips from leaf to leaf, and Ludi and Reo delight in taking one of the droplets onto their fingers and watching its tension melt into their skin. The ground beneath their feet becomes damp, and the air begins to smell clean again.

Everyone removes the waterskins from their backs and stops walking to hold them under the wet leaves, patiently collecting the drips from their tips. Shaye fills her waterskin to the very top. She doesn't want to give Ludi any of the river water to drink unless there is nothing else. It hasn't made anyone ill yet, but everyone is uneasy now. They think it is only a matter of time before something foul in the silt poisons someone's blood.

It is a relief at first, to feel the air cool and the pressure of the cloud blanket lift, to breathe the damp green scent of the forest drinking deeply of the streams of water dripping between the grooves of the bark; but then Shaye remembers the river. She looks at it uneasily, a muddy snake slithering past her in the wrong direction, stripped of the proper undulation of its tides. Silently, she begs it not to rise further. And then, full of shame, she begs the sky to stop the rain, even though she can feel the delight of every living thing in the forest at the slaking of their long thirst.

I wish it wasn't raining, says Gai Gai, and Shaye is startled to hear her own thoughts echoed. Gai Gai has her hands clasped under her belly, holding up the weight of the baby. She's dropped back from Vesti and put her spindle away in her pouch. Although we need it.

Shaye murmurs her agreement.

Do you think he'll be alright? Gai Gai asks, her voice lowering to a whisper. No one will speak of Cherl now, they would not even like to hear his name spoken. He abandoned the group, so they have abandoned him.

Yes, Shaye says firmly, and she means it. He's doing what he thinks is best.

Gai Gai pauses, and Shaye looks at her, shoulders straining to hold her weight back, face damp with sweat, lips thin and white with the effort of walking. He won't be there when we come back, will he?

Maybe. I hope so.

He'll never see the baby.

Shaye is silent. She imagines Cherl, alone in the clearing when the frosts and then the snows come. She imagines him trying to keep a fire alive while looking after his traps and digging for roots, all on his own, no one to share the work with, no one to give him anything from their pouch if he is hungry. She imagines him huddled under a fur, ice crystals forming in his beard, shouting out the old songs and stories just to hear a voice, and to keep the beasts away.

She cannot answer Gai Gai, and there is nothing more to say. A chill guilt spreads across her back, and she turns around, expecting Cherl to be standing behind a tree, a fierce look of blame directed at her. She wonders if he knew how much she wanted to go walking, how much he had guessed after what the guest had said about the hunting party. He never liked Marl much. Gai Gai used to laugh when she said that and say that Cherl never liked anyone much, but Shaye noticed the narrowing of his eyes whenever Marl spoke, and she knew what it meant.

The rain has passed, and clouds are drifting away in fat white clumps to reveal the sun beginning its descent towards the horizon. A chill whispers through the damp air and Ludi creeps back to her side. He's eager for more food than the occasional bramble bushes can provide. Shaye gives him a handful of nuts from the store in her pouch, and brushes the dirt from a garlic mustard root for him. Gai Gai is nibbling at one too, picking the fine hairs from the moon-like tuber and crunching it loudly between her back teeth.

Will we be there by sundown, Ma? Ludi asks between bites.

No, sweet one, Shaye says. We've got a lot more walking before then. She sees a clump of chickweed and bends to pull it from the ground. She picks the mud off between her thumb and forefinger and shares it between Ludi and Gai Gai.

How much walking?

Oh, many sunrises. It depends on how quickly we walk and whether there is enough to eat along the way.

Ludi considers this for a while. How will I know when we get there? Shaye stops to tug another root from the ground, rolls it between her palms to rid it of most of the dirt, then gives it to Ludi.

Do you remember I told you about the sea? Ludi nods. Well, when we get there, you'll smell it, and you'll see the big blue, like I said, and you'll start to feel sand beneath your feet.

Ludi crunches his root. Reo said we're going to do dancing and singing for the spirits.

Shaye smiles. He's right. She reaches for his face and swoops his hair back. His forehead is sticky with drying sweat and his cheeks are pink.

Is it because of the river?

Yes. Shaye hesitates. It's because the land and the river are sick, and the spirits need us to attend to them.

The land is sick too? Ludi finishes his root and tosses the leaves to one side.

If the water is sick then everything has become ill, or will be soon. Everything in the world is made of the same spirits, so even if only one of them is not thriving, it is as if they are all dying.

Ludi nods his head thoughtfully. Shaye dreads more questions, as she doesn't know how to explain the river's bloat even to herself, but Ludi says nothing more. She gives him another pile of nuts and they occupy his tongue for a while.

The pace of walking is slowing, and nobody is talking anymore. They are tired; from where she walks at the back of the group, Shaye can see that everyone's feet are heavy. Yael is trying to disguise a limp; Reo is hanging onto Ayla's arms and dragging his feet in the mulch. Shaye's own feet are sore too, and there is a dull ache in the small of her back which she can't stretch out because of the way she's tied her waterskin.

Brig, walking just behind Sala, stops suddenly in the shade of a young alder. Shaye watches her long grey braid swing as she raises her arms.

Sala! she calls, and everyone stops as though their names have been called too. Brig throws her waterskin to the ground. Enough walking! I will sleep exactly here tonight. I don't care where you all go, but I tell you I won't move another step along this path until sunrise tomorrow.

Shaye smiles. Brig can always be relied upon to be the first to say she wants to stop walking, and it makes them all feel as though this is a normal journey to the oak grove or back again, one where they would take their time and sing as they walk.

Brig says it's because she's the oldest, and when they're all grey and achy like her they'll know when to stop walking and bed down for the night too, but the other elders laugh and say she's always been lazy. But Brig's decision to stop walking frees everyone else to rest too, and nobody hesitates to unpack their waterskins, now mostly empty of the rainwater, remove their pouches and sink onto their haunches in relief. Ludi comes to hover by Shaye, waiting for whatever she might give him to eat. He sits with his chin resting on his knees, eyes heavy with sleep. He takes the root she gives him and chews on it.

My feet hurt, Ma, he complains.

Everyone's feet hurt, Shaye replies. We've been walking all day. You'll get used to it soon. But she sits Ludi down to inspect the soles of his feet. She checks he has no thorns stuck between his toes and presses the pads of his heels, still so soft, but hardening each day.

Dusk is settling, and Shaye rolls out three sleeping mats side-by-side at the top of the ridgeway. Gai Gai sinks onto hers gratefully, pressing the heels of her hands into the arches of her feet.

If you think your feet hurt, you should try carrying what I'm carrying, she tells Ludi.

I can take your waterskin tomorrow, Gai Gai, says Ludi. It won't be too heavy for me, I promise.

Gai Gai smiles and reaches out a hand to stroke his hair.

No, sweet one, I can carry my waterskin fine by myself. You concentrate on collecting lots of nuts for your Ma and me. That's your special job when we walk tomorrow.

Ludi nods seriously, and lies down on his side facing Gai Gai.

I will. I'll find loads for you and Ma to eat, you'll see.

Shaye likes sleeping out in the open, where the canopy of highest branches does not obscure her view of the sky. It is a clear, still night, and she lies on her back watching the light fade and the stars appear in the blue-black sky. There are only a few ruffles and whispers. They are all too tired from the day's walking. Shaye's own legs feel heavy, her skin buzzing faintly. She stretches along the mat, her heels pushing into the ground, and listens to Ludi and Gai Gai's gentle snores.

Shaye lies with her eyes open to the darkness for a while, watching the stars. Mice scuffle in the undergrowth and bats' wings flutter as they scare from a high branch overhead.

But then a closer sound catches her attention, something scratching just by her head. She holds her breath to listen better, but all she can hear is the thumping of her heart. She hears the scratching again, louder than the banging of her pulse, and she fights the urge to fling herself onto Ludi. Perhaps a lynx has come out of the deeper forest, she thinks, perhaps the animals are scared of the river too. She hears the scratching again, the sound of claws on her mat now. No, not a lynx, for a cat would be quieter. A fox maybe, or a hare.

She hears the creature breathe and snuffle, and slowly, as gently as she can, she rolls over onto her front, away from Ludi and onto the forest floor, and stares into the twin star eyes of a badger.

She blinks, but that is the only part of her body that she moves. She is lying uncomfortably on her arms and they begin to tingle but she daren't shift her weight off them. She doesn't know where this badger's young are, and she doesn't want to find out by moving too quickly and scaring her.

Hello, friend, Shaye whispers.

As if given permission, the badger shuffles forward and places her nose to the ground, sniffing at the mat.

I've got nothing to give you, she says softly. I have to keep it for my own boy.

The badger raises her head again and stares at Shaye. She looks sad, and Shaye wonders if she is worried about the river too, if maybe their sett has already been flooded out.

Go back to your babies, Shaye says. We're all asleep here.

The badger doesn't move for a long time, and Shaye's heart begins to trip again. She cannot see if the creature is fat or thin, how shiny its fur is, how hungry she might be. She can only see the eyes, fixed on hers. A pair of mothers awake in the stillness of night.

The badger's eyes disappear into blackness as the animal turns her face away, and Shaye listens to her shuffling feet get quieter as she moves off. She stays in her cramped position, a little on and a little off her sleeping mat, until she is sure the badger has moved away into the night and is not planning to return. The pressure of her body has numbed her arms, and it is starting to hurt.

She turns onto her back as quietly as she can and gazes at the sky. She places a hand on her chest to calm her heart and wriggles her fingers to bring the feeling back. Her face is hot, as if she has been running. She cannot shut her eyes now. She is too alert and listening for the sounds of stray animals, wondering what else, more dangerous than a badger, might be displaced because of the high river.

The moon is just fatter than waxing crescent, and as if the sight of it reminds her body what it should do, she feels a prickle of discomfort tug at her belly. She will bleed tomorrow, or tomorrow tomorrow.

When this moon swells to its greatest shape, it will be the thunder moon of plenty. Then they will have a whole other moon cycle to reach the oak grove, before the ceremony on the darkest night after the ancestors' moon. She imagines waking up the morning after the ceremony to find the river shrunk to a trickle, all the many people gathered at the mouth of the river weeping with joy, falling to their knees to kiss the earth and thank the spirits for saving them. She thinks about how she will sit on the sands with Marl during the frosts, making nets, showing Ludi how to cast them far into the water. She thinks of the three of them scrambling over the rocks at low tide, sucking sea creatures from their shells, collecting long strands of kelp to lay out along the beach for drying. She imagines them walking back along this path when the hungry moon rises full, Marl hoisting Ludi onto his shoulders when he gets tired, everyone fat enough from the time spent by the ocean for the men not to have to go hunting. She hears the songs and stories around the fires they'll set along the way, transformed by the deep timbre of the men's voices added to the women's. She sees them returning to their plenty-time place just as the blackthorn is blossoming, setting up a loom again, eating the young sorrel that Ludi will bring her. Then she imagines Marl coming to her, exposing the pale veins on the insides of his wrists again, and her stomach swoops with joy. She sees him leading her away from the fire and pulling her down on top of him.

She falls into a restless sleep, finally, and the gleam of the badger's eyes fades away. Her fingers stretch for the body of a man who is still far away, her heart full of the hope that he finds his fingers longing for her too.

> • <

They walk for many sunrises. Shaye walks at the back of the group each day, sometimes with Gai Gai, and sometimes alone. Whenever Sala turns to check on her kin walking behind her, she catches Shaye's eye and cocks her head to ask the wordless question: are we alright? And each time, Shaye nods her head slowly to answer yes. We are yet.

Each sunrise is a touch colder than the one before. Most of the time a misting rain tumbles through the canopy and Shaye walks with her waterskin open and held in front of her. The ash leaves are starting to grow patches of orange, but they are not falling yet, and underfoot is only the soft mulch from the falling season before, and the occasional early acorn she picks up and adds to the nut store in her pouch.

She stops for a moment whenever she sees spongy patches of moss, spreading over dampened boulders or entwining with the bark of a tree. She brushes it off and stores it in her pouch, and when the expected bleeding comes, she places it inside her wrap. She buries the bloodied moss in the soil so the animals can't get at it, like footprints she's leaving behind her on the path. The blood of her womb, returning to the womb of the world.

She prefers to walk alone and have time to think. Ludi runs back to her now and then with a handful of orange cap mushrooms or a sprig of rowan berries. Reo brought Sala a sprig of rowan on the first day of walking, and she praised him for bringing good luck upon their journey. Now the boys grab whatever rowan berries they can find and bring them to the grown ones. Shaye finds the fruits too sour to eat all in one go, but Ludi is so proud when he finds them that she has to eat whatever he gives her and smile her pleasure, even as she wants to screw her face up.

She remembers the spring when Ludi was only just walking, how she left him with Gai Gai to jump the fire at the Bel ceremony with Marl, then disappeared into the thick undergrowth to press her aching body to his and await the sunrise together. Then the next spring, when Ludi's babble was starting to shape into words, they jumped it again, but there was already something distant in his eyes when she came to him. He often went on small hunting trips with other men, staying away from the plenty-time place for as much as a moon. And when he came back, he would spend long days whittling and carving, with no time for her. She began to discern a restlessness in him. When she spoke to him he answered curtly. He did not speak to others any differently to how he spoke to her; if anything, he reserved any drop of affection he could muster for her and Ludi, and snarled at all the others. He showed his wrists to her less and less, and when he took her into the darkness he was no longer playful, no longer delighted by the folds of pleasure between their bodies.

He let her anoint him before he left for the last hunt, the one that none of the men returned from, but he did not meet her eye. She thought then that it was because he was itching to get away into the trees, longing to scent a doe's fear and bathe his hands in his kill's blood. But now she wonders if it had something to do with the river.

But after the ceremony she will have her man back, and the thought of it slides over her body like she is slipping into the cool ocean. She floats on it so that she barely notices her feet moving over the roots and the occasional stones. She has to blink to concentrate again, to look for stray nuts or seeds, or even some shy plants bearing edible leaves to fill her belly as she walks.

As she walks she lets her mind bloom with imaginings of what it will be like, next spring when the men will return with them to their old place of plenty, and she will jump the Bel fire with Marl again. He will smile again. He will take Ludi's hand in his own and they will walk off into the forest to check on their traps and climb the higher trees. Perhaps Cherl will still be there, she thinks, perhaps he will have survived the frosts and be waiting for them.

She can hear a blackbird singing at its mates above the noise of footsteps and conversations, and if she hangs back from the group and lets all the talking fade ahead of her, she thinks she can even hear the soft wingbeats of the swallows, flitting around the sky before they leave their own plenty-time places to escape the coming frosts. Shaye has always wondered where those birds fly away to when the nights begin to draw in. When she was a child, her mother told her that they spent the winter in a land where every single tree groaned with berries of all the colours of the rainbow, and the little birds ate them all up until they were so fat they had to sleep for at least a moon, waiting to become light enough to be able to fly back to where it was plenty time again. When Gai Gai was born and dedicated to the owl spirit, Shaye was jealous. She thought that meant the baby would grow up with wings, and would fly away to that other land without her. It was only when Gai Gai began to walk on her legs like everyone else that Shaye began to love her.

When the thunder moon rises almost full, Sala tells them they will stop walking for a while. They will stay in this place to fill their food stores again and rest their bones.

Brig and Yael murmur their appreciation at the place Sala has chosen to rest; a patch of thinner forest, where there are pools of sunlight reaching the ground. Butterflies dance in the slanted rays of the late sun, piercing the layers of leaves, and the boys chase after them, creeping up on them as they perch on the ivy flowers and the feathery petals of old man's beards, with their painted wings folded away. Reo finds a pair of damson trees laden with fruit so ripe it falls from the branches with a thud. The boys sweep huge armfuls of sweet purple flesh into their arms and tip the fruits into Shaye's lap, leaving sticky trails of juice all over their skin.

Brig takes her fishing net from her pouch and gives it to Rilk.

I want eels, you hear me! she calls after them. Get some proper meat for the babies in these bellies!

Sala begins to twist her spindle stick to create an ember, and Shaye prepares a bundle of kindling and sets it beside the stones that mark out a firepit. She stands up and moves away from Sala. Fires can be shy and do not like too many eyes on them as they are trying to birth. She directs the boys to the patches of dandelion leaves.

Not the ones in the sun, do you hear me? she tells them, over and over again.

We know, Shaye. Reo rolls his eyes and Ludi giggles.

They're too bitter and nobody will eat them. Only pick the ones from the shade.

Shaye goes to the river and helps Rilk drag the net in. The river is thick with eels, as Brig knew it would be, and Rilk is slipping on the silt as they writhe inside the net, lashing their tails to be free.

Ma will be pleased, Rilk pants as Shaye grabs the other end of the net and hauls. She loves eel meat.

Shaye gathers her end of the net and lifts the eels from the water, watching their flickering tails become still.

That'll be enough for tonight and for smoking, Shaye says. Let's get them on the fire.

They drop the writhing net next to the growing fire and Shaye tests her flint on her thumb. She takes an eel from the net and runs her hands over it. It smells clean, of river dirt and reeds. There is no sign in this animal of the disease that afflicts the water.

She slices her flint along the black belly and cuts around its head, breaking through the backbone with a quiet crack. Then she tugs at the head, her thumb covering its slimy, sightless eye, and pulls out the spine and guts. She excavates the belly with a finger then hands the flesh to Sala, who arranges it on the fire. The clearing begins to smell like home.

Later, in the gloaming time, they all sit together by the fire. Smoke drifts towards the sky, listing slightly to the north, and Sala passes around the white flesh of the eel, the dandelion leaves and damsons. Every so often, Ayla or Sala pluck the nuts that have been picked along the path from their roasting pit and place another handful in. They leave the roasted ones to cool, then tie them tightly in a bundle. It is a tedious, watchful job, tending to the nut stores, but when the hungry days come with the frosts and everything is barren, the soot-blackened fingers and the occasional burns are forgotten.

Quietly, Brig asks how the river is looking.

No lower, Rilk replies.

Higher still, it seemed to me, Vesti says.

Shaye's mouth becomes dry. It is easy to forget about the river until someone mentions it.

When everyone is licking their fingers to catch the drips of the damson juice and the boys have started to get restless, Sala begins to sing. She opens her mouth and lets the sound meander among the humming midges who are coming out to dance in farewell to the sun.

Ludi has come to sit in Shaye's lap. She can feel his heart chiming with hers through his warm back pressed to her chest, and their twin heartbeats keep time with Sala's song.

Now Sala is singing a song of mourning, only ever sung to say goodbye. It is sung to the corpse of a person to ease their spirit's passing from this world, and also to places when they become too barren for people to stay there. It is to lessen the grief of the spirits of that place at no longer being able to provide, and to balm the ache in the hearts of the people left behind.

Shaye closes her eyes. She remembers singing this song, Gai Gai's sweaty hand clasped in hers, on her knees beside the empty body of her mother. She remembers rocking with the melody and the skin of her knees becoming rough and scratched from the twigs and bark. She remembers the smell of her mother's body beginning to rot, like mushrooms in the springtime, and the rhythm of the earth dropped on top of her in the grave, like the drumbeats at the oak grove. They had not returned to that plenty-time place after the frosts, and Shaye had known at the time they were not just singing for her mother but also for the barren bramble bushes, and the dying hazelnut trees, and the ugly twisted roots they dug for. She had just had her first bleeding, and she had the feeling that just as she was blooming into life, everything else around her was dying.

Brig joins her voice to Sala's, tears gathering in the corners of her eyes. The boys hum along, swaying with the melody. Shaye begins to sing too. Despite its sadness, there is a something light in the centre of the song, the way a seed sleeps in the earth during the frosts in order to burst into life in the spring. Although the song says all things must die, it also says the spirit of a person will soon live again in another body, and there will be another plenty place somewhere near. It tells them the place they are leaving will not be abandoned forever, for maybe one day when their children are grown, they will return. And by then it will be green and lush, and the trees will be laden with fruit and nuts, and ready to receive people again.

Sala lets her voice fade, and Shaye notices Yael brushing his fingertips past his cheeks. The crickets fill the silence and chatter their news to each other. The light is dying.

A charred branch tumbles from the top of the fire, an owl hoots. The sky is purple like a mallow flower. Brig is the first to leave the fire and disappear behind a sycamore, where she has left her mat and her pouch. Ayla follows her, prodding the fire to make it slumber, taking her son by the hand and leading him away to sleep. Shaye helps Gai Gai to her feet, and Ludi follows them to the place under a silver birch where they have laid out their mats. Ludi is tired, and he stumbles as he walks. He falls asleep as soon as he lies down, and Shaye arranges his heavy limbs in a way that won't make him grumpy come sunrise. Shaye falls asleep quickly; she barely sees the stars blink before she is dreaming of the ocean, of swimming deep under the water and chasing the bright lights she finds there.

It's hard not to feel that the road is a kind of scar across the land, and the forest is like the new pink tissue forming beneath the old wound, knitting the body back together after being rent apart. Shante thinks of the faint lilac scar across her belly from the C-section giving birth to Locke, and the way that even now a stray finger of Zeb's across the jagged skin will send shivers through her body, her skin sewn shut but the nerves connected differently, an electrical circuit still functioning but fusing every now and then, just for attention.

She'll wear that mark for the rest of her life, forever branded as the woman who held this boy in her womb. What mark will this land still bear of humans in a hundred years? They abandoned this road not a hundred years ago and already green things have arrived to reclaim it as theirs. The same thing would happen to her city, if its fate wasn't to be drowned. As soon as the last footprint has faded from the pavements, spiky green shoots would crack through the grey shell of the concrete, vines would creep up apartment blocks and strangle them and trees would rip the roads apart. In ten years' time, the city would be unrecognisable; in fifty, there would be nothing left of it.

Yes. Nature will win. Like she is winning now.

She's been winning for years. For as long as Shante has been listening to or watching the news bulletins, there've been reports on sea levels, small islands in the middle of the ocean being swallowed up, hurricanes and floods and abandoned seaside towns all over the world. Documentaries about flood defences in big cities, levees, barriers, millions spent on drainage systems and desalination plants and special spongey pavements that let water drain through into the sewers. New subsidies announced for solar glass, just before the blackouts started, and government statements every day saying the faults in the grid had been found and fixed. The sea's been drifting into the river for as long as she can remember, and it seems that now it's only just beginning to matter.

Mum? Locke's voice cuts through her thoughts. I'm hungry. Is it almost lunchtime?

The shade has shrunk to cover only one lane of the old road, and they have followed it, but Locke's forehead is shiny with sweat and Grainne has large patches spreading from under her arms where the straps of her backpack chafe.

I think so. She drags the suitcase to the very edge of the concrete and sits on her haunches to lay it down and unzip it. Let's sit down for a rest.

Her legs ache and to let herself sit down, even on the hard surface of the road, feels like a gift. Her feet are hot, and part of her sock has rucked up between her heel and her shoe. She takes them off and lets her wrinkled toes breathe.

There's not a lot to choose from to eat, and she doesn't know how much she should ration it. There's hunger rumbling in her own stomach, but it's bearable. She'll wait until she really needs to eat. That'll make it last longer.

She gives Locke a packet of crackers and a fruit bar. She takes a bottle of water out of her handbag and sets it down in front of him too. Although food is a worry, it's water she dreads running out of. Three days, she knows that much. Three days without water and it's all over. She wonders if that's the same for children, or if they have even less time.

Are your feet okay, sweetheart? Not rubbing in those shoes?

Locke shrugs. I'm okay. Bit tired. He tears open the fruit bar with his teeth and eats it in two bites. But I want to get to Dad so I'm okay.

Grainne unzips her suitcase and opens another packet of crackers. She offers some to Shante, who allows herself four, just to put something in her stomach. She watches as Grainne eats five then puts the packet back into the suitcase.

They share a bottle of water, Locke has one to himself. Thirst drags at her throat even after she's sipped her share of the water. It's too hot for walking. They're going to need so much more water than this. The hum of anxiety that's been thrumming since the train stopped ratchets up. The base of her skull is aching. Perhaps it's because of the thirst.

I think we should limit ourselves to one bottle a day, each, Shante says. She knows Grainne has counted the bottles, she saw her when they opened the suitcase just now.

What are we going to do when we run out? Grainne asks in a low voice.

A small burst of fury explodes in Shante's belly. How dare she say it out loud, as if she isn't already strung out with worry about that.

No idea. Dehydration makes you irritable and flustered, she knows that, but it's hard to control her feelings when her tongue is sticking to the roof of her mouth when she swallows.

Maybe we'll pass a river or a stream or something.

Maybe, she says, fighting to keep her voice even. And the water will probably be brown with silt and raw sewage, she thinks, and writhing with bacteria.

Or maybe it'll rain.

Maybe. She hopes it will rain. That's the best-case scenario, that cleanish water will fall from the sky and they can turn their faces upwards and open their mouths to let the water splash onto their tongues.

Grainne waves the empty plastic bottle. Shall I keep these, to fill them up if we can?

Shante nods. She doesn't trust herself to speak.

Grainne packs away the empty bottle into her suitcase. At least there's less to carry now. That's something, at least.

They watch Locke for a moment, licking crumbs from his fingers.

Dad would like to see this, Grainne says quietly.

What, this forest?

Grainne nods. He'd love it, wouldn't he? All his stories.

Shante doesn't reply. She misses Charlie with a fierce ache. If her father were here, he'd know what to do and where to go. He'd be in charge, he'd make all the decisions. He'd find water, he'd get them food. He'd tell them about their mother, bobbing up and down in a dinghy crossing the ocean with no idea what was on the other side of it, and he'd tell them they were strong and lucky.

Let's get going again. Shante pulls her damp socks back on and ties her shoelaces. She zips the suitcases, pulls them upright and straps the lute to her back. Her left hand falls to the folder in the bag by her left thigh, the place where she's keeping those magic talismans. They're useless out here. She can't eat or drink them. The trees don't care which city they came from or which one they're going to. It's hard to know exactly what the trees care about.

Her legs are stiff, and it takes a few minutes to ease out the aches in her calves. She walks closest to the trees, protected by their shade, with Locke in between her and Grainne. He's telling her one of his stories that has no ending, a parade of statements linked by and, and, and. Grainne's half listening, and murmuring, Really, oh, that's great, when she thinks she should.

Shante listens to the trees, their eerie whispers in the faint breeze. She also listens for the telltale hum of a camera drone, or the crash of heavy boots on the soft undergrowth, or the sirens of a patrol. Nothing. She can't remember the last time the air around her was so quiet. There are so many noises in the city, even at night, that she never felt alone.

They follow the road for hours, and it changes little. In the mid-afternoon it begins to slope upwards, but soon after that it slopes downwards again and then it flattens out. They pass a few more of the bridges they crossed as they left the old station, and each time Shante approaches them fearfully. They're a reminder that the human world still exists out there, and she half expects to see someone walk over them and join them walking on this old road, perhaps dragging suitcases behind them too. As she passes, she sees the same suspended concrete paths extending left and right into the woods. She wonders where they go, how far into the trees they get before the soil swallows them completely. The whole territory must have been like this at some point, she thinks, roads and paths and streets criss-crossing the land like veins and capillaries on a sagging thigh. How did people know which one to follow?

They pass a twin set of buildings covered in green-grey fungus on the southern side. They're connected by another bridge over the road, this one bound in dirty glass. Some of the rectangular panes are smashed, making jagged black star shapes.

What's that, Mum? Locke points to either side of him at the buildings.

Shante shrugs. It seems rude to look too closely at the old buildings, like stopping to examine the wrinkles and liver spots on a hundred-year-old woman shuffling past you on the street. Although the dark, silent mass of the trees is unsettling, these periodic signs that humans once lived and built in this place are worse. She thinks of her flat at home, the laundry basket sat quietly in the corner of the room as though she's coming back tonight to pack some of it into the bag to take to the laundrette tomorrow, the bed with sheets creased in the hollowed out parts of the mattress.

She has the sense that someone is watching them from behind that glass, and she draws closer to Locke. She feels as though she should not speak as they pass under the bridge, as if they are walking past a graveyard of a thousand writhing ghosts.

The sun is setting and the heat softens. There are tiny insects humming around their faces now, not biting but insistently existing. Waving them away from her face does nothing. She walks straight into their blizzard, becoming thicker and thicker as the light fades. This time yesterday she was worried about their visas not arriving, walking home from that wedding along the river, listening to the clanking of the pumps and watching the rubbish float in the water. In twenty-four hours she's lost her home, her father and maybe her chance of getting to Zeb, but these midges don't seem to care.

Look. Grainne points to her right, where the sun is becoming a warm glow through the top of the trees. The sun's setting to our right.

Shante follows the direction of her finger. So?

It means we're definitely going in the right direction. If that's west, she points ahead of them to the route through the trees, then that's definitely north.

Finally some good news! Shante thinks. Everything's awful and I'm dying of thirst but we've made one good decision today.

She says, We should stop for the night, find somewhere to sleep.

Grainne looks around her into the trees and waves her hand helplessly. Is one place here better than another? It all looks the same to me, just trees trees trees.

We should get off the road at least, it'll be more protected in there.

They leave the concrete surface and climb up the bank into the trees. Maybe they can find a soft leaf drift to lay a few clothes on top of and lie down on. She and Grainne spread out, looking on the darkening forest floor for something they're not sure they'll recognise when they see it.

What about here? Grainne calls. Shante drags her suitcase over to where Grainne stands at the foot of a huge tree. A trunk wider than her arm span, standing taller over them than she can see in the indigo sky, its leaves have formed a soft carpet all around its roots. It's no better or worse than anywhere else, so Shante sits down and unzips the suitcase.

She drinks more than she intends to, a whole bottle of water to herself. Locke has a whole one too, and Grainne most of one. She counts the bottles left in both suitcases. Thirty-eight. If they have one bottle a day each, that gives them twelve days at most before they're completely fucked. Will it rain soon? The weathercasters have been saying that it's going to rain for weeks now, but there's been nothing more than a showy crackle of lightning and a few showers. She licks her lips; she craves that water. Perhaps that's the one thing she has in common with these silent trees. The ground beneath her is hard and dry; they're as thirsty as she is.

She brushes the salt off the peanuts before she gives them to Locke. Crackers, another fruit bar and a few dried apple rings are all there is to eat. The rice and dried beans felt like a good idea when she realised they were going to have to walk, but they need water to cook them.

Should she make a fire? She took matches from the train guard's carriage, but perhaps she should save them too. Frustration makes her ball her fists as she listens to Grainne and Locke chewing, the plastic wrappers rustling as they dig their fingers right in, trying to scoop up every last crumb in the packets. She doesn't know what to do. She wants to screw her eyes shut and will herself back to this morning, and when the lady in the blue uniform behind the desk asks her if she wants to get on the ten past eight train or the eleven thirty, she will say, The eleven thirty please, and they'll wait in the station, maybe get a sandwich and a juice for breakfast and watch the freight being unloaded, speak to Zeb, maybe even ring Charlie and try to persuade him to change his mind. Then they'd have got on the train, maybe with other passengers so they'd be safe, and by now they'd be in the north, probably sitting in plastic chairs in some room with an immigration official looking through their paperwork, but Zeb would be there, or on the other side of some glass, waiting for them, longing for them, getting ready to take them home.

Locke is yawning, his eyelids drooping and his chin dropping towards his chest.

I need the toilet, Mum. He says it quietly, as though he's embarrassed, and she has a kick of guilt that she hasn't asked him if he needs a wee all day.

She needs to relieve herself too. She realises she hasn't been all day, and now she sees she's going to have to piss here in the woods like an animal.

She stands up and holds out her hand. Come on. We'll pretend we're bears, and we have to go in the woods.

Grainne snorts. I'm trying to digest here, Shan. Do you mind?

She leads him around the shadows of the trees. Darkness is stalking closer and closer, and she needs to get everything done and be tucked up inside their pretend bed before it is fully dark. She doesn't want to stumble around this forest, hands outstretched to grope the rough bark of trees to guide her without the last of the sun.

You go there, and I'll be just on the other side of this tree. She's chosen a thick trunk where they'll each be able to have a measure of privacy.

Locke looks doubtful. What do I do?

It's almost funny, but she feels the same strange panic about this wild defecating that she can't quite pinpoint.

Just go to the toilet.

He looks around him. But there's nothing to sit on.

You're just going to have to crouch, like this. She drops to her haunches to show him and he sighs, heavily, like an adult weary of the world he's found himself in.

Go on the other side of this tree.

When Locke is out of view, she unzips her jeans and pulls them down to her ankles. She crouches again, pulling the denim out of the way. It takes a couple of minutes to relax enough to let a thin stream of urine out, splashing onto the leaves below her. She has never peed outside before and there seems to be nothing to recommend it.

Finished! Locke calls.

She's reminded of toilet training, clapping wildly at the sight of a small brown shit in the plastic potty, her enthusiasm completely bewildering to Locke who would have pooed wherever she told him to, without the curtain call or the little stickers she gave him.

Great, come on then.

But... er... His voice is small and worried. Mum?

What?

What do I wipe myself with?

A bubble of laughter rises in her. How ridiculous that they should be here, shitting in the woods like the past thousand years never happened. Dogs never mind, they just cock their legs in front of anyone and leave their shit on the pavement for some other idiot to pick up. Cats are more discreet but they still leave it out for someone else to deal with. They're being cats. Hiding to shit, but leaving it all the same.

Just grab a handful of leaves. She hears a rustle as he picks some up, then scraping as the leaves brush against his skin, and she has to bite her lip to keep from laughing.

He appears from behind the tree, holding his hands splayed in front of him and frowning.

What about my hands, Mum? He shows them to her as though she's going to inspect the germs on them. How can I wash them?

No hand washing out here, sweetheart. They're going to be filthy as rats in no time, but they can't spare the water. You'll just have to wipe your hands on your shorts and be dirty.

He bends down to pass his hands over the leaves, and keeps stopping to do it again as they walk back to Grainne, who is gathering bundles of leaves and patting them into mattress shapes at the foot of the giant tree. Shante gets out some shirts from the suitcases and lays them on top, tucking them underneath. There's nothing to pull over them as a blanket, but the air is hot and still and she hopes the trees will insulate them from any unexpected wind chill.

They lie down, Locke in between them, shifting to get comfortable. Shante lies on her back, looking up at the sky. Her eyes are wide open but now there's no difference between having them open and shut, the darkness is just as dense. She knows there are thick limbs of this old tree suspended above them, she saw the branches black against the indigo sky when they were eating, but she can't see a thing.

It's the noises that keep her still and terrified on her bed of leaves. The forest seems to have come alive as the sun set, animals crawling out of their daytime holes like club kids queueing around the block with their pills tucked into their waistbands. Birds hooting, snuffles and scratches, noises that seem to come from all angles, amplified by her blindness, no sense of where they're coming from or how far away they are or what's making them.

She doesn't know what animals live out here. Might she wake up with the light to find some rodent has gnawed Locke's face off, or dragged their suitcases off into some hole? The food. Her chest constricts, then she remembers that she saw Grainne zip the suitcases shut as they went off to their pee tree.

She hears wings flapping against the air and the sound isn't soft like birds' feathers, it's harsh and scratchy. Bats. She shudders and shuts her eyes. She has never seen a bat except on her tab. She knows nothing about them except that they hang upside down to sleep and when they're surprised they rush at you to slap their slimy wings all over your face and tear at your hair, and if Shante raises her head even a fraction off this leaf bed they'll swoop down on her and beat at her until she's screaming with madness.

There's no way she'll be able to sleep. She can hear Grainne breathing slowly and knows she's already drifted off. Good for her, that she doesn't feel worried about what's out in these woods.

Mum? Locke whispers. Are you awake? His voice is conspicuous in the night-time orchestra; there is no other forest sound like it.

She rolls over onto her side, facing him. What's wrong?

I can't sleep. He pauses. She can hear him chewing some words, deciding whether or not to say more. He lowers his voice again, now he's so quiet he's only breathing the words.

I'm scared. It's too dark.

His voice seems untethered from his body, and Shante reaches out to feel him, to reassure herself that he's still there.

She shifts over on her bed of leaves and tucks Locke into her body. He should be close to her, so she can protect him.

I know. But there's nothing to be scared of. She feels like a liar saying that, lying here terrified of the not knowing just like him. Everything here is just the same as it was when the sun was up, we just can't see it anymore.

I miss my nightlight. That orange street light that stands right outside his window back at their flat, the glow that no curtain has ever been able to fully block and no electricity blackout has ever turned off; since before he was born, all the street lights in the city have been solar charged.

Well, let's see if there's a moon out tonight. She turns her neck so she can face up to the sky again. That can be a kind of nightlight while we're out here.

There's no moon, or perhaps it's in a place in the sky where they can't see it, but in looking at the sky so intently Shante sees that the blackness is sprayed with pinpricks of light, illuminating the far distance. The sight is beautiful, and she's never really appreciated that before. All those worlds out there, and all that black space between her and them.

Maybe the stars can be my nightlight.

That's a good idea. Charlie used to sing a song about stars, stardust, something like that. He said his grandmother used to sing it to him.

What are they made of?

I have no idea.

Do we have stars in the sky at home?

Yes, we just don't see them very much because we've got other lights on and you need it to get very dark like this.

What's that one called?

I can't see which one you're pointing to.

That one there.

It's a naming question again, the ones she dreads. She has no idea what these stars' names are, although she always thinks of them as being romantic.

Benjamin, she says.

No it's not.

How do you know?

Benjamin isn't a proper name for a star.

Who says?

He hesitates. I'm going to ask Dad when we see him.

She smiles into the darkness. Good idea. Dad'll know for sure.

They are quiet then, watching the sky that doesn't appear to change yet seems endlessly new. She feels him begin to fall asleep in her arms, his neck going slack, his breathing slow, and then his legs twitching as he yields to his tiredness. She strokes his hair softly, and when he is fully asleep she rolls him away from her onto his own bundle of leaves as gently as she can. So much of motherhood takes place when a child is asleep. She remembers the first few weeks of his life when she would sometimes think she had forgotten the exact shade of his irises, and wait by his cot for him to wake up so she could look one more time, and fix it in her mind.

She looks up at the stars again. One is moving swiftly across the sky in a single determined line and she recognises it as a satellite, not a real star, only a few miles up from the end of the planet's atmosphere. It makes her think of her tab, just as far away from those space shuttles as they were at home in the city, but now insolently quiet. The steady pace of the satellite through the mass of ancient stars, some of which might not even exist anymore, reminds her that there are still humans on this planet, billions of them, carrying on with their lives even as she is lying in the woods. She thinks of all the people who have gazed up at the night sky over the centuries and felt less alone, those who believed that they would one day solve the mysteries of deep space, those who believed in alien lifeforms, and then those – like her – who only liked to think of those same stars glittering on the people they loved, people who were far away and people who they might never see again. She wonders if Zeb is looking at these stars now. Maybe you can see them better in his city, maybe the street lights aren't quite so harsh there. She wonders if he can somehow sense that she's looking at them too, and thinking of him, and just in case he is she sends a message up to the satellite, now soared far away out of her vision, the way she supposes her tab does: I'm here, I'm safe, I'm coming to you. She chants it over and over again in her head as though she's trying to learn a new piece of music, and when she falls asleep it echoes in her dreams of giant trees wrenching their roots from the earth and walking alongside her on this endless, ancient road.

Shaye is woken by the sun screaming.

No, it is Gai Gai screaming. She rolls over and blinks her eyes open, shields them from the bright sunlight with her hand and sits up. Gai Gai is sitting on the other side of Ludi, a pool of clear fluid spreading across her mat, her mouth stretched open in panic.

It's coming! she says, looking at Shaye. Gai Gai's hands are pressed on her knees, her knuckles white. It's coming now! It can't come now, I'm not ready, we're not at the oak grove yet!

Shaye smiles and reaches across Ludi, who is stirring on his mat. She squeezes Gai Gai's shoulder. Her eyes are wide and her mouth is tight. Tiny lines appear around her lips.

I wanted it to wait until we got to the oak grove, I wanted it to be born there.

The spirit comes into the body when it thinks the time is right, Shaye says, and she feels wise like Sala. Something must have been passing in the night and liked the look of you.

Gai Gai closes her eyes and places her hands under her belly. She looks as if she might cry, and Shaye climbs over Ludi and kneels in front of her, just in front of the puddle of womb fluid.

You need to relax, Shaye tells her, cupping her face with her hands and stroking her cheek. It's going to be a while yet before it comes, and the more you fret, the more it'll hurt.

The news that Gai Gai is going to deliver her baby lends an air of joyful activity to the sunlight place in the woods where they've stopped. Sala can't help pressing her hands to her heart when Shaye tells her Gai Gai is beginning her birthing, and despite the greater danger of a baby being born on the path than being born in a settled place, she cannot do other than smile wildly. She begins to direct everyone to get wood, cloths, food. Her voice is commanding, and everyone obeys her without grumbling. If all goes well, there will be a new baby among them by the time the sun rises tomorrow, and the thought makes their throats itch to sing. There is no better sign from the spirits that all will soon be well.

Shaye's thoughts turn to the water they'll need. They're nowhere near the holloway of hawthorn and blackthorn with its sweet-tasting spring she had hoped they could use, and there's no other spring nearby. What was left in the waterskins from the rain is almost gone. There is only the river water left.

Shaye gives her waterskin to Rilk to fill. Ludi hovers around her, now reluctant to scamper off into the forest with Reo. He stares at Gai Gai, resting at the foot of a silver birch with her eyes firmly shut and her hands on her belly.

Is she going to be alright, Ma? he whispers as Shaye moves their mats, and begins to shake out the cloth she had packed for this very time. Will there be a baby soon?

She takes his shoulders and moves him out of her way so she can spread the cloth across their mats.

Gai Gai's going to be fine, I'm going to be helping her and so is Sala. She runs the back of her fingers across his forehead. You'll get to see the baby as soon as it's born, and then we'll all sing for it.

Ludi nods, then his eyes drift back to Gai Gai, groaning softly, and he looks scared again.

Go and collect some nuts for Gai Gai, Shaye says, turning Ludi around so he can't see her. Do you want me to give you my basket? Give you something to put everything you gather in?

It is a shameless bribe, to give him something to think about other than Gai Gai being in pain. He nods shyly, he loves the responsibility of holding her basket. Shaye retrieves it from her pouch and hands it to him. He puffs up with pride.

You can have that one to keep, she tells him, and he is so pleased he presses himself to her, throwing his arms around her hips and kissing her where his mouth lands on her belly. There is no time to relish the feeling of his small, warm body near to hers, she has to think of Gai Gai. She leads him over to where Reo is dragging at a hazel branch. She places a kiss on the top of his head and leaves him. It's a dance, motherhood, just like any other thing, she thinks. He needs me when I've got little to give him and he forgets me when I long for him.

Shaye picks up Gai Gai's sleeping mat, and places it to one side for washing later. She brings a length of cloth to the tree where Gai Gai is on all fours like a wolf, trying to stand up.

I don't want to be here, she says, and Shaye takes her under the elbows and helps her to her feet. I want to go to the river, the baby wants to be near the water.

Shaye can't imagine wanting to be near the sick river, her heart twists every time she thinks of it. But perhaps this child, still living in the murky world of spirit, knows better.

Sala appears at her side.

She wants to go to the river, Shaye says, and without a word, Sala takes Gai Gai's other arm and they walk away from the clearing towards the water.

Gai Gai leans on Shaye heavily, and together they stumble forward. The cloth slips from Shaye's shoulder onto the ground and they have to pause to gather it again. When they get to the riverbank, they see Rilk and Vesti coming out of the water, the hems of their skirts wet and dripping, the waterskins full. Gai Gai convulses with a contraction of her womb, and cries out. Her nails dig into Shaye's arm, and she winces along with the labouring woman. Shaye begins to feel like a tree struck by lightning, guiding the immense power churning in Gai Gai into the ground where it can be safe.

It's beginning, whispers Sala, more to the spirits than to anyone else.

They settle Gai Gai down on patch of earth cleared of leaves and twigs and Shaye sits behind her, one leg either side, their fingers entwined. She insists on facing the river, saying the first thing the baby wants to see is the water. Shaye recognises the birthing trance from her own labour with Ludi. She remembers the humming strength she felt throbbing in her veins, that feeling of invincible power that began the second she felt the womb fluid running down her legs and has never truly left her, only faded under the weight of everyday matters in the time since. She holds onto Gai Gai's hands and pushes her strength back when Gai Gai leans into her.

Sala sits at her feet, rubbing them, checking on the opening of her womb. Gai Gai is naked, her skirt and belt left back with her mat for washing. The dome of her belly heaves with every flush of pain and her heavy breasts fall to each side, the dark nipples erect and waiting.

Rilk, Ayla and Vesti come and go, with food, with water, with motherwort for Gai Gai to chew on to ease her pains. Sometimes she wants to walk around, so Sala and Shaye heave her to her feet and walk up and down the riverbank, weaving around the willows that stand with their roots waterlogged. Their heads crowd close together as they walk, a dark one flanked by a fiery red on either side.

When the sun is at its highest, Brig appears holding a grass snake by its neck. She shows it to Sala and Shaye, and its tail swings as she holds it high above her head.

For tomorrow, or tomorrow tomorrow, she says. Sala nods her appreciation.

Brig is the best snake catcher Shaye's ever known, and it's always she who manages to get one for a ritual. Cherl used to say it's clear why Brig has that particular talent, because she's as lazy as a serpent and she meets them when she slips off to a sunny place to laze around. He used to say it before every ritual, and everyone used to laugh because it was true. She remembers Cherl's words now, and catches Sala's eye. It makes her throat ache to think of him. She wonders if Sala is thinking of Cherl too.

Brig places her hand on top of Gai Gai's sweaty head, and murmurs a blessing.

I'll bring you something to eat, she says, and returns shortly after with a birch basket filled with damsons and grey-spotted mushrooms. She also lays two flints and a knife made of antler on the pile of cloth next to Shaye. Sala thanks her with a smile, Brig leaves to join the others, and the three women are alone again.

Sala looks relaxed, and so Shaye realises everything must be going as well as it can go. She remembers the deep furrow between Sala's eyebrows when she began to labour with Ludi, it was twilight and a new moon. Not good, not favourable, Sala had muttered, to labour in the darkness. She had stayed by the fire that long, cold night, and when Ludi arrived, red faced and squalling just after dawn, Sala had pronounced him a child of fire immediately.

Sala hasn't said it yet, but Shaye knows they are both thinking the same thing. This baby will be a child of the river, dedicated to the sweet water like all people are dedicated to one spirit or another. There are worse things to be dedicated to, thinks Shaye, than to the river. Especially if it is going to become good and clean again.

And for the first time since the water began to rise in the spring, Shaye feels a huge swell of hope rise in her belly, and it seems to flow into Gai Gai through their linked hands. This baby will be of the river, there will be new life in this sad old water channel and when they have danced for the spirits and the ancestors at the oak grove the water will subside again, the birds will come back, and the sky will no longer be heavy on her shoulders.

Sala and Shaye eat, but Gai Gai refuses food. She only wants to drink the water Sala tips into her mouth between pants and she doesn't seem to care about its musty, slightly salty taste. She doesn't even want to pace the distance between the birch trees on the bank, she just sits, propped up by Shaye behind her, her eyes tightly closed and breathing long and slow.

Shaye sings, to pass the time and to give Gai Gai something outside of the pain twisting in the centre of her. Sala joins her in whichever tune she is singing, and Shaye feels a powerful pleasure in choosing the songs. The elders always choose the songs, for they know best which melodies are suited to which spirits at which times, but now Sala is following Shaye.

The pressure is building in Gai Gai. She's close, says Sala, peering between her legs with a smile. Not long now. Don't stop singing.

Sala helps Gai Gai roll over and position herself on all fours. Shaye moves onto her knees, hunched over like a mole, her forearms flat on the ground with her hands still clamped in Gai Gai's. She begins to sing in a whisper. Gai Gai moans, an unearthly sound that makes the leaves shudder. It won't be long now, Shaye thinks. The baby can see the world and it's rushing towards it.

You're almost there, Sala calls from behind her, a hand each side of her wide hips. You're doing so well, keep going.

Gai Gai shakes her head from side to side and groans again. Her forehead is speckled with sweat, strands of hair have escaped from her braids and stuck to her face. Shaye untangles her fingers and pulls Gai Gai's braids to the side. Now her hair is spooled on the earth like a vine, heaving with every breath. Shaye puts her hand back on Gai Gai's forehead, to give her something to push against. Her back aches from the pressure against the tree and the long day of sitting down. She wiggles her toes and adjusts her hunched position. Nearly there, she whispers to Gai Gai in a pause in her song. You're so nearly there.

Gai Gai has not said a word since the morning, has barely

opened her eyes, but as a chill breeze drifts towards them from the river her eyes flicker wide open and stare at Shaye, bright and unseeing. Her mouth falls open like a yawn before caving in on itself again, and she hisses a breath out between her teeth. She seems to say something in that gasping breath, but Shaye can't make it out before she hears Sala's voice.

Alright, Gai Gai, Sala calls, it's time to push.

Gai Gai screws up her face and howls. Shaye's hand becomes purple where she is squeezing it, and she pushes against Gai Gai's pressure in her hand. Sala is sounding triumphant, she shouts that she can see a dark head just like hers.

A breath, a cry, an enormous push. Shaye takes her hand from Gai Gai's and places the heels of her palms against her shoulders. Gai Gai's fingers claw and tear at the earth. She shakes her head from side to side as though the inside of her skull itches.

Push against me, Shaye says, I'll hold you. She isn't sure if Gai Gai hears or understands what she is saying.

Another breath, another cry, another enormous push. Sala's voice, low and calm.

Just a little bit more, you're almost there, I can see it, it's coming.

And Gai Gai screams, with a last heave into Shaye's hands, and Sala cries out. There is a soft slap of wet flesh into Sala's arms, and a splash of blood onto the ground behind Gai Gai.

Shaye waits, not breathing, her thumbs pressing into the tough ridges of Gai Gai's shoulders. She gazes at Sala, who cradles the small figure streaked with blood. She notices the twilight midges dancing around her head, and she sees that they are dancing slowly, crowding around to welcome the child, descending curiously towards Sala to smell the new being and pronounce it alive.

A girl! Sala says quietly, and Gai Gai releases a sob. She drops onto her elbows and presses her forehead to the ground. Her back is quivering.

It is as if Sala has given the baby permission to speak. A wail pierces the air, impossibly loud, and Shaye feels an answering release of held breath from the trees. She had not realised they were silent while Gai Gai was labouring, she had not noticed the lack of wind, the distance of the animals, the quiet listening from the place where the others were gathered. But now the forest sounds come to life again, the wind picks up and makes the canopy rustle in celebration, she can hear the buzzing of the midges, she can even hear clapping and stamping and shouting from the other people. Shaye smiles, and strokes Gai Gai's hair.

They're shouting for you, they're welcoming the baby, can you hear?

The baby keeps up a constant wailing while Gai Gai turns over onto her back. She lies in Sala's arms, her face ridged with wrinkles like tree bark, the birthing cord still pulsing blue at her belly.

Good girl, Sala says, and she rests a hand on Gai Gai's blood-streaked thigh. She cradles the baby expertly in one elbow and peers between her legs. You were fantastic, I'm so proud of you.

Shaye settles herself in a seated position again and Gai Gai leans back into her. They are like one person now. Gai Gai rests the back of her head on Shaye's shoulder and Shaye arranges her braids and picks the sweaty strands of hair from her face. Gai Gai gulps air as though she is thirsty.

I can't see her, she whispers, her voice tight. Can you hold her up to me?

Sala smiles and lifts the baby with both hands around her belly. Gai Gai sobs again, and she reaches for her child. Sala tips the slimy body into her arms.

Have a rest, Sala says, and she sits back on her heels. You're almost done.

The baby stops crying as soon as she sinks into Gai Gai's chest. Her lips pucker and her tiny fingers move. The women stare at her in silence, listening to her snuffling and her quiet sucking noises as she roots for Gai Gai's nipple. Tears spring to Shaye's eyes, and she sniffs loudly. She looks up to see Sala crying and smiling too. She cannot take her eyes off the baby and neither can Shaye. Babies always drag everyone's attention, Shaye thinks, staring at the now calm features. You can't help but gaze at them and watch all the tiny changes on their faces.

There's something on her back, Gai Gai says, but she sounds dreamy and content, there is no hint of anxiety in her. She's marked, there, on her back.

It takes Sala a while to respond, lost as she is in contemplation of the miracle she has just ushered into the world.

It's just blood, she replies. We'll wash you both off soon and then you can sleep.

The contractions of the afterbirth begin. There is an anticlimactic feel to it, the meaty mass of blood just slips out, Gai Gai doesn't even pass her daughter to Shaye.

Sala examines the afterbirth carefully, prodding at it to make sure it has been delivered whole. The air fills with the scent of womb blood, which is so different to any other kind of blood. It smells secret and sly, like damp crumbly soil. Dank and vital. As it gushes from Gai Gai along with the afterbirth, it sinks into the earth as if it has been longing to get back there. She doesn't seem to notice, she is still staring at her baby. Sala is watching the entrance to the womb with narrowed eyes, standing sentinel to guard against too much of that secret blood flooding out. Stay in there, Shaye imagines her chanting to herself. Stay in there, birthing blood, we have no need of you out here.

And stay strong heart; and stay away infection; and stay cool fever, Shaye mumbles to herself. Gai Gai is strong and she's carried the baby easily these past moons, she has a better chance than many of living to nurse her daughter. Still, the birthing spirits are capricious and mean. They can make you think all is well and slit your throat while you sleep.

> • <

Her incantations worked, because as the light begins to fade Sala declares Gai Gai healthy and fit for now, and takes the sharp flint Brig left and slices through the cord. She ties a knot in it, her fingers slippery and clumsy. Gai Gai pays no attention to anything Sala says or does, she has retreated into her own bliss with her own baby. She places her big finger in the little palm, and gasps when her daughter closes her own tiny fingers around it. She begins to hum softly.

Shaye moves away from Gai Gai, and stands up. She stamps her feet to bring feeling back into her legs, she feels bruised all over.

She takes Gai Gai by the waist and helps her stand up. She guides her to a fallen birch a little distance away, where she can sit down again and rest.

Are you cold? she asks, brushing the backs of her fingers over Gai Gai's skin. Shall I get you something to cover you?

Gai Gai doesn't answer, just shakes her head and keeps crooning to her child. She is exploring her baby's body with gentle fingers, examining the creases in the elbows, in the knees, passing her thumbs over her baby's wrists, the folds of skin at her neck, her two eyes which are just dark slits. Shaye crouches to kiss Gai Gai on the forehead, then goes back to the place where the afterbirth lolls on the ground.

While she digs a hole to bury it, Sala fills the two waterskins with river water and washes mother and baby. Shaye listens to the gurgling of the baby as the water touches her skin and tips the afterbirth into the hollow she has made. Before she covers it over with dirt, she thanks the shiny mass on Gai Gai's behalf, and she tells it to rest now. She thinks of the place where Ludi's afterbirth is buried, just outside the stones marking out a firepit in the old plenty-time place. It was Brig who buried it and thanked it for her then, while Sala washed her and Ludi off, just as she is doing now for Gai Gai. When they had come back from the oak grove the next spring, Shaye had looked for the spot eagerly. Ludi was crawling by that point, and she wanted to take him to his womb twin to greet it. But the earth was no longer charred where the fire pits had been, it was covered with a fresh, lush growth of sorrel and chickweed, and she couldn't quite tell exactly where it lay.

Shaye! Sala calls. Come and help me wrap her up.

She hurries over to Sala, who has the length of cloth slung over her shoulder. She lifts Gai Gai by her armpit, and helps her stand up. Gai Gai whimpers, and Sala pats her shoulder.

I know, you're sore, she says softly. But you did the hardest part, you'll start to heal now.

Gai Gai shuffles her feet apart gingerly, clutching her baby as if the pain in her seat might make her drop the bundle. Sala and Shaye pass the cloth between them, around Gai Gai's hips, underneath her womb opening and around the tops of her thighs. She is still oozing blood, but less than Shaye has seen at some births.

Then Sala wraps the baby in a smaller piece of cloth and gives her back to Gai Gai. Let's take you back to your mat, you need to sleep now. It's almost dark, that time of the sun's journey across the sky when it's hard to see colours. Sala puts her arm around Gai Gai's waist and leads her away from the river. Shaye yawns, picks up the two waterskins, the flints and the antler knife, and follows them.

The fire is still bright when they reach the clearing where all the sleeping mats are laid out and everyone is gathered expectantly in a tight group around the blaze. Brig springs to her feet when she sees them. Sala's wide smile emerges from the shadows of the trees into the light of the fire, and Brig claps her hands joyfully.

Blessed be the spirits! she calls, and everyone else scrambles to their feet. Shaye squints at the smaller figures to find Ludi, but before she can make out where he is, she feels a hard body smack against her legs and she drops the things she is carrying to wrap her arms around her son. She crouches to press her nose into his scalp and breathe the smell of him as Sala and Brig begin to sing.

They are not singing any of the sacred songs, that will come later. This is just a song of pure joy, a celebration of the life that Gai Gai has brought to them, but also a song to thank the spirits of death for returning Gai Gai to them from the threshold. Shaye remembers Brig and Sala greeting her in that way too, as the dawn rose and she held a tiny Ludi in her arms. She felt as though they nodded to something over her shoulder, something she couldn't see but could feel very clearly, thanking it respectfully for her life and sending it away for another time. It made her feel invincible, the way that presence receded in the moon after Ludi's birth. It made her feel as though she could outrun any beast, heal from any disease, win any fight. She looks at Gai Gai, swaying slightly but standing with her feet firmly rooted in the ground. She looks as though she knows what that presence is, now. She looks as though she is outrunning it.

There is some food saved for the midwives and the new mother, and Shaye sits on the ground to eat, hungrily swallowing bites of mushrooms and beechnuts while Ludi talks at her, his words tumbling out of his mouth, in a hurry to tell her all the things that have happened to him while she was away.

She stifles a yawn as he is speaking and lets his chatter wash over her. There is an excited, shrill feeling around the fire. Everyone is impatient to see the baby but there is no light left in the day now. They will have to wait until tomorrow to come to Gai Gai and peer into the little girl's face to exclaim how beautiful she is. Vesti places her hands on the dome of her belly and eyes Gai Gai with a mixture of envy and worry. She will soon return to a fire pit as a heroine too, clutching a tiny bundle of new baby, but she knows she will first have to pass through thorns of agony to get there.

As soon as Shaye swallows her last mouthful, she stands up and takes Ludi by the hand. Some have already left the fire to sleep, some are settling the younger children down with muttered lullabies and hushes. Shaye yawns again, then she walks slowly with Gai Gai on one side and Ludi on the other back to where they left their sleeping mats that dawn; such a long time ago now. She sees that someone, likely Brig, has arranged for Gai Gai's mat to be cleaned and dried.

She kneels on the middle mat, and directs Ludi to the side away from Gai Gai. He doesn't protest as she expected him to. Every night of his life so far he has slept either curled up in her arms or on his own mat in between her and Gai Gai, but perhaps Rilk has been telling him stories about what you lose out when a new baby is born, and so he knows that his time sleeping in the protected nest is over. He curls up into an acorn shape, lying placidly in his new place as elder child. Shaye lies beside him, and in the darkness she fumbles to help Gai Gai arrange herself too, first kneeling, then lowering herself to the ground, then rolling onto her back with a whimper. Shaye hears the baby snuffle then latch onto the breast and begin to suckle, and she hears Gai Gai give a long hiss.

Shaye lies on her back and reaches her hand out to Gai Gai's mat. She gropes for her hand, and Gai Gai gives it, grasping her fingers almost as tightly as before. She has been almost silent since the baby was born. Shaye recognises the feeling. The pain, the endurance of it. The shock of having what was inside you tumble out and become its own being. The reshaping of your heart to cradle around the tiny breath of the new being. She remembers that she lost her tongue for a while too.

It won't hurt forever, she whispers. She's not sure if Gai Gai can hear the chuckle of experience in her voice, or if she minds. You did so well today. I'm so proud of you.

Gai Gai sniffs. I wish Cherl could see her, she whispers into the darkness.

Shaye tries not to let herself imagine him back at the old plenty-time place, his mouth set tight as he watches the river from sunup to sundown.

He will see, she says, squeezing Gai Gai's hand. Next spring, when we come back from the oak grove.

Ludi shifts on his mat beside her.

Goodnight Ma, he says softly, and Shaye reaches her other hand to her other side to stroke his hair. Goodnight Gai Gai, and goodnight baby. See you when the sun comes back.

Shaye feels overcome by the sweetness of Ludi's sleepy call, the innocence and the contented joy of it. Tears spring to her eyes, but she doesn't wipe them away. She stays as she is, one hand wrapped in Gai Gai's and the other resting on her son's warm head, listening to the baby's suckles subside. The tears trace a cool, wet line as they fall towards her ears as she falls asleep, her body heavy on her mat, and she feels as though there is nothing in this world or the next, not even the sick river, that can break the happiness of her family.

〉•〈

Shaye is woken by her aching legs and buttocks. Her body is stiff all over, as if it is she who has given birth. She rolls over and sees that Gai Gai is still asleep, the baby tucked into her elbow, snoring softly. She sits up to see Ludi is awake too. She puts a finger to her mouth and beckons to him. He stands up quietly, moving slowly so as not to rustle his mat and wake Gai Gai or the baby, and follows Shaye away from their mats and into the forest. Shaye is ravenous and she wants to make sure Gai Gai has a feast waiting for her when she wakes up.

Ludi takes pleasure in gathering as much as he can for the new baby's naming feast, and he fills Shaye's basket with mushrooms, damsons and plantain leaves until it is full to the brim. Shaye fills herself with blackberries and chews on one of the mushrooms as they go back towards the fire pit.

Everyone is awake already, and Brig is tending to the fire. Shaye places the basket beside her.

I've sent the net to the river, Brig says, examining what is gathered in the basket. We're going to eat so well today you'll only be able to roll to your mat. Shaye laughs.

Is Sala with Gai Gai?

Brig nods. Ludi has already run off, his dark head bobbing alongside Reo's as they throw a puffball mushroom to each other.

She returns to her sleeping mat and sees Sala kneeling in front of Gai Gai, lying on her back with her knees facing the sky.

It's all looking alright, Sala murmurs, no infection and the usual amount of swelling. She takes a wad of comfrey leaves and crushes them between her fingers. She places them between Gai Gai's legs and holds them in place with a length of cloth.

Now let's see the little one, Sala says, and Gai Gai sits up, unwraps the baby from her swaddling cloth and holds her up by her belly.

They see it before Shaye does. Shaye can only see the baby's face, her eyes tiny black slits, her little mouth opening wide for a yawn. She has perfect rosebud lips and she looks like their mother. Shaye feels a tug in her belly that she recognises. It is the tug of fierce love that tells her she would happily die for this child. When Sala and Gai Gai gasp, it takes her a while to drag her eyes from the sleepy face and look at what they have seen.

The baby has a red mark snaking across her back. It starts at her shoulder, then dips towards her spine, dancing across the mottled skin until it reaches her hip on the other side. It looks like a snake winding its way along her body.

Sala reaches out one finger and touches the mark gently. It is not raised from her body but a part of her skin, painted into it. It is lighter than blood, more like a flame, or the colour of a friction welt.

Sala sits back on her heels. She does not meet Gai Gai's eyes, but begins to chew on her bottom lip. Her hands are shaking, so she clasps them together so that neither Shaye nor Gai Gai can see them quiver.

My baby, my little girl, Gai Gai says. Her voice is no more than a whisper, and she is staring at Sala with terrified eyes. Shaye looks from one to the other, Sala not meeting Gai Gai's gaze. Shaye remembers Hoel, who gave birth to a child with twisted stumps instead of feet some frost times ago. She remembers that Sala and Brig took the child to the river and let it sink into the water to feed the spirits there. She remembers how Hoel moved after that, thickly, as though wading through fog. She let her long dark hair clot into thick clumps and joined another group after the ceremony at the oak grove that shortest day.

Shaye reaches her hand out to Sala, to grasp her arm. She wants to say that Sala cannot do that to Gai Gai's baby, that this red snake is not the same as having a pair of twisted stumps for legs. A lump sticks in her throat. She wants to find Ludi and drag him onto her lap and hold him tight.

Sala shakes Shaye's hand off, and stands up.

I need to speak to the elders, she says briskly, and holds out her hands for the baby. Brig should see this.

Gai Gai hesitates. She does not want to give her child away, not yet, not the dawn after she has met her. She looks at Shaye, who nods gently. Sala cannot harm this child, Shaye thinks. She will not harm her.

Gai Gai hands the baby to Sala and stands up awkwardly, her limbs fighting her. She stands as if in a daze, looking at her child.

You should come to hear what they say, Sala says as she walks away with the half-swaddled baby, and Gai Gai follows her, limping slightly, as listless as if she has already been told that her child will have to die.

Shaye sits on her haunches and watches them leave. A chill runs over her back, and she hugs her arms around herself. She cannot move, even though she is cold. There are things to do. She could go to the river and make sure any fish caught in Brig's net are healthy, she could tend to the fire in the next copse. She could set some traps for hares and mice, or she could spread all the skins she has packed in her pouch and start piecing them together for their frost-time clothes. But she cannot move. Fear tethers her to the same spot she crouched in when she saw the mark on the baby's back, and all she can think of is that little face disappearing into the bloated river's new shallows, and Gai Gai becoming sullen and dirty like Hoel.

It is Ludi who shakes her from her stupor. He bounds over to her, stands with his hands on his hips. His ankles have tide marks around them where he has been paddling in the river, and a line of silt shimmers on his arches.

Ma, where's the baby? he asks. Shaye closes her eyes. Everything feels too bright. I want to show her to Reo, he wants to say hello to her.

Shaye rocks a little, then stands up. Her vision crumples, her head spins.

Reo can see the baby later, she's with Gai Gai now. She places both hands on Ludi's shoulders and guides him away from their mats. And you know you're not going to be able to play with her yet, she's too little.

I know, Ma, but I just want Reo to see her.

He will, he will. She turns him around and gives him a small push between the shoulder blades. Go and play, I've lots to do. If you see good firewood, collect it and put it by the fire.

He runs off, unperturbed by his mother's strange behaviour. He puts it down to the river, Shaye thinks. Perhaps he just accepts us all being slightly mad, and he thinks it's all the river to blame.

Shaye sees the pile of bloody cloth from the day before lying in a heap by their mats, and gazes at it for a moment as though she can't quite remember why it is there or what to do with it. Then a strong gust of wind lifts stray strands of hair from her face and it stirs her to action. She doesn't want to think of what the elders might be deciding, she wants to move. She sweeps the stained cloth into her arms and treads carefully towards the river, the way treacherous and slippery with mud.

She works herself into a sweat as she rubs at the cloth, knee deep in the river, slapping it against the trunks of submerged trees to work the stains out. She hears voices approaching from the path, and ducks under the fronds of a willow so she cannot be seen. She waits. She hears Vesti and Rilk chatting, and she listens for any hint of shock in their voices. There is none; they are talking of the oak grove, of the moots and the men who the initiate said will be gathered there from the last hunts. Shaye lets the cloth dangle and drift in the water so she can be silent. She doesn't want to talk to them, she wants silence in her thoughts and emptiness in her mind.

She lets the women leave and their voices fade before she ducks under the willow fronds and out into the river again. A shiver passes over her shoulders as she wades out of the water and steps up onto the bank. She is sorry to leave the cocoon of the willow. The dappled green light and swish of the wind as it gently lifted a frond to weave around another had been as comforting as a womb. She hopes the baby is not scared. She hopes that if Sala has to bring her to the river, she will duck under this willow frond to return the small body to the water, then at least the baby might feel as though she is returning to the place that held her so safely before she came into this cruel, cold world.

By the time she hangs the wet cloth over a tall branch to dry and returns to the fire pit, she realises everyone knows that there is something wrong with Gai Gai's baby. Ayla won't look at her as she turns the fish over and over on the spit, and Vesti is sitting to one side, hunched over her spindle. Shaye doesn't know how they know, as Sala and the others are tucked away in the thicker trees where no one can see or hear them, but she guesses that someone, probably Vesti, saw Sala carry the newborn to Brig and guessed at what was afoot. Or maybe it was Ayla who told, having understood the tender expression of grief in Gai Gai's tired eyes.

When Shaye appears, the whispers stop and the silence gets loud. She looks for Ludi, ignoring the way their eyes slide away from her. He mustn't hear of this, she thinks desperately, he mustn't get this from Reo, he won't understand. She imagines Ludi running wildly to her, confusion marring his face, trembling as he tells her that the others say there's something wrong with the baby and she can't live, and what will Sala do with her, Ma, why can't she live with us, why can't she grow up?

But Ludi is not there and she is grateful. She wants the elders to come back to the fire pit before he does, she wants to know what is to happen to the baby before he finds out what it is that could happen.

Shaye crouches by the fire and busies herself with skinning some of the hares that lay there. Nobody talks to her. It is as if she is back under the willow fronds again, and no one can see her, but this time the feeling does not make her feel safe.

Then, before she has gutted the first hare, Gai Gai

appears from the gap between two pines. Shaye cannot see her face yet, she grips the hare flesh tightly in one hand and a flint in the other. Sala appears behind her, then Brig, then Yael who stands, frowning deeply. They do not look exactly happy, but none of them look grave either. They look troubled, but this is the way all the elders have looked since the river first began to rise, so Shaye can't tell what it means. Gai Gai is carrying the baby, who is tightly swaddled again, but she isn't looking relieved. She looks shocked, as though she has been told something impossible. There is stillness around the fire pit as everyone else watches Gai Gai and the elders. They wait, as Shaye does, for Sala to turn to them all, acknowledge their anxious wait, and tell them whether or not to continue with their preparations for the naming feast.

But Sala makes no such announcement. She places a hand on Gai Gai's cheek, then turns away to walk to the river. Shaye sees that she avoids the curious eyes that follow her and keeps her eyes on the leaf cover of the earth. Brig disappears into the woods too, her antler knife tucked into her skirt, and Yael comes to squat next to Shaye to skin the hares, returning to what he was doing before Sala summoned him to look at the baby.

Shaye takes this as a sign that the little girl will not be going to the river for anything other than a wash, and so does everyone else around the fire pit. There is a soft sigh of relief, so quiet that only a wolf would hear it, and there are noises of movement again as everyone goes back to their business, although not without a new set of questions in their minds. Shaye feels their wonder burn as they try not to stare at Gai Gai too hard.

Gai Gai fusses with the baby for a moment, and Shaye sees her cheeks flame. She places the hare on the pile of other carcasses; someone else can take its skin and prepare it for the meal. She walks over to Gai Gai, standing with her legs far apart. It was only yesterday that Gai Gai was in labour, struggling to bring that tiny new being into the world.

What did they say? Shaye peers into Gai Gai's face and places a gentle hand on her shoulder. What are they going to do?

Gai Gai turns from the fire pit and leads Shaye off into the woods. She cradles the baby as they walk among the elms and beeches, damp twigs crunching underfoot. Shaye does not have her pouch with her, it is lying by her sleeping mat back beyond the fire pit, but she is not thinking of her nut store now. She picks a handful of black berries and tips some of them into Gai Gai's palm.

They looked at her back, Sala, Brig and Yael. Gai Gai begins. Her voice is low, and she half turns around in case she can be heard. They were quiet for a long time, Shaye, just looking at her. I thought I would go mad, I couldn't breathe, could hardly stand up.

Shaye says nothing. She stares at the earth in front of their feet. They continue to wander, slowly, not trying to get anywhere in particular but just to move away from the confusion that has infected everything since the dawn.

Anyway, they decided quite soon that it wasn't a curse, that she could live and grow up. Gai Gai takes a deep breath. But then they couldn't decide what it did mean. They touched it over and over again, and she didn't like it, she started crying and she wouldn't stop. I think she knew—

Gai Gai breaks off.

Ludi knew, I remember he was very sensitive to what people were saying around him, Shaye offers. Gai Gai nods absently, as if this is not much comfort, as if she wants to be told that babies cannot hear or understand anything.

Anyway, Brig said it was like the snake, and she thought it meant that the baby should be dedicated to the snake spirit. But then Sala said she was sure the river spirit called her, and maybe this was a sign about the river rising?

Shaye feels something flip over in her belly.

She said she wants the initiates at the oak grove to look at her and decide—

Decide if she should go into the water? Shaye cannot keep the horror from her voice.

No. Gai Gai smiles suddenly, as if she has only just realised that won't happen. No, she's definitely not going to go into the water. Thank the spirits.

She shifts the baby onto her shoulders so she is carried upright. Shaye sees that she is asleep, her tiny pink mouth puckered.

But Yael said something about the initiates taking special children and raising them at the oak grove. Sala tried to change the subject, but you know how he is. Once he gets an idea in his mind he can't let it go. He said she's a sacred child, and he thinks the mark isn't a snake at all, but a river.

A river? Shaye tries to recall what she saw that morning on the child's back, the shape of it, where it marred the soft skin. She can't. She only saw the red welt quickly before Sala bundled her up again.

Gai Gai nods. That's why the initiates might be interested in her.

Something occurs to Shaye, but she tries to chase the thought away. She doesn't want to put it in Gai Gai's mind, not if it hasn't already occurred to her too.

I asked Yael if he thinks they'll want her for the ceremony, Gai Gai continues. Her voice is carefully steady but Shaye winces. She cannot think of that. Somehow it is much worse than her going into the water.

But he said he doesn't think so. Gai Gai's frown softens so it is no longer so deeply etched in her skin. So we're going to have her naming feast today, and she's going to be dedicated to the river.

Gai Gai sighs, and she stops walking.

But they're worried, the elders. She shifts the baby again to cradle her flat, and she looks away from Shaye, at her daughter's face. I don't know why. She shakes her head. I don't want to know why. Not yet.

Shaye holds her hands out towards the baby. Can I see the mark again?

Gai Gai glances over her shoulder, just briefly, but the hint of fear Shaye sees in her face makes her worried. Nobody else will ask to see the mark, but when they get to the oak grove everybody will be looking to catch a glimpse of it, and stories will spread from mat to mat about what will happen to her as she grows.

Gai Gai kneels and places the baby across her lap. She unwinds the swaddling as though unspooling thread from a spindle, and holds the baby against her chest. The baby's fingers twitch as she feels a sudden breeze dance across her skin, but she doesn't wake up. Shaye crouches in front of Gai Gai, the baby between them, and she looks carefully at the mark. It is no different to how it appeared that morning, but the skin around it is less mottled, turning the same colour as young elder bark, just like them. Shaye doesn't want to touch it, but she is afraid she will offend Gai Gai if she does not, so she passes her thumb over the place where the mark fades into the skin and then fights the urge to wipe her hands on her skirt.

She smiles at Gai Gai and shakes herself.

If the elders tell you not to be worried, then let's not be worried! She stands up, and holds the baby as Gai Gai winds the cloth around her again. We've got a naming feast to cook for, come on. Shaye gives the baby back to Gai Gai, and takes her hand as they return to the place where the fire is already twice the size it was yesterday, and the air is already beginning to smell of roasting hare.

> • <

A naming feast is one of Shaye's very favourite times. Full moon fires are not special enough, they happen too often. The hawthorn blossom festival of Bel used to be wonderful, back in the times when Marl showed his wrists to her and took her off to be alone, but that has not happened for a while now, and at the last one there were no men left who hadn't gone on the hunting trip, so she had left the fire early and gone to sleep between Gai Gai and Ludi as usual, dreaming of Marl's hands on her body. The longest day is always marred by the itchy bites all over her body, and the night of the ancestors is sad, while the ceremony of the shortest day at the oak grove is never something to look forward to.

No, it is a naming feast, however humble, that makes Shaye's heart glad. And she has been looking forward to this one since the day during the last frosts when Gai Gai had whispered that she had missed her bleed twice in a row.

As she takes her place around the fire, with the light beginning to dim and a belly fuller than it has been for a moon, Shaye remembers that moment. She remembers the way that Gai Gai had turned back to Ker, who had been sitting on the other side of her, leaning forward so the heat from the fire glanced off his face. She had nuzzled her head into his long black beard, sliding her hand under his hide cloak to scratch at his belly.

Ker left with the rest of the hunting party when the frosts began to soften, the one that didn't return. Cherl had steadily grown in wrath with each day of the spring and plenty time that passed without the return of the men. He used to sit on a log he had carved into a comfortable seat, whittling his knives and spindles and keeping watch for the men when they might come. Some joked that they wouldn't come back for fear of the scorn Cherl would unleash upon them, others worried that something terrible had befallen them, a horrible hunting accident perhaps, or a pack of wolves which had claimed them all. Gai Gai never seemed to be worried about where Ker was. Shaye used to wonder sometimes if the only thing that caused her to remember him was her growing belly, for she could not stop thinking about Marl.

Shaye holds onto Ludi's wrist to keep him next to her, but she doesn't need to. The boy is rocking back and forth on his heels in excitement, but watching Sala and Gai Gai carefully.

Sala raises her hands to the sky, and all the murmured conversations hush. The air becomes thick, and there are no more crackles of twigs and leaves on the ground as everyone stands very still, their eyes fixed on the women next to the fire.

Here we are gathered around our sacred fire to welcome this new soul into our world.

Sala stretches her fingers as if she might grasp a star in her palms, and for a second all the tension of the day melts from Shaye's mind, and she closes her eyes. She takes a deep, full breath of forest air. Air that smells like the burning branches of the fire, the loamy earth underfoot, and the damp heaviness of the leaves that Shaye has only ever thought of as smelling of the colour green. A chorus of blackbirds begins, and distantly there are some crickets squawking at each other. She opens her eyes again and focuses them on Gai Gai, and the baby in her arms.

This girl child was born on the first dawn after the full thunder moon, Sala says, loud enough for everyone standing to hear her. What do we call her?

Gai Gai swallows, and a slow smile spreads across her face.

Her name is Nata, dedicated to the river.

Shaye has been expecting some surprise, but it seems that everyone already knows which spirit the baby is born of. There are no sharp breaths and no wide eyes. Only smiles of pleasure.

And who speaks for Nata of the river? Sala asks. She is using her loud ceremonial voice, but her eyes are soft.

I, her mother, Gai Gai of the owl, Gai Gai replies.

And who speaks for Gai Gai of the owl? Sala calls, half turning to Shaye, who steps forward in anticipation.

It is I, Shaye of the mistletoe, she replies, then steps back to her place, gently pushing Ludi forward.

And who speaks for you, Shaye of the mistletoe? Sala calls.

Ludi, who can hardly breathe his chest is so puffed up with pride, takes another step forward so everyone can see him.

It is I, Ludi of the fire, he shouts, and there is a low chuckle among the grown ones. Shaye takes his shoulders and gently pulls him next to her. She holds him tightly to her, her throat thick with emotion. He is quivering, and eagerly watching everyone step forward to name themselves and their spirit. It is the first time he's done it for himself, and Shaye can see the gentle power of the ceremony is thrumming in him exactly as it does every time for her.

She's been telling him about the naming ceremony since Gai Gai's belly first began to expand and droop over her skirt. She's told him all the stories of why the people he loves are dedicated as they are: that Gai Gai is of the owl because it was the first thing Sala heard when she delivered her; that he himself is of the fire because it was the only light in the world he first came into; that Shaye is of the mistletoe because her mother gave birth to her at the foot of a great oak entwined with the sacred plant. She knows he will ask questions about why baby Nata is dedicated to the river, but for the moment he is caught up in the occasion, and she puts the worry of what she will tell him out of her head.

Shaye listens, and kneads Ludi's trembling shoulder, as one by one everyone names themselves and their spirits. Like Ludi, Reo is naming himself for the first time and, like Ludi, he is throbbing with the pleasure of it. Rowan and blackbird; fox, woodpecker and sea kelp: they are all invoked with their name, and Shaye feels as though every living thing in the world has come to sit with them to see the new baby, and sing her spirit into being.

It is Brig's turn to name herself.

It is I, Brig of the snake, she calls, and she walks softly towards Gai Gai and Nata, the dead rope of the snake she caught yesterday in one hand, and an antler knife in the other.

Gai Gai has unwrapped Nata from her swaddling and slung the length of cloth over her shoulder. She cradles her, but away from her body so that when Brig slices along the length of the snake, the sacred blood does not fall on her own body.

Softly, so that no one really hears it over the infant's thin wail, Sala mutters, And I speak for Brig. I, Sala of the rains.

Brig lets the blood drip on Nata's belly, squeezing the body of the snake to draw more from it. Sala begins to sing, and before she has finished the first couple of notes everyone has joined in, even the children for they all know the naming song. It is one of those songs that is not so sacred that it is never taught, but also not so common that a heart can become lazy to its joy, and never quicken with pride and happiness during a naming ceremony when everyone present opens their mouths and lets their voices soar into the sky.

Brig tucks the knife into her skirt and with one finger smears the blood around Nata's skin. She sings as she works the blood into the creases around her elbows and under her armpits, then across the fat lumps of her knees. She dips a finger into the carcass of the snake, then passes it over her lips, down her cheeks, and across her forehead. Nata is no longer crying. Gai Gai is rocking her and singing her daughter's name and spirit to the tune of the ancient naming song. The baby seems to like it.

When the baby is covered in the drying paste of the snake's blood, Brig tosses the snake carcass into the fire with a murmured prayer of thanks. Gai Gai holds Nata up, high above her head, and turns slowly so that everybody can see her. Shaye remembers when she held Ludi up for everyone's cheers. She had thought her heart would burst with the perfection of him.

Gai Gai lowers Nata into her arms and swaddles her again. Shaye puts her forefingers in her mouth and whistles, catching Gai Gai's eye and sharing a smile. That starts all the noise; everyone starts cheering and clapping, stamping their feet on the ground and making a ruckus fit to wake the dead. Birds jump into the air, startled from their perches by the sudden commotion, and Shaye sees the tail of a red fox as it slinks away from them, wanting some peace from the strange shouting.

Gai Gai is flushed with pleasure, her hands trembling as she finishes wrapping the baby and gathers her to her breast. She lowers her eyes as she turns again, smiling at everyone whooping and shouting for her baby. Tears gather in the corners of her eyes and drip down her nose.

Shaye takes Ludi by the hand and walks towards the fire. Gai Gai crouches so that Ludi can see the baby's face, and he leans forward, his hands twisting as he tries to contain himself.

Hello, Nata of the river, he whispers. I'm Ludi of the fire. I'm your kin.

Shaye squeezes his hand and tries to swallow the spiky lump rising in her throat.

Hello, Nata of the river, she whispers. The baby's eyes are peacefully shut, despite the noise of the welcome, and Shaye brushes her lips against the soft skin of her cheek. I'm Shaye of the mistletoe.

Shaye feels everyone pressing in behind her, eager to get their chance to greet the baby. She withdraws to let Vesti get close to the baby, her eyes shining with delight at the tiny toes, and takes Ludi away from the fire.

Will Nata play with me, Ma? Ludi asks as the light dims and the noise of the cheering and clapping is replaced by the whispers of the greeting and the rustles of people retiring to their sleeping mats. He yawns and leans into her as he watches Gai Gai smile at the last few people to greet Nata.

She will one day, Shaye murmurs. When she's bigger and older.

I'm going to show her everything I know, Ludi mumbles. His eyes are drooping, and Shaye lifts him to his feet and leads him to their sleeping mats. He is far too big to carry now, but his limbs have become soft in their tiredness and easy to guide.

I'm going to show her which nuts are good, and I'm going to help her climb trees. Shaye rolls him over onto his side and lies down next to him. And I'm going to pick blackberries for her, and I'm not going to tell Gai Gai if she's naughty.

Shaye sweeps a lock of hair back from his forehead.

Shhh. Go to sleep now, she whispers and Ludi begins to snuffle. You'll see her in the dawn. She strokes his head softly. We'll all see her again when the light comes back.

›•‹

The next dawn, Sala comes to examine Gai Gai again. She clucks approvingly as she looks between Gai Gai's legs and changes the comfrey compress.

How do you feel? she asks. Do you think you can keep walking?

Gai Gai nods. Yes, I can. I'll be fine. She looks towards Shaye with a faltering smile, a smile that betrays some of her shock. On the night of the fruit moon fire, she was still pregnant. Now she has a baby who is honoured by the spirits, a baby who might be favoured by the initiates at the oak grove. There is some distance between there and here, thinks Shaye, so she gives Gai Gai an encouraging smile back.

Good, says Sala. We'll start walking today then. I'll tell everyone to start packing up.

Shaye follows Sala until Gai Gai cannot hear them. She places a hand on Sala's shoulder and the older woman turns as if she has been expecting this talk. Is it her imagination, or does Sala stiffen as she turns to face her?

Please tell me, I won't tell Gai Gai but at least I could start to prepare her, Shaye whispers. What will the initiates do with the baby?

Sala shakes her head, softly.

Nothing bad. It's a blessing, for a child to be born on the path, to be born in a time of change like this, says Sala, her voice so deliberately comforting that Shaye wonders if she is lying. She narrows her eyes, tries to see the meaning lurking beneath the words.

And this mark is a blessing too, I can feel it.

Will the initiates want her? Shaye looks carefully for any falter of her smile.

Sala opens her palms. I can't know that. We will certainly show Nata to them when we get there, but I don't know what her mark means. Honestly, Shaye.

Shaye nods, and smiles tightly.

I'm going to pack my things, Sala says and she turns away. But when she thinks her face can no longer be seen, Sala lets her smile fade and be replaced by an expression of what her heart truly feels. Shaye sees her mouth drop into weariness and worry, and for a moment she sees how the mask of the kind and watchful elder takes its toll on the face underneath. Sala's true face, lined with exhaustion and etched with the same vague panic that infects them all.

Get ready to leave, Sala calls over her shoulder, and Shaye can tell that her mask of confidence is back in place, ready to display to anyone else who calls upon her. We'll be walking again as soon as everyone's set.

It's the birds that wake her, a twittering choir of chirping that drags her from sleep, confused. She wonders if Grainne has changed the sound of her alarm, but no, she's not in her own bedroom, the light's too bright, and kind of green too. She tries to pull her duvet up but there's nothing covering her and her hands only clutch at a T-shirt and some dried leaves.

She opens her eyes and the memory of where they are and why fills her mind. Dread fills her stomach, and she rolls over onto her side. Her neck aches, the muscles taut like the strings of her lute, and her legs feel like a stuffed toy, ragged and woolly as she tries to stretch out.

Locke and Grainne are still asleep, or they're both just lying with their eyes closed and pretending they can sleep through the chatter of the birds. She wonders what makes them sing like that. Perhaps they're unusually scared of the dark, and each morning they're so relieved to see the light again they have to get together and have a sing-song about it. Perhaps they're catching each other up on all the news of the night-time, gossiping and spreading rumours.

She sits up, reaches her arms up and ignores the protests from the places on her shoulders where she carried the lute yesterday. Her eyes are gritty and she feels the light-headedness of being so tired when you went to sleep that your brain can't catch up with all the rest it needs. She slips her feet into her socks, then her shoes. She struggles to get her shoes onto her swollen feet, and they feel tight and hot when she shoves her toes right to the end of the shoe. She loosens the laces then shuts her eyes for a moment. This can't be happening. How she'd like to open her eyes and find that it was all a dream, back in her bed next to a sleeping Grainne, ready to get up and start their real journey to the north.

She gets to her feet, hips cracking, knees groaning, and stumbles to find a large tree to hide behind so she can piss. As she pulls down her jeans and crouches, she wonders if this is the same tree she led Locke to at dusk last night, if perhaps she's standing in the puddle she made of her own waste last night and peeing into it again. She's surprised to find that she doesn't much care. Watching the newscasts of the flood refugees, the long lines of people leaving their homes in river deltas or coastal cities and living in their makeshift camps, she's always been struck by how dirty they are, how quickly people become raggedy and dishevelled when they are flung from their homes. She's always known that she would look like that if she were in one of those camps. But she never expected to be. She thought she would be safe.

She slept in her jeans and the T-shirt she put on yesterday morning, and she's planning to wear them to walk today. Her skin is covered in a layer of dirt, sweat and all the other body secretions she doesn't ever think about but automatically washes off each morning. A shower, even a cold one, would go quite some way to making her feel like herself again, but the water in the thirty-eight bottles can't be used for anything as trivial as washing. Perhaps she already looks like those bedraggled people on the newscasts, the ones she used to watch with a detached pity, then turn away to do something else. At the thought of water running over her naked skin, her mouth becomes dry. She's thirsty again.

Locke and Grainne are awake by the time she gets back to their beds. Grainne has packed away the T-shirts that doubled as sheets, and there are three bottles of water standing around a packet of biscuits.

Breakfast, says Grainne, gesturing towards the food. She looks bleary-eyed too, and she's rubbing her neck with a grimace. Locke looks brighter than the pair of them and he tears into the packet of biscuits, opening the plastic with his teeth when he gets frustrated with his fingers. Shante knows he's hungry, it's obvious from how quiet he is, but he doesn't say anything. A rush of guilt makes her dizzy for a second. She takes one biscuit and nibbles at it. She has two gulps of her water bottle and then tucks it into her handbag. She'll ration it throughout the day, have one gulp an hour or something like that. It'll be something to look forward to, something to mark the passage of time.

When the packet of biscuits is finished, mainly by Locke, there's nothing to stop them getting going again. Shante checks her watch; only seven thirty, they've got more than twelve hours to get as far along this road as they can before darkness threatens. She passes her handbag diagonally across her body, then shrugs the lute bag onto her back. It jangles as she bends down to zip up the suitcase, and there seems to be something defiant about the sound; discordant but definite, as though it has come to a decision. Maybe she'll play it tonight, to help Locke to sleep. That'll make her feel like herself, like a human being.

Ready? she asks Locke. He nods, his thumbs tucked into the straps of his backpack.

She glances at Grainne, who sighs. Off we go then. She begins to wheel the suitcase over the bumpy leaves, slightly downhill towards the road.

This is how it will be, every morning until they see the gates of the city. One step after another, day after day, until they come back to civilisation. This is an endurance game, there's nothing strong or smart about it. She has to be a tortoise, not a hare. She's never seen either of those animals but she knows the story. Step. Step. Step. Here she goes.

> • <

For the first couple of days, she keeps expecting to come to the border at any moment. She walks with her eyes on the horizon, looking out for gates or guards or buildings. She goes over and over a map of the territory in her head, has endless discussions with Grainne about where they might be. All fruitless, as they have no idea where the train stopped. After three days of squinting into the distance, she gives up looking. It is too tiring, and there's too much else to be worried about. They have twenty-nine bottles left, and a large, fierce hope that they will get there before they drink them all.

She gets used to the thirst. She drinks one bottle of water a day and pees twice, once in the morning when she gets up and again before she lies down on the leaves to go to sleep. Each time her pee is yellow and strong smelling, but she's still alive and still walking, and that seems to be the only thing that matters now.

She gets used to being dirty too. After a few days she stops noticing that she smells of sweat and sleep. She keeps her hair tied up in a pile on top of her head to keep her neck cool, and when she gets used to the smell of her unwashed body she notices that her scalp no longer itches.

When her period comes, with the accompanying dull ache in her back, she is shocked. She had forgotten that her body does this, and it seems strange to her that everything inside her skin has been carrying on as normal. Her tab would usually warn her, counting down the days with a special red graphic. She retrieves her silicone cup from the bottom of her suitcase and squats in the forest to place it inside her, and she ducks off the path every few hours to empty it. She clears some leaves and pours the blood onto the dirt before kicking the leaves back over the wet patch. She can't use the water to rinse out the cup before she puts it back again, or wash her hands. This disgusts her at first, and she uses a spare T-shirt to wipe her hands, leaving pink streaks all over it. She bundles it into a plastic bag and stuffs it inside the suitcase, but there is still blood left under her nails and cuticles. She picks at it as she walks, trying to clean her own blood from herself. This forest is turning her into an animal.

The road never changes. Occasionally, a giant steel structure like a thin pyramid will loom to one side of them, far taller than the trees, reaching up to a point far above their heads, almost scratching the sky like the buildings at home. Locke asks if it's a climbing frame like at the playground at home.

They're old electricity pylons, she tells him. She remembers learning about them in school, drawing diagrams of how the territorial grid used to work before the cities shut. They used to carry electricity in the old days, before solar glass and wind farms.

Locke nods, only mildly interested. It's hard for him to imagine a world different to the one he lives in now, he thinks things have always been the way they are for him. The curse of humanity, Charlie used to say. Doomed to cycle through the same mistakes until we fall off the wheel.

But mainly, it's just the road and the trees. The grey concrete shimmers in the midday heat and the white paint of the lane lines flakes off under their steps. It feels like they could be the last humans alive. Perhaps the train guard died because of some calamity back in the city, a war perhaps, or a really bad blackout that knocked out the network and the servers and everything that keeps the world going. Perhaps this is the end of the world, and all there is left is miles of trees, tiny rodents with bushy tails and birds. She knew from Charlie's stories that the forest was a lonely place, but she didn't know that it sucked the life from you, made you feel part of the forest itself and no longer human at all.

Shante's beginning to notice that the trees are all different to each other. Some of them have smoother trunks that look more like stone, as if they'd be hard to cut down and slow to rot, but some of them have trunks that look softer. Their wood is more ridged, with dark crevices in the bark that smell like the soil in the morning. Shante imagines all the insects that probably make their homes in those holes, those that come out each day at dusk to skitter around their heads.

What do you think they're doing? Grainne asks as the first of them appear while the sun sinks behind the trees.

They're coming to say goodnight to their friends before they go to bed, Locke says. He bats them away from his face. They're having fun.

Grainne laughs. After that, she and Locke look forward to the time each day when the tiny buzzing insects appear and they have pretend conversations with the insects, asking them if they've had enough to eat, what they learnt at flying school that day. Talking like that makes Locke laugh, and Shante feels a little lighter every time she hears his giggle.

Grainne keeps taking the tabs from their bags to charge them, connecting them to the solar batteries and laying them out in the sun while they sit down in the shade of the trees to have some lunch. Shante never tells her that it's probably futile because it seems to give her some hope, but no matter what she does, they never get back online. Their smooth black surfaces stay cool, no matter how hot it gets, and the screens only say one thing: Disconnected from the network.

Leave them, Grainne, they're not coming back on while we're out here, Shante says, but her sister shrugs and fiddles with them anyway. When they're fully charged they bleat and say, Disconnected from the network. Locke starts to repeat it, mimicking its high-pitched, robotic voice. Disconnected from the network, disconnected from the network. Shante tells him to stop.

It seems more practical to put her effort into worrying about the other things they brought from the city, the food and the water. They each drink a bottle of water a day, and store the empty ones in their suitcases. Perhaps it will rain soon, but Shante can't tell when. The sky is the same brilliant blue it was when they were in the city. She thinks of it like a cold, hard diamond encircling the world; beautiful but indifferent.

The trees seem to care though. They seem to nod politely to her as she passes and urge her onwards. When there's a breeze they shiver and their leaves all sing. She thought it was quiet out here when they first left that station and walked along that suspended path, but now she hears every movement of every creature and leaf. The birdsong too, that's different. It used to seem like a chorus, lots of animals singing to a crescendo with a single loud voice, but now she hears it as an orchestra. The birds as musicians just like her, playing at different pitches, harmonising with each other and letting the different parts come in to have a solo every now and then. There can be no conductor, and they're following no score, but their music is complex and never the same twice. Shante never gets bored of it. She listens as she walks, and tells herself that when they stop for the night she'll get out the lute and try to mimic the birds, but she's always too tired and the light fades quicker than she expects. Melodies keep tumbling through her mind, and she hums them to try to remember them.

She gets used to the hunger. It gets easier to handle, less maddeningly distracting to her walking. It hums quietly in her belly, receding like a shadow at midday when they sit at the side of a tree and eat their biggest meal: nuts, crackers and occasionally a fruit bar. But still, thirst torments her without relief. Her mouth sometimes so sticky that she can hardly speak.

Grainne and Locke are hungry too, getting bored of the same food and tired of her tucking packets of crackers back into the suitcase when they're still hungry.

On the day when they have twenty-one water bottles left, Grainne says, Maybe we can pick things in this forest to eat.

Shante looks at her, surprised. Have you seen anything we could eat here?

Well, no. But the animals have to eat, don't they? We should eat what they do.

Shante is silent for a bit. Neither of them have seen any of the animals. They know they're there, they've seen the scat and the chewed-up remains of prey, and they've heard the night-time scuffles, but everything in the forest seems to know to keep away from them. Shante's glad. She doesn't want to worry about wolves or foxes or whatever, as well as everything else.

Think about it, how did people ever find out what to eat? Grainne says. They just tried it and waited to see what happened.

You can't be serious.

I am. I'm hungry, Shan, aren't you? And there must be loads of food out there. She waves her arm towards the trees. I don't think we need to suffer like this anymore. Grainne looks around her and sees a clump of a bright green plant with tiny white flowers growing just on the edge of the road, where the concrete dips off and becomes earth. She pulls at a handful. It's springy, and with another tug it comes away in her hands. She brushes the dirt off and holds it up.

Is it alright to eat? Shante asks.

I don't know, but it's green. Greens are good for you. She holds it to her nose. It doesn't smell poisonous. She holds it out to Shante. Here, smell it.

Shante sniffs. She's hungry, and it occurs to her that this

green plant surely has some water in it. It smells bright and clean, a bit like the salad leaves you could sometimes buy back at home.

We could call Granda, Locke says. He'd know.

Shante and Grainne do not look at each other. They try not to think of Charlie, but the fact is that Locke's right, he probably would know if they can eat this green thing or not. Or, if he didn't know, he would certainly tell them how to find out.

Fine, let's taste it, see what happens. Shante feels nervous but her mouth is sour with the sudden rush of saliva.

Grainne picks off one tiny leaf and puts it in her mouth. There's hardly any chewing to be done, but she moves her mouth again and swallows it. Shante waits, worried, then feels her stomach unclench as nothing happens.

Do you think it could be some kind of slow-acting poison? Shante says. Maybe it'll only affect you tomorrow.

Grainne laughs and puts the rest of the plant in her mouth. I think it's fine, it's yummy. She pulls another handful from the edge and gives it to Shante. Here, you have some.

Can I have some too? Locke asks.

You wait until I've tasted it, Shante responds, and fills her mouth.

It's an instant relief from the thirst and she chews and swallows it easily. It tastes a little bit like a freshly cut lawn. They've been eating nothing but bland, white food for days now and her stomach seems to sigh with relief.

Yeah, I think it's good, she says, and picks a clump to give to Locke and another for herself. It feels so right to eat this stuff, she can't stop herself. They pull up all of that little white flowered plant they see on that edge, and eat it all.

When they start walking again, they keep their eyes fixed on that place between the concrete and the soil, looking for more. When they find it, Locke shouts out and pounces on it as though it might run away, and they pull it from the ground and share it out. For the first time since leaving the train, Shante goes to sleep that night with her thirst slaked.

After that, they look at the forest more closely, trying to find something they can eat. The day after they found the tiny leaves, Locke finds some kind of dark purple berry on a bush with thick stems spiked with thorns and eats it before Shante can inspect it. He groans with delight and picks some more before she can stop him.

They're delicious, Mum! he says, picking another and thrusting it at her. Try it.

It's tart at first, but then the taste relaxes into sweetness. Best of all, it's wet and soothes the itch of thirst in her mouth. Before she has swallowed the first berry she picks the next one. They spend an hour at that bush, stripping it of every single berry, climbing over the thorns to get to the ones underneath and scratching their arms up to the shoulders.

Your tongue's black, Auntie! Locke shouts, pointing at Grainne as she opens her mouth wide to fit in a whole handful of berries. Grainne laughs, and Locke sticks his tongue out at her.

Is mine black too? She nods, and they giggle together, showing each other their tongues after they eat more and more fruit. Shante laughs with them.

That night Shante feels her intestines gurgle with the unexpected weight of all that fruit, but she's less thirsty and that loosens the knot of worry tying up her stomach. She lies listening to the nocturnal animals going about their night-time business and feels a kinship with them. She's eaten wild food and felt her belly expand with nourishment; she's like the squirrels and the foxes now. She feels as though the animals know this; there's something friendlier about their footsteps in the dark now, and occasionally they catch a glimpse of a red-tinged tail flicking behind a tree, or the glossy black feathers of some bird in a high branch before it flies away.

Yes, the forest is their friend now. They eat the tiny stretchy leaves and the dark purple berries when they find them, and they chat about the stars before they go to sleep. Locke is no longer frightened of the absolute blackness of the night. Sometimes they watch as the satellites draw their straight lines across the curved sky, but she no longer connects the fact of their presence in space with her own tab, whose silence she is beginning to forget about.

It's actually peaceful, isn't it, Shante says one day to Grainne. Not taking your tab out of your bag every five minutes to check it, no beeps, no notifications, no nudges to input your data?

Grainne makes a face. I don't miss all that, but I wish we had some way of knowing what's happening in the news. I'm worried there's been some kind of mega-blackout, and that's why the tabs are down.

Aren't we just too far away from the masts?

Maybe. Grainne pauses. I've always thought the masts are inter-city and inter-territorial, but maybe I was wrong.

Shante looks at the trees. She feels sure they don't know which city just had a coup, which river just flooded or which old nuclear station exploded. They're still, and change so slowly that she thinks you could sit and watch one for a whole day and never see its growth. Like Locke. She turns to him sometimes and sees that his hair is longer, the bottom of his shorts higher from his knees and his jaw a little less chubby.

I'm glad we've given it a rest with the doom and gloom, she says. I don't need to know all that bad news.

You can't just bury your head in the sand, Shan, Grainne says. Wouldn't you rather know about something catastrophic before we get to the border?

What can we do about it? We're just trying to save ourselves, Grainne.

The only thing that feels real now is the road under her feet and the watching trees.

And the sky, the endless blue sky. She watches it the way she used to watch the newscasts, scanning it for any hint of change or omen. They need the rain to come. She collects the empty water bottles in the suitcase and waits to see a cloud. At night she lies awake and makes bargains with the blackness above her. If you rain I'll be kind to everyone I meet, forever. If you rain I'll donate money to the refugees of the river deltas, if you rain I'll volunteer at a refuge when I get to Zeb's city, if you'll only rain I'll do anything, I promise, just tell me and I'll do it.

Locke distracts her from her deals with the sky with his chatter about the forest. He usually walks a little ahead of them in the mornings, picking up twigs, stones and little green nuts in pitted shells to fill his pockets with. After lunch he whines until Grainne gives him a piggyback, and then he pulls at her shoulders to stop her when he thinks he's seen an animal, telling them all to shush when they are already quiet.

Stop! he shouts on the day they have nine water bottles left. Let me get down, Auntie, I want to see that plant there.

Grainne dumps him on the ground and he runs off to a patch of straggly green plants in the gap between the two sides of the old road. He puts his face in the wild tangle, his nose a fraction away from the leaves.

Mum! He runs to her, grabs her hand and drags her back to the bushes. Come and look at this.

He points to the tiny pods thronging the stem and Shante leans forward with a sigh.

Wait, Mum, watch what it's going to do.

Before her eyes, the pods throb and release little puffs of yellow dust.

Locke shrieks. Did you see it? Did you see that, Mum? He presses his face close to the edges of the leaves, serrated like a breadknife, entranced. Shante murmurs that she did see it, wasn't it lovely, let's get walking again now sweetheart, but she is entranced too. She didn't know that plants could do anything like that, almost breathe as though they are alive. She feels as though she's witnessed the living pulse of the forest in that tiny breath of dust from that pod, and the thought is big, too big to fit inside her mind at one time, like thinking of the scale of the universe and feeling dizzy. She can't think of the throbbing dust of the stinging plant too much without feeling as though she's falling into some kind of urgent but horrible truth, the way you can't look directly into the sun.

He walks for the rest of the afternoon, collecting fallen leaves from the ground and laying them out in a line in front of him as he eats his dinner crackers.

Mum, what type of tree is this leaf from? He holds up a

small, vaguely oval-shaped leaf with rounded lobes on each side. A naming question. She has no idea, but she recognises the type of leaf, they're everywhere and they fall from a tree that seems to grow outwards as well as up. They often sleep under those trees, there's something solid and comforting about them.

She could be silly, make him laugh, deflect his question with a joke as she always does. But now there is a curiosity building in her about the names of the trees that make up the forest around them, a forest which now seems to be looking after them in the way the world at home never did.

It's from a spreading root tree, she says. She calls it that because she's seen that those trees often have roots that extend far away from the trunk, often forming hollows which they can pile leaves into and curl up to sleep.

He seems pleased with that, and repeats the name to himself. She feels a tiny pang of guilt but pushes it away. They'll be at the city soon and he'll never see any of these trees in one place again.

And what about this one? He holds up a leaf with five large lobes, tightly serrated at its edges.

That's a star tree. She says the first thing that comes into her mind. Because it looks like a star, can you see? He nods, and places it gently next to the other one on the road.

And do you know what type of tree this comes from? He holds up a piece of bark, brown on one side and silvery white on the other. She recognises the tree again, one of those slender ones that grow straight upwards and close to each other like strands of spaghetti in a jar, their tiny leaves dotted against the sky like one of those ancient pointillist paintings.

That's called a silver string tree, she tells him with confidence, and he looks at the strip of bark with a new wonder, and gently tucks it away inside his backpack.

It's like she's said the words of a magic spell. These things he's picked up off the road have been named now, and they seem to have a new importance for him. They finish eating, pack away the food and start walking again. As she's going, she sees the trees that she named for her son, and when he sees them he points them out to her. She feels the effects of the magic naming spell too, now she feels as though she knows each of the trees that she gave a name to, and recognises them the way she'd recognise a person she knows. Privately, she gives names to the other types of tree too, and then she feels as though she is walking among friends.

She never says anything like this to Grainne, but she can tell she feels something of the same quiet comfort in the solid, still trunks. On the morning of the day when they have six water bottles left, Shante sees her sister pressing her forehead to the trunk of what she calls a spreading root tree as she leads Locke back from going to the toilet. She appears to be talking to the tree in a whisper, her palms pressed against the rough bark. Shante stamps on the leaves to signal their return, and Grainne jumps back as though she has been caught doing something wrong. Shante says nothing, but she feels a rush of love for her sister that reminds her of when they were children, and she would go to pick her up from her class downstairs at school, take her by the hand and lead her out to the playground where their mother would be waiting. For she sees that Grainne has fallen in love with the forest as surely as she has, Locke too, and she is praying for rain with a strange but sure faith that the trees somehow know how to make it happen.

Sometimes, if Sala has heard a wolf or seen a track that tells her a pack have been close, they walk in a tight group, keeping the children close by. When the forest thins and they can see through the trees for a long distance all around, they know nothing can sneak up on them and they spread out again, allowing the boys to dawdle and wander. Sometimes there is nothing to pick the whole day, and they have to build a fire at night and take Brig's net to the river; but if they pass blackberry bushes that groan with fruit, then the forest is lively that night with everyone trying to find a private place to empty their guts. They do not try to hunt the herds of bison they see among the distant trees; Ayla itches to hurl her spear and see what she hits, but there's no time to stop and butcher any animal she might catch.

The path is flat at this point, dotted with small stones that Shaye kicks out of her way as she walks. The river lurks just out of sight, and Shaye notices that everyone is happier when they can't see it. When last fall time's leaf litter gets thin underfoot, thin mud squelches between Shaye's toes, but mostly the path is dry, the deer and lynx tracks dusty and indistinct. The trees grab what little moisture they can and suck it down deep into their roots.

The river has become too salty to drink now, it tastes exactly the same as the sea. There is only the dawn rainwater and the occasional spring to drink from. Every morning when she opens her eyes and sees there is a misty cloud cover, Shaye thanks the sky spirit, for without the pitiful rain there would be nothing to drink at all. Some say it's a sign their luck is changing, for there had not been rain for many moons before. Now the rains come just as we become unable to drink from the river, they say. The sky spirit is protecting us.

Sometimes Ludi walks beside her, asking questions about the oak grove, about the river, about the baby. She gives him a waterskin to carry, reminding him to hold it the right way up and not tip out the gathered droplets. Often Ludi runs with Reo, only coming to her with a dirty palm held out when he gets hungry. He is growing. His skin is stretching its fat stores to grow up and out, and he looks less and less like a baby. He moves easily now, dextrous in his limbs, hopping over splayed roots and ducking under spiky branches without seeing them. Shaye remembers the last journey to the oak grove, his hand clamped tightly in hers, the hood of the hare-skin cape she had made for him pulled firmly over his forehead.

Mostly, Shaye walks at the back of the group. She senses that Sala wishes her to. Sala and Brig still walk at the front. They talk quietly, rarely letting anyone other than Yael into their conversation.

Gai Gai walks with her. She has recovered well from the birth, and there is a lightness to her now that Shaye is pleased to see. The grunting woman of the visions and demand for the river has faded in her. She carries Nata in a sling on her front, and the infant lies close to her mother's skin to listen to her heartbeat as she sleeps. Gai Gai chews on bramble leaves as she walks and tells Shaye how much milk Nata is drinking, how long she sleeps, and how heavy she is getting. Shaye listens attentively, although she can see all those things for herself. Gai Gai never mentions the mark on Nata's back, although when she rewraps the baby's swaddling Shaye has seen her trace her fingers over the red welt, as if she might be able to pick it off the way she picks off the flakes of dry skin on Nata's scalp.

Shaye tries not to think of Nata atop one of the stone pillars in the oak grove. She walks quicker every time the image pops into her head, as if she can outrun it and leave it behind. There is no reason to think it will be Nata, Shaye tells herself, sometimes aloud. It has never been a baby before.

If she is alone, Shaye spins. She tucks a combing paddle into her skirt and lets the spindle drop on her other side. She moistens the nettle with spittle or runs her fingers along the edges of a wet leaf to catch the drops. She spins until all the fibres she's dried over the plenty time are spun into thread, and she keeps it all wound tight into fat balls tucked away in her pouch. As she lets the thread gather on the spindle and grow fat, she thinks ahead to when they will make this journey the other way, when the spring is beginning. She will have a pouch full of thread to weave next spring, and she can make Ludi a new, bigger wrap. When she has spun all her nettle and put away her spindle, her fingers tingle and hang thick and useless by her sides. She misses the way spinning keeps her hands busy.

Once, she manages to trap a couple of pigeons, purely by accident. They are old and slow, and warbling so loudly at each other that they do not hear her creeping up on them to wring their necks, nor her mutter of thanks to the pigeon spirit. Sala roasts them and shares out the flesh as fairly as she can. There is not much meat to be had when walking on the path. It is harder to trap or hunt when you have to follow the river, not the winding sneak of prey.

One night, they stop near the place where she had hoped Gai Gai might give birth. While the others set a fire, she takes Ludi by the hand to visit the spring along the holloway, showing him the hard unripe berries of the hawthorn and blackthorn dotting the leaves like red and purple stars. They listen for the gurgling of the spring, and when they find it they kneel and press their faces to the earth to drink deeply.

Ugh! Ludi spits out his mouthful, screwing his face up. It tastes bad, Ma. Like licking a rock with a red bleed.

Shaye laughs. It's good for you! It's special water, it makes you strong. She fills her waterskin to the brim and drinks again. There's a special spirit that lives here and gives protection to all who drink from this spring.

Ludi looks suspicious, but he takes a sip. Later, everyone comes to visit the spring and fill their waterskins. None of the young ones want to drink it, they miss the sweet dankness of the river, but the adults drink deep and thank the spring.

As she walks, Shaye sees way markers from previous journeys, forgotten until the moment they pass her vision. There is the boulder where Gai Gai cut her foot as a little girl, that oak must be the ancient one Cherl climbed to shake the acorns from. There was a time, many frosts ago, when they slept in that grove of pines off the path, and there used to be good honey mushrooms found there by that gnarled elm with the knot in the trunk. When she was pregnant with Ludi, Marl caught a pony while they walked this path, and they butchered it together. The waterskin she carries now is from that animal. She wonders if Marl still has the one he made for himself.

Shaye feels the sweetness of moving across the land in her feet, the same tingling happiness she felt on that day more than a moon before when the guest came. Sometimes, when her hands are busy with spinning nettle or shelling nuts, and she hangs back from the others to let their conversations becoming a boring hum, their words blending into a drone just like the chatter of the midges, she can soar out of herself like a hawk, and see them from the sky as a bird might do. She sees them snaking through the trees, one line made of many dots, like ants, walking towards the great blue ocean. She imagines the world as the hawk must see it, a mass of blue then a mass of green, separated by a line of yellow sand. Like a man and a woman making love, the beach the skin that cruelly divides them.

The initiates at the oak grove teach that the world is a couple entwined; half forest, half ocean. Half light, half dark. Half fire, half snow. The forest seems eternal when you are walking through it, Shaye thinks, the trees watching as people pass, witnessing the babies grow and turn into elders. But then you get to the ocean and it seems even bigger, even older.

She begins to see signs that others have travelled along this path before them, other groups of people coming to the coast to dance at the oak grove. The grasses are flattened from sleeping mats, there are fresh ashes in piles of stones and sometimes there are only the small, hard berries left on the bushes. Sometimes bones stick out of the ground, half dug up by the squirrels and the voles; sometimes she follows a trail of ants with her eyes to a place just off the path where a carcass writhes with maggots.

She wonders if the same initiate from the oak grove went to all the peoples of the forest to tell them of the early ceremony. If it was the same man as the one who appeared in their plenty-time place a moon before, then how could he get to everyone so quickly? Nobody can move faster than their own two legs. Although Shaye heard as a little girl that the initiates of the oak grove can take the form of any animal they wish, so perhaps the guest who came to them had flown the long journey as a bird. A hawk, perhaps.

In the darkness, Shaye lies awake listening to Nata suckling on one side of her, and Ludi's restless legs twitching on the other. Night after night, she watches for the clouds to part and reveal the moon. She watches it shrink to nothing after the thunder moon, and then wax into a crescent again. On the night of the full fruit moon, they make a fire and sit around it to sing. Brig leads everyone in a song about berries and nuts and carpets of good mushrooms, and because everyone has eaten well recently they are all happy to join in.

The season is beginning to turn. Now there is a chill in the air at dawn and dusk, and Shaye has begun to sew the skins in her pouch into frost coverings for Ludi, Gai Gai and herself. Ayla has made hers already, and she walks with her cloak draped over her shoulders. Vesti and Brig are stitching theirs as they walk, cursing when they trip over roots. The fires at night are welcome, and warm them right through to their bones.

Soon, they will arrive at the oak grove. Probably before the dark moon, Shaye thinks, if they do not stop for too long again. She imagines Marl looking up at this same moon and calculating when she will arrive. She pictures him scanning the faces of all who arrive at the oak grove for her face, squinting at the children running in between the half-built dwellings to find Ludi. I'm coming, she says to her vision of him, quietly at first, then shouting in her mind. I'm coming and I'm bringing the boy and everything will be alright.

There is something different about the sky when Shaye wakes up after the dark moon. It's heavy, and the same grey as Cherl's flints. The clouds are sitting on top of canopy and pressing hard. Shaye has a headache, the air is still, and her skin is moist with sweat.

Something is tight between Sala and Brig as they pack up their sleeping mats, a worry that has descended on them in the night. Sala tells them all that they will stick to the path through the forest, and not make the usual detour to the salt marshes.

They'll be too flooded to pass over, Sala says. Shaye glances at Brig as Sala speaks, but her eyes are shut. A raindrop gathers on her nose and she brushes it away. Shaye will not miss that grey-green expanse where the horizon blurs into the land, the light shimmering with spirits. Not with the weather coming, although there is often good samphire and purslane there. She prefers to stay under the protection of the forest for as long as possible. She remembers the last time they made this journey, when the falling season was well underway and there were huge drifts of dead leaves to soften the ground underfoot. Ludi loved leaving the path to forage in the marshes, giggled helplessly as she held him over the still pools to gaze at his reflection and watched the billowing clouds wander across the sky above him. She will take him there on the way back, she thinks. After the frosts, when the flat patches of tufted grass wriggle in the wind again.

The midges that draw the thunder are fluttering in the air, and Shaye draws Ludi close to her as lightning flashes. Everybody stops still, waiting for the boom to follow. Ludi trembles to hear it. The elders tip their faces right back to face the sky spirit. They close their eyes, sniff the air.

The rains are late, says Yael. Should have had these storms in the last moon.

Nothing is as it should be, Sala replies. She turns away as though disappointed with the sky. We'll start walking and hope the rains pass. She does not say that she is worried about where the river will rise to with all this tumbling water. Shaye sneaks a glance at where it lies, hidden behind the trees. Don't come to meet us, Shaye asks the river spirit. We'll come to you.

The rains do not pass. Sala leads them through the forest and Shaye takes her place at the back of the line. Ludi walks next to her. Everyone is now wrapped in their winter skins. Vesti's and Gai Gai's are only half made, the stitching hasty and incomplete but better than nothing. Shaye pulls her hood right up over her head and holds Ludi's hand as they walk. The ground is fast becoming slushy with mud. The water is fierce, pouring from the leaves and splashing on the ground, making pools where it lands. It roars as it smacks at the leaves and at the tree trunks, and the pelt of it on Shaye's cloak makes her head pound harder.

Are your feet alright? She turns to Ludi. His face is wet but he's not writhing as though he is damp inside his cloak. He is silent, gripping at her hand and careless of the water dripping down his arm from their clasped hands. He nods, his mouth a pinched line, and she sees he is afraid.

Are you wet inside your cloak? He looks up at her, his eyes squinting against the droplets, and shakes his head. He does not speak, but he grips her hand tighter as the sky flashes again, leaving the world dark and gloomy as the thunder rolls after it.

Shaye is wet and muddy up to her knees, her calves thick with churned mud from the path. Her skirt clings to her legs and makes the flesh there cold. Her hair is damp on her back and tiny droplets of rain find their way inside her cloak and make seams of dampness down her back.

She glances at Ludi every so often as they walk, but she does not speak. She doesn't want him to hear the tremor in her voice. She passes him a handful of damp beechnuts from her store, only enough to let his teeth crunch on something. They are not very good eating, but they will have to do. She picks some burdock leaves, swollen to giant food by the plenty time, and hands them to Ludi to chew on. Give him something to fill his belly, Shaye thinks. He'll likely get nothing else for some time.

She keeps her eyes fixed down on the forest floor to watch each step she takes. Her heels slip and sink as she places each foot in front of the other. The whole group is getting slower, their legs aching with the effort of wading through this mud. She can no longer see the worms and the slugs, the only creatures in the world that delight in rain like this, but she knows they are there, writhing joyfully in the dirt, not caring that the weight of any footstep could make them explode into mush.

No one speaks, and there are no conversations in the branches above them from the birds. Once, Shaye looks up into the branches, brushing the droplets of water from her hood, to see a blue tit sitting just above her head, sheltered by the thick branch of a beech. He follows her slow progress past him, unruffled by the presence of so many people. She watches him twitch the gathering water away from his neck, and the tiny droplets fly off into the air. He looks miserable, the way she feels. Shaye wonders where his family are, if he is cold like she is, if he knows when the rains will stop and is waiting patiently under his beech bough.

Twilight comes early, as the clouds block out the late sunlight and bring the darkness roaring in. Still, it rains. There is nowhere dry to roll out the mats; only puddles of silted water and the mud banks in between.

Sleep wherever you can find a place, Sala calls over the noise of the water on the leaves. She shrugs helplessly as her kin unroll their mats, press the earth to see exactly how much water it exhales, stare upwards to check the cover of the leaf canopy. We won't be here long, we'll get walking again at first light.

Shaye is shivery and dizzy with exhaustion. Her cloak squelches on the mat, and the cold damp seeps through the hide and towards her skin. A hunger pang grips her belly, and she takes a swig from her waterskin to ease it. She shivers, and curls up on her side to gather all the heat her body can muster. Gai Gai lies next to her, Nata tucked inside her cloak, suckling gently. They do not speak, for there is nothing to say that can make them feel any better, and too much to say that will make everything seem worse. She falls into a fitful sleep, curled around Ludi like a nest around an egg. The rain beats down on her hood, pulled right up over her ears, and although she knows she is safe, that no wolves or lynx will come hunting in this weather, no matter how hungry they are, and they are far enough from the river that it cannot swell and drown them overnight, still there is something alert in her that prevents her from falling completely under the spell of her dreams. Perhaps it is the relentless drumming of the rain on her head, booming as it hits her hood as if calling her to a ceremony at the oak grove. Perhaps it is the wet chill creeping up her legs, or the hungry burn in her belly. Or perhaps it is the vague feeling of dread that has crept upon her as she walked today, that all will not be returned to normal after the early ceremony, that Marl will not be cured of his strange sadness, and that something in the world will never be the same again.

In the feeble dawn, Shaye wakes to find the rain abated, but still falling. Now it is a shower with occasional squalls. Shaye packs up her mat, blinking away the blurred sleep from her eyes, and follows the group along the path. Her eyes feel gritty, like a stray grain of sand is lingering, and her head is thick. The lighter rain is a small reason to feel better, but she does. They are one dawn closer to reaching the oak grove, where there will be shelter.

She sees she was not the only one visited by night terrors as she slept. All around her are the drawn, crumpled faces of those who have drifted between wakefulness and restless sleep all night. Ludi shows his back teeth as he yawns and takes her hand again. There is no tree-climbing or shouting, not today. Only the tired focus of one foot in front of the other and the longing for the solid walls of the cave shelters at the oak grove. They are close now, close to the long stretches of golden sand to run across, heaps of kelp and seawort to lay out in long sheets and prod at until it dries, and waves, always the waves, to watch and chase and run from in a never-ending game.

Shaye tears each burdock leaf she can find, even the smaller ones, and passes them to Ludi and Gai Gai. She chews as she walks, but their bitterness seems to empty a cavern in her stomach that makes her more hungry, not less.

They walk at a steady pace, mostly silently, only stopping by a blackberry bush to strip it greedily of its yield. Shaye starts to plan how many hares she will need to catch and skin to make another cloak to replace Ludi's, then hers. Perhaps Marl will help her trap, and this thought is like the sun piercing the cloud to let a shaft of light through her thoughts. Yes, she thinks. Marl will help me.

The river has risen further with the rains, swelling so grotesquely that Shaye can see the water from the path. She sees ahead that Sala has stopped walking, staring at the river. A murmur begins. Shaye can hear the voices but she cannot hear what they say. Ludi tightens his grip on her hand, and she draws him closer.

The wind has picked up, and occasionally it blows rain

into her face. It is the smell she notices first, brought to her nostrils by the wind. A smell of rotting. A smell of death.

Sala leaves the path to walk towards the thing she has seen, towards the smell of death. Brig and Yael follow her, but everyone else stays on the path, leaning on the trunks of the sturdy oaks to rest themselves. Ayla looks on the ground to find places where they might all sit down, but the ground is too boggy. Gai Gai hangs back, her nostrils flaring and her lips pressed in a tight line, alert to something she doesn't want to bring Nata anywhere near.

Should she go with the elders to see what is found, or should she stay with the others on the path and wait? She hovers, letting Ludi's hand loosen in hers. A curiosity builds in her. She wants to see the source of the dead smell herself, she wants to know. She's been walking at the back, she's been the tail of the group for more than a moon now. She should go to see the dead thing. She should take part in the rituals, whatever they will be.

Shaye untangles her fingers from Ludi's hand and leads him over to Gai Gai, leaning against a tree with Nata suckling at her breast. She looks weary, but smiles gently at Ludi.

Stay here, she says, and makes to turn from him, but a whimpering noise of protest stops her. He looks panicked and tries to follow her, but she catches him by the shoulders and leans to whisper in his ear.

You have to stay here, she tells him. I need you to look after Gai Gai and Nata for me.

He gazes up at her solemnly, nods, then turns back to hunker next to Gai Gai, facing the river like a watchful wolf pup.

The earth among the thick trees is even more squelchy with mud than the path. The water is closer here. She sees the line where the watery mud becomes muddy water, the line to which the river has spread, ever expanding into places it has not reached before. These trees are standing as if in an ocean, their roots and lower branches submerged.

Shaye hears the murmurs of the elders as she gets closer and closer, their voices bleak.

Why would someone sleep so close to the water? Brig says, shaking her head. Why would you risk it?

Shaye leans over to see what they are staring at. Bodies. A man and a woman, elders. They are curled on their sides, facing each other, their fingers tightly entwined between their faces. The water covers them to their waists like a blanket, tucked almost lovingly around the furs their skin is wrapped in. Their faces are turned towards the mud, the water lapping at their noses and mouths. The long, grey braid of the woman is draped over the man like a snake protecting its eggs. Shaye's belly flips over, with sickness or sadness, she cannot quite tell.

Sala heaves a long sigh. Shaye glances at her and sees that tired, hopeless expression again, the same one she saw after Nata was born. Shaye thinks of all the nights they've laid their mats down in places where the river was only just out of sight, the way Sala always hesitates, looks all around her before nodding her assent to a stopping place.

Perhaps it wasn't that close when they lay down to sleep, Sala says quietly. Perhaps they couldn't see the river properly. It was hard seeing yesterday, with that rain.

They are all quiet at this. To think that they could have made a mistake as deadly as this one, to think that some of them might have woken up this morning to find the others sickly pale and blue-lipped like this couple, their skin already mottling to the same grey colour as the murky river. It silences them. They are still, gazing at the dead. The wind gusts and a spatter of heavier rain hits their cloaks, and the sound of it is too loud in the hush.

We'll have to bury them, Sala says quietly. We'll have to say their rites.

Brig looks to Sala and frowns. It was the dark moon last night, she says. We can't stay for too long. Shaye knows she is thinking of where they will sleep tonight if they are caught by the darkness in this place. She is wondering how far off the path they will have to walk to find a place safe from the greedy river.

We'll see them off, then we'll leave. There is a hint of impatient authority in her voice. Shaye recognises it from when Cherl refused to leave the old plenty-time place. They have no other kin, Brig. Sala passes her hand over her eyes, ringed with pink from sleeplessness. I would want others to do it for you.

They work quickly, for there is truth in what Brig says. They want to be away from here as soon as they can. Shaye gathers a large branch and begins to clear away the earth beside the woman's curved back, carving a womb in the silt that will become their tomb. It is easy going, only tricksy when the water rushes into the cavern and makes it a muddy mess.

No one says it, but it is silently agreed: no need to dig too deep. The river will take them soon enough.

Shaye and Brig tip the woman into the hole, then roll the man on top of her. There is already stiffness to their flesh, and Shaye is relieved to feel it. They looked as if they were only sleeping in the arms of the river, before. Not as if they were ready for the grave.

She remembers seeing her mother in a tomb like this one. She remembers reaching out to touch her hand, just to test if she was really gone. She had been shocked by the icy feel of her skin, the sensation that the body was no longer her mother but something else, just a sack of skin that pretended in a grotesque way. She saw Gai Gai do the same thing, next to her, and she wondered if she should stop her, wanting to save her from the momentary disgust that had made her recoil, her memory of her mother's warm flesh replaced with the corpse's cold finger. But Gai Gai did not seem worried. At that point she had not yet had her moon blood initiation, and Shaye had wondered if she had really understood it, the finality of the cold body.

When the grave is roughly filled in, the displaced earth kicked over the bodies enough to hide them from buzzards, Sala begins to sing. Shaye closes her eyes and sings with the elders, the song pitifully quiet with only a few voices, competing with the drumming rain. Again, she remembers Sala and Brig and the others singing the mourning songs for her mother, she and Gai Gai kneeling by the mound of earth letting their noses drip with aching sadness. She remembers that Cherl howled as they sang, beating his fists upon an oak until they were bloody. She thinks of him, alone in the old plenty-time place, and she has a sudden vision of him lying by the new line of the river as this couple were, face down in the mud with the water enveloping him. The words of the mourning song stick in her throat. Who will bury Cherl if he dies there, alone? she thinks. Who will sing these songs for him to ease his passage back to the great spirit, whose voice will guide him there? She cannot clear the vision from her mind, so she begins to sing instead for Cherl, in case there is no one else who can. A tear escapes from her eye and runs down her cheek. She can only tell the difference between her tear and yet another raindrop because the tear is hot, and leaves a memory of warmth as it wanders down her face.

They leave, and begin to walk again. Shaye takes Ludi's hand once more and tries to rid her hand of the cold feeling from the corpses, rubbing at her son's fingers, trying to warm them both. She thinks of the way she saw those elders curled up together, the way Sala found them. It wasn't a mistake that they lay there next to the river, thought Shaye. Neither did the water wash them up from somewhere else. No, the further she walks from their shallow tomb, the more she becomes convinced. They lay down in the mud intending for the water to take them, she thinks. They wanted to die, and they wanted to leave the world in each other's arms. She cannot decide if the thought has a terrible kind of beauty, like the flexing muscles of a wolf come to kill you, or if it is the saddest thing she has ever heard.

As she lays down that night to sleep, in the soft mossy hollow between the roots of an oak, she wonders at the peace required to shut your eyes, knowing you will never wake up, not wanting to wake up. She lies awake until sleep sneaks up on her, wondering at the couple who knew they would die, wiggling her fingers and toes every so often just to feel the heat creep into them, just to remember that she is still alive.

They are down to their last two bottles of water. For twelve days they've walked and walked and walked and passed only rusting pylons and the occasional bridge like the one they walked on when they came off the train. What began as a grim knowledge that they would have to find water at some point has become an aching panic that she will not be able to keep her son alive for much longer if it doesn't rain in the next few hours. Grainne has counted the remaining water bottles every day, as if she's been hoping someone might have slipped an extra one into their suitcase overnight, and when she finds that there's exactly the same amount as she expected, she purses her lips and turns away, swallowing hard.

They've passed no rivers or streams and they don't know what to look for to find one. The sky has been nothing but blue since they left home, which feels like it was a different lifetime now. We could follow the animals, Grainne suggests, but they dart away as soon as they hear them coming. The squirrels and foxes are quicker than them, and this is their land to know every tiny part of. Perhaps I should be happy we've made it this far, Shante thinks. Twelve whole days out in the wilderness of the edgelands, and we're still alive. But she can't be grateful for their survival if they're only going to die of dehydration in the next three days. The cruel sky, keeping them alive with the water bottles from the train, giving her hope each morning that today is the day a grey cloud will come, letting them die slowly of hope as much as thirst.

That night she presses her hands into the dirt and claws at it until her fingernails are black with mud. Tell me, she begs silently, half in the floating space between sleep and dreams. Tell me where there's water, tell me what to do. But the earth says nothing back, only lies cold and hard beneath her, punishing her for a crime she does not know she has committed. She falls asleep with tears tracing a line between the outside corner of her eyes and the top of her ears, and the last thought she remembers is cursing herself for crying and wasting precious water in despair.

She is woken by something on her face. She shoves it away, but there it is again, and again. She opens her eyes but it is not yet fully light, just that grey time before the sun appears that makes the world seem drained of colour. There is a constant, loud noise she can't place. It's not the birds, and it's not the usual night-time parade of foxes either; it's like distant applause or a building crackling into flame.

The thick boughs of the spreading root tree above her are illuminated in a bright burst of lightning, and then, a moment later, a heavy groan of thunder.

She sits up quickly, pushes her hands into the ground to stand up. The leaves under the T-shirts she was lying on are wet, muddy droplets clinging to her hands.

Wake up! she shouts, and as if the sky hears her the rain gets heavier, its splashing on the leaves noisier. Grainne! It's raining! Get up!

She lurches to the suitcases and unzips them both, her hands trembling. Grainne is at her side in a moment, her T-shirt already soaked through and clinging to her skin. They take a bottle in each hand, unscrewing the lids, and run out into the middle of the road where the rain is falling in sheets. Shante can barely see the trees on the other side. Like tiny bullets, the water hits the road and bounces off; already there are channels of muddy water flooding the sides of the road, puddles filling up in the previously invisible depressions in the concrete.

They set the bottles upright to fill and run back to the suitcases to get more. Locke is awake, standing by the suitcases and shaking water out of his hair. Shante grabs a whole armful of water bottles and runs back to the road. Locke copies her.

When all thirty-six empty bottles are standing in the road, slowly filling up with rain, Shante drops her head back and opens her mouth to the sky, letting the rain pound her tongue. The water is warm and she swallows it in gulpfuls until her belly swells, over and over again, letting the rain drip down her chin and neck. She gathers handfuls of water and splashes it onto her face, rubbing at her palms and fingers to rid herself of the dirt and the old menstrual blood that she can still see staining her skin.

The water tastes the way the city used to smell, as though it's passed by something burning. It's not the fantasy of pure crystalline rain and she knows there's probably a million poisonous particles swimming in every droplet, but she doesn't care.

When she's finished drinking, she wipes her mouth with the back of her hand. Locke and Grainne are drinking the rain too, standing with their faces tilted up to the sky, their tongues splayed, catching as much water as they can and swallowing it. Grainne starts laughing and stamping her feet in a puddle. She shrieks with joy when it splashes back at her. Locke takes her hand and splashes with her, leaving streaks of clean skin along his arms and legs. It's impossible not to join in. This rain has loosened something in her, drenched that hard, dry spot that's been calcifying these past twelve days of walking and worrying about the water. Shante grabs Locke's hand on one side and Grainne's on the other to form a tiny circle, and pulls them around so that the three of them are spinning.

She howls into the rain and Locke copies her. They spin and spin, rain dripping down their arms towards their clasped palms and making them slippery. She can hardly breathe with the naked pleasure of it; how good, how wet, how perfect this rain is.

Grainne shouts and screws her eyes shut, letting them both go at the same time so that they burst out of their circle and fall to the ground in a wet, giggling heap. She whoops, lifts her hands to the sky and from her position sitting on the wet concrete next to Locke, Shante sees her sister as one of the witches from Charlie's old stories: beautiful, knowing and completely at one with the eldritch powers of the old forests.

The water bottles are almost full, and Shante screws on the lids as they begin to spill over. The water inside them is faintly grey, but she's gleefully, gratefully full of wonder for this water falling from this generous sky.

All thirty-eight bottles are full and the rain is still falling, but it's colder now and she shivers as she screws on the lid of the last bottle. The sky is light now, but blanketed in metallic grey cloud that holds on to the darkness. She shivers. It's the first time she has been really cold since they've been walking.

Locke is sitting on his haunches, wet through, wiping rain away from his nose and lips. There is a crack of lightning forking through the sky. Locke stands up quickly, grabs at her hand. She waits, listens for the answering call of thunder. One… two… three… Charlie told her to count the seconds between lightning and thunder when she was a girl… four… so that she wouldn't be scared if she was caught out of the house in a summer storm… five… there it is, the roar's back. The storm is moving further away from them, the rain will end soon. She sticks out her tongue for another drink, but her mouth takes a while to fill with water.

The rain is beginning to slow now, although the sky is still heavy and grey. They pick up the bottles and take them back to last night's sleeping place under the tree with the spreading roots and the thick branches. The suitcases are shut but not zipped properly, and there are damp patches on their clothes. Shante checks the lute, but it's completely dry in its hard case.

She takes out a change of clothes for her and Locke, and they change right down to their underwear. It feels like setting the clock back on their journey, starting afresh. The water has renewed them, brought them back to the point they started from. She rifles in her suitcase to find the water purification tablets she slung in there before leaving the city, and crumples them into as many bottles as she can. The water fizzes a bit, then settles into the same faint grey as before.

She packs the bottles into the suitcases, zips them and stands them up. They're going to be heavy to drag behind them again, but strength has flooded through her veins with the storm. She feels as though she could pull anything now.

The rain has become a damp mist. The pitter-patter on the leaves has stopped and the ground is already drying up, the puddles in the leaf drifts disappearing like bathwater down a plughole. The water is sinking into the thirsty soil, the roots of all these trees gulping the rain just like them. Shante drags her suitcase out into the road, where the puddles are glistening. Water runs in tiny rivulets between the cracks in the concrete, down the camber of the road and into the mud. The sky is lighter now.

Come on, let's get moving. She adjusts the lute bag on her back and starts to walk. Grainne follows her, and for a moment the only sound is the trundling wheels of the two suitcases on the hard concrete. They each hold the wet clothes they've been wearing since they left the train draped over their arms, shaking out the shirts every few minutes to get rid of the drips.

I can't believe our luck, Grainne says.

I know. Shante exhales. They've never talked about the water, just watched each other counting and re-counting bottles. We learnt that from Mum, Shante thinks, she never wanted to name things or describe the way she was really feeling. Even on the day she died, their mother gave her a shopping list for dinner, insisting that she would cook for them that night.

Something's looking out for us, Grainne breathes, and she turns her eyes skyward for a moment like the people in the old paintings, always looking and pointing to the heavens like they thought whoever lived up there could hear them.

Shante doesn't respond, but she's been thinking the same thing. It unnerves her that it rained just as they had run out of water. She thinks about how she pleaded with the earth, making her bargains, and she wonders if something out beyond the sky actually heard her and made it rain to save their lives. She doesn't know what that force could be, apart from the forest itself. It needed the rain as badly as they did.

Or, it occurs to her now, it could have been their mother. Her ghost, her soul, whatever you want to call it, following them and manipulating the weather to save them. She would have been so heartsore to see them now, wandering into an uncertain future.

As they walk, Shante thanks the trees, and as an afterthought, thanks her mother's spirit as well. She thanks each tree her glance falls on individually, and then she extends her thanks out into the entire forest. Thank you, she whispers as they move along the road, which is already dry in some patches. Thank you thank you thank you.

Walking is different now. There is still the same footstep after footstep, the unchanging road, the trees and the endless sky, but now she walks with triumph. She has snatched their lives from the jaws of death, and there is a warm wind at her back, pushing her onwards. Her optimism has risen so high she starts to look for a border on the horizon again.

The clouds clear by midday and leave the sky the same brilliant blue as before, and the forest steams with humidity as the water evaporates into the heat that returns after the storm. The road is completely dry again by the time they sit down to eat, their meal made more substantial with some more of those dark purple berries and some long leaves with jagged edges, growing around a tough looking yellow flower. They're bitter but they fill her up, and Locke likes them so much he keeps looking for them as they walk, pulling them up and munching long into the afternoon.

She's no longer thirsty, for the first time since they left the train. It takes her a while to get used to the feeling of her tongue moving smoothly around her mouth. She knows they'll get thirsty again, it's back to the one-bottle-a-day rule, but now Shante feels invincible. The sky is looking after them.

Granda would have liked that storm, wouldn't he, Mum? Locke holds a fistful of those long, bitter leaves and he has half-chewed pieces of green stuck in his teeth.

Yes, he would have. Shante exchanges a glance with Grainne, and then her sister turns her eyes to the road straight ahead. They don't talk about Charlie like they don't talk about the water.

Do you think he'll come and visit us when we get to Dad's city?

I hope so sweetheart. She wonders what Charlie is doing right now. She thinks he's probably assumed them to be dead, and maybe Zeb has too. Perhaps he's mourning them now, his grief made unbearable and aimless by not knowing exactly what has happened to them, or knowing where their bodies went. She imagines him going to the spot along the riverbank where he let her mother's ashes slip into the water, and asking the water where they are and if they can possibly still be alive.

I miss him, Locke says, and he is so matter of fact in his tone that it makes Shante's heart twitch. I know he had to stay at home and be close to Mimi, but I miss him.

I know. She is quiet for a long time. He should have come with them. They should have made him, they should have waited for him to get used to the idea and persuaded him it was the best thing to do. She's not used to making her father do anything; she obeys him, not the other way around. But life is a cycle, as she's beginning to see, and a caring parent becomes a cared-for parent in the end. Perhaps it was the moment to insist, back in his flat looking at his wall map; perhaps it was time for her to tell him what he had to do, the way she'd tell Locke, and she'd missed it.

I think if he was here, he'd know where all these trees came from, Locke says, waving his hand. He'd tell us stories about the rain and magic things. I bet, if Granda was here, the animals wouldn't hide from him.

The complaining note in his voice makes her smile. As always, her son is a marvel to her. The separateness of him, the way he came from her own body and was fed from her own breast and now the essence of him lives inside that head, shut away from her.

I know where all the trees came from, she wants to say. I know things about the rain and magic. But she doesn't. It's only luck that they are still alive, she knows that. She knows nothing of this road, this forest, the world outside the city.

I know about those things, she says. You can ask me. Locke raises his eyebrows at her, and for a moment he looks so adult, so like Zeb.

Alright then, he says, sceptically. What about the rain, where did that come from?

She thinks for a moment, and Grainne turns to her with an amused, what's-the-point-of-this look. She tries to think of the kind of poetry Charlie would come up with for his grandson about something like the rain.

There's a huge giant who lives in the sky, she says, improvising wildly. And the clouds are his bed. When he has a bad dream he thrashes around in his bed, and that's the thunder, and when people make him happy he cries, and that's the rain.

Locke narrows his eyes at her for a moment, cocking his head as though he suspects her of making fun of him.

Is that a real story, Mum, or did you just make it up?

Grainne laughs, and Shante reaches out to cup her hand behind his head. It's a real story, sweetheart, I just made it up.

He looks to Grainne on his other side, still suspecting a trick.

I mean, did Granda tell you that one?

Shante pretends to consider. Granda told me, she says. She feels a wave of longing for Charlie, for what he would say if he were here. Fragments of things he's told her drift through her head: a seal woman who slips off her skin to dance on the beach; a woman who slept for a hundred years; a wolf who led a little boy through an enchanted forest. It's all silted, like the dirty river at home, settled into sludge at the bottom of her memory.

Locke points to the sky. What about the sun, then?

It's the giant's son. He eats fire all winter, and then in the summer he blazes hot and high until he's burnt himself out and needs a rest.

And the moon?

She hesitates, and Grainne jumps in. It's the sun's baby

sister and she chases him around the sky over and over again to try to make him play with her, but he never wants to.

Locke smiles. That's something Charlie would have said.

Okay then, Mum. Tell me where the fox came from, then.

She is getting into this now. She takes a bottle from the pocket on Locke's backpack and has a swig of water. It tastes grey despite the tablet she crumbled into it, like there's some chemical decaying invisibly in between the molecules, but she puts it back without thinking about it too much.

The fox used to be a human, a very clever man who tricked the sky giant into giving him a lot of food to eat and got turned into a fox as a punishment.

And the owl? Grainne says. Why does the owl hoot, Shan?

She remembers something Charlie once told her. The owl was once a woman. Her husband made her out of flowers, but she didn't love him back. When she went off with another man the husband turned her into an owl, and she's been hooting her sadness ever since.

My turn, Auntie. Locke smiles at Shante slyly as though he is about to checkmate her. The road. What about the road, Mum?

She bites her lip. The road is the curse of a witch. She lived in a house made of bones and some people came along and burnt it down. To punish them, she drew these roads all over the territory and made the people walk along the roads for ever and ever.

He stops to pick up a smooth black stone about the size of his fingernail, and tucks it into his pocket. Shante and Grainne keep walking and he skips a little to catch up with them.

So that's why we have to walk, because the witch cursed us?

Shante looks at him, trying to see if he's joking still, but she can't see his face properly. She shouldn't have said that.

No sweetheart, she says, we're not cursed. I think we're very lucky, actually. And I think Granda, if he was here, would say the same.

And this is true, she does think they are lucky. They were lucky to get their visas, and they've been lucky not to run into any patrols yet, and they were lucky with the rain coming when it did. But she's known for years that the ultimate luck would be to have been born long before the water started to rise, before the War, back in a time when the world was better, kinder and everyone was happy.

Grainne glances at her above Locke's head, hoping to share one of those adult-only looks, but Shante doesn't look back. She looks at the surface of the road, like Locke, trying to see it as he might; littered with tiny hunks of treasure left there just for him. She points to a crystalline bit of stone just in front of them and Locke hurries to crouch in front of it and pick it up. He can't, it's attached to the concrete, and she stops to watch him try to tug it out of the ground before giving up. A story about the little piece of rock pops into her head, but she doesn't say it out loud. The time for stories seems to have passed.

For the rest of the day there is a feeling in the air around them that Charlie is with them. It's as if she's conjured his quiet presence by telling stories like a magic spell. Though they don't discuss it, they each have the impression that Charlie is gliding silently behind them, somewhere just beyond their suitcases, looking after them. Each time she looks around to check there's no one there, but occasionally she catches the back end of a squirrel darting up a tree, or a flash of bright tail feather from some bird moving behind a branch, and she wonders if he knows they're still alive, the way he always used to know if they were lying.

That night the ground is still damp from the rain shower, and there's a chilly breeze sweeping through the trees. The three of them huddle together for the first time since they left the train, pulling jumpers from the suitcases and swaddling themselves in them before they sleep. The wind makes the trees hiss all night and Shante barely sleeps. She feels as though the wind is trying to tell her a change is coming, and if she'll only listen carefully enough it'll tell her how.

By the time the bulging moon is spied at sundown, nestled in a gap between the heavy clouds, they are almost at the oak grove. They hear the first squawk of a gull and with it the imagined crash of the waves. Shaye closes her eyes for a moment, relief seeping into her tense shoulders and neck. Nearly there. The gulls are calling them, encouraging them onwards and singing the praises of the ocean.

It rains, still, and Shaye is so wet by now that she cannot remember ever having been dry. Her furs, and Ludi's, and everyone else's, stink as they rot from the damp. She had planned to rebraid her hair this close to the oak grove, and Ludi's too, make them both look nice for the moot. But the incessant rain has bedraggled them both, and sapped her will for anything but putting one foot in front of the other and making sure her son has something he can call food in his belly.

They spread their sleeping mats out at the foot of the tall cliffs and sleep at the bottom of the sacred oak forest. There is an atmosphere of relief as they settle down. They are so close to proper shelter, so close to the wisdom of the initiates for comfort. It is easier to sleep than on other nights. By the next time darkness falls, they will all be warm, and probably dry. And hopefully lying down with full, satisfied bellies.

Tomorrow, Shaye whispers to Ludi as she curls around him. We're going to walk up the cliff to where the initiates live, and we're going to see all our kin.

Ludi makes a sleepy noise, and Shaye pulls her knees closer to her.

And we're going to be dry again, she whispers, but Ludi doesn't respond.

And we're going to see Marl, she thinks, and her heart begins to tumble inside her chest, making her breath catch in her throat. We're going to see your Ba, she tells Ludi silently, willing herself to fall asleep sooner so that the dawn will arrive without her even noticing; and with it, his familiar face, and the slow grin when he realises she has come.

> • <

The shortest day moot always seems like chaos at first. After the cool silence of the forest, the mass of people and bodies is confusing, loud and boisterous. Ludi cried inconsolably the first time she brought him here, carried in her pouch facing outwards to the world as she climbed up the hill towards the cave settlements, terrified by the noise of so many voices, singing, the ringing of stone against stone as men refreshed their flints' sharp points. He had buried his face in her neck rather than look at so many unfamiliar faces, and she had had to coax him out so that she could show him to the kin she hadn't seen since the last frosts.

But Shaye has always enjoyed the moot, even feeling twinges of sadness when the frosts begin to melt and they leave to begin the journey back. There is something celebratory about it, something wild. She can walk down the other side of the hill to where the cliffs lower to the sea and go fishing on the beach there without recognising a single face. The anonymity of it thrills her, and at the fires each evening she bathes in the feeling of being part of a hive. The caves are always warm, heated not only by the fires but also by the constant chatter. Shaye imagines the words as tiny fireflies, soaring around the caves. Words of new babies, recent deaths, good plenty times, good hunts. Stories of wolves spotted, of bears tricked, of seals in pup. Plans for young men to hunt with another group, plans to trade these flints for those skins, plans for naming or initiation ceremonies. It wasn't until she was older, when she brought Ludi for his first moot, that she realised how many of the great events of her life had happened, or begun to happen, here. It was here that Marl had started to lay his mat down in the same part of the cave system as her and then decided to join her group. It was here that Gai Gai met Ker, and he came back with them in the frost melt. It was here she had said goodbye to the boys she had run and climbed trees with as a girl when they'd left to join other plenty-time places.

As she walks up the hill, her thoughts turn to what will happen here this moot. It is here that Nata will receive her judgement from the initiates, and perhaps be promised to them. It is here that they will do the ceremony to push back the tides, begging the spirits to save their world. And it is here that Ludi will leave her to hunt with others, a time that will not come for a good few frost times yet, but will surely come before she has looked for it.

Although the cliffside and the forest around the cave settlements crawl with people, like a rotting log infested with lice, there is a hush muffling any of the laughter or lightness that usually accompanies the beginnings of a moot. Something mournful but urgent swirls around them all, and as they come closer, and nod to these distant kin in greeting, Shaye sees that they are not the only ones to suffer, not the only ones to arrive wet and starving. Sala leads them straight to the caves where the great shelter carved into the trees covers the fires kept burning constantly by the younger initiates.

There is food there, heaps of roasted fish and plump mushrooms ready for eating. Reo and Ludi find a last reserve of strength in their legs to run to the huge birchbark baskets to have a handful of hazelnuts, then dip their hands into the stores and let them run through their fingers over and over again, their desire to play returning. Something releases in Shaye's heart, something she hadn't known was caught, to see her son eat more than just leaves. He is safe, they all are. There is food, here. All will be well now.

It is a relief to step into the dry darkness of the opening cave. She peels Ludi's hare skin from his body and he brushes his chest and arms, glad to be rid of it.

It started to itch at me, Ma, he says with a grin. She takes her own off, and holds them both over her arm. They are impossibly heavy. She wonders at how doggedly they walked with them on their backs for so long.

I know, but we're going to get dry now. She follows Sala deeper into the caves and it becomes drier and even warmer. The skins on her arm start to steam as they get deeper and deeper underground.

The caves are as old as the world itself. No one knows how they came to be there, although the story goes that the chalky rock spirit dug them out to hide from a storm. Caverns, each tall enough to stand up in, each one with openings into more caverns, then still more beyond them. Cherl showed her a mole burrow once, when he was showing her how to trap. It's just like the oak grove! she exclaimed to him, and he had grunted his agreement. Where do you think the rock spirit got the idea from, girl, he said.

Most of the caverns are lit by holes carved in the roof, and some sunlight struggles through to make the cave walls grey. There are many entrances, although the one with the fires is the biggest and most used, and Shaye has never found them all. The floor is packed earth, a relief after so long trudging in ever deeper mud, although it will not be very soft to sleep on.

Sala leads them through the caves, searching for an empty, unclaimed place they can make their own. The air inside these rocks smells of musty sleeping bodies and damp skins and furs, and then beneath it all, a tang of the sea. Not the sea as she smelt it from the river, but the real sea. Saltwater spray and dried seawort and fish smoked on the fire until perfectly tender. The light is dim, but every so often it strikes a wall of one of the caves Sala leads them through to illuminate a painting etched on the chalk walls with a deeply charred stick. A pony, a bear, a wolf. A snail, a snake. Men running in the hunt, women grunting in labour. The walls are smudged grey from where others have drawn in times before, probably since the chalk rock spirit itself came here. Shaye looks out for pictures she hasn't seen before, looks where Ludi points. He is fascinated by the images. He doesn't remember it here, she thinks. He thinks he is seeing it all for the first time. And because he is, she feels as though she is too.

Shaye keeps half an eye on the faces they pass, looking for Marl. She doesn't think she'll be able to find him tonight; there are too many people here and that would be a luck too far, but she'll start searching and asking tomorrow. Sala finds an empty cave and declares it theirs to sleep in. Her face bears a hint of triumph. There is still the moot to come, where she will have to speak for them all and answer questions from the initiates, and of course the ceremony. But she has kept her people safe, and that is what matters most now.

Shaye spreads out their mats and begins to unload all the things she prepared for carrying, that day moons ago when they left the old plenty-time place. She lets Ludi eat the last of the nuts in her store, and spreads out their skins hopefully. She takes off her waterskin and the bundle of cloth she brought with her, soaked like everything else. She spreads that out on the mats too, planning to change her skirt when the new cloth is dry enough, for she is muddy up to her thighs. She gets out all the nettle she has spun, lays that out to dry alongside the spindle and paddle, both slimy with rain, and brushes off her flints. She feels lighter in her spirit now she doesn't have to carry this. She will return here each night to sleep among these things that are hers, next to the things that are Gai Gai's. She feels that just with the simple act of laying down the things she carried, she has created a birthing cord from her roaming self to this dark corner of the caves.

They fill their bellies deeply that night, deeper than they have in a while. Shaye sits between Sala and Gai Gai around the great sheltered fire, munching slowly on the plentiful mushrooms. Ludi sits in front of her, sharing handfuls of nuts from the basket and picking the bits from his teeth. She hears snatches of conversations that she knows Sala is listening to as well; people swapping stories about where their river rose to, when they last saw a heron, what berry bushes or hunting grounds were lost to the insistent floods. She listens to people from the forest, just like her, who mourn their drowning trees. She listens to people from the marshes who have been at the oak grove for a while, for they were the first to be flooded out, their lands now a flat, salty lake. She listens to the fishing people from up the beach talk of the boats they have lost to the high tides, how the seals did not visit them this year. The air is saturated with loss. The sadness of all the peoples gathered around the great fire swells and rears until it covers even the tallest oaks. Shaye begins to ache in her chest for all that may not come back.

She sleeps soundly that night, for the caves are quiet and warm and it reminds her of curling up next to her mother when she was a little girl. Her hair is drying out and she is warmer than she has been since the fruit moon. She places a hand on Ludi's ribs and feels his breath move his chest. Her son is safe. She feels a little bloom of pride at that thought. My son is safe. My son is alive and healthy. She lets a smile gently crack the dry grooves of her lips.

Grainne sees them first. She points at the horizon where the road dips slightly and slows her steps. They're walking along one of the road's rare straight sections, where the concrete stretches out in front of them like an arrow.

Can you see that, Shan? There's a wobble in her voice that takes Shante by surprise. She looks quickly at Grainne, and then at the horizon.

Shante stops walking. She squints into the distance, her eyes screwed up against the sun. She sees the glint of something shiny and metallic in the sunlight, and then huddled shapes on the pavement. She sees their stillness rather than their form, they draw her eye among all the undulating trees. The air is shimmering, playing tricks on her eyes so she can't see exactly what it is, or how many there are. Her heart slides to her stomach and she grabs at Locke's hand.

They continue walking, their eyes fixed on what's lying in the road. Shante dreads arriving at it. It pulses with threat, and the avenue made by the trees begins to look like a corridor leading to something that will trap her at the end.

Locke grips her hand tightly. He walks so close to her that some of his steps bring him swerving into her path, and his backpack and the lute case bump together. They don't speak, and as they come closer and closer they see that the huddled shapes are two bodies, lying face down in the road. Just in front of them is a bicycle, lying on its side with one of its wheels detached and missing its tyre. That's what was sparkling in the light: the places on the frame where the paint had chipped off to expose the gleaming steel underneath.

She pulls on Locke's hand to keep him close and he presses himself to her side. She wants to cover his eyes or pull him behind her so that he doesn't have to look at whatever's happened to these people. She thinks of the train guard all those days ago. She wonders how many people have come across his body since they left it, if it's bloated and wormy yet, if the poor man had a decent burial.

Stay by the bike, she says to Locke as she and Grainne creep forward. See if you can find anything useful on it. Try to get the tyre off, or something.

She lets go of Locke's hand and the handle of her suitcase. She and Grainne part to walk around the bike and approach the bodies. She hears Locke following her and turns back to him quickly, holding out a panicked hand.

Stay there! He stops, his eyes fearful and flicking to what's behind her. She unclenches her jaw and lowers her voice. I need you to look after the suitcases, she says, trying to be calm. Me and Auntie are just going to see what's happened.

He turns away from her and crouches by the bike. Shante watches him for a moment. There has been so much death in his life these past few days. It feels as though the whole world is rotting from the surface in.

She smells them as she comes close and puts a hand over her mouth, pinching her nose shut. Grainne gags softly and claps her hand to her face too. Shante opens her lips reluctantly. The air must be too dirty to breathe. How could it not be if it smells like this?

The bodies are both men, lying face down, dressed in dirty jeans and T-shirts with a scattering of belongings spilling from backpacks next to them. Their clothes are wet from the rain last night and tight with bloating. Shante leans closer, looking for a mark on either corpse that will tell her about the violence of their deaths, but she can't see anything. She can't make herself touch either of them.

She glances at the silent trees. You all know what happened here, she thinks, you saw it but you won't tell me. She looks back to the bodies and the damp skin on the back of her neck prickles. She wonders if they're being watched by someone hiding behind the thick trunk, if someone is waiting there to hurt them too. She glances at Locke, crouching over the bike with his back to her. She looks into the woods again, scanning the dark trees for any sign of a person. She can't see anything, no scrap of cloth fluttering behind a trunk or flicker of movement drawing her eye.

But there's something else here, something present that isn't accounted for by these corpses and their smashed-up bicycle.

We should leave, Grainne says, and Shante nods, but they don't step away from the bodies.

She drags one of the backpacks away from the body and looks inside. It was already unzipped, and somehow that's better than having to open it herself and admit that she's looting the possessions of a dead man. Grainne does the same with the other bag and they don't talk about it. They probably never will.

She finds two packets of unopened crackers and a fruit bar that she stashes in her own handbag. There's no water, just two empty plastic bottles. Three days, a person can go without water. Maybe less in heat like this. They might have died only hours before the rain shower, like a vicious joke. If it was thirst that killed them.

Shante puts everything else back into the bag. The rest of it is all stuff like in her own suitcase, photos and a change of clothes and personal things that make no sense to anyone but the dead man who packed them for his new life. Shante glances at Locke and the bicycle again. Did they have just the one between them, or was there another? What happened to the other bike then, and did these people die for it?

She turns to Grainne and sees that she has a tab in her hand, the screen alive with images. Shit, Grainne says with a long exhale. Look, Shan. This tab is on the network.

Grainne turns the screen towards Shante so she can see the screen illuminated with the dead man's most recent data points. The sight of it brings the real world of the city crashing around them. The city is still out there somewhere, the network is still live, everything that used to be theirs is carrying on without them.

Grainne puts it carefully on the ground. She slides her own rucksack off her back and unzips it, rooting around until she pulls her own tab out. She prods the screen with a fingertip, expecting something to flicker into life, then sits back on her heels.

Nothing, she says. Mine's still disconnected. Check yours.

Shante slips her tab out of her handbag and swipes her thumb across the screen. No, she says, her hope deflating as abruptly as it had swelled. Still nothing on mine either.

Grainne picks up the dead man's tab and slides her thumb over it. The images start to move, and Shante steps around the dead men's legs to peer over her sister's shoulder. The screen has a crack through the centre of it, a sign that they might not have been legal. Most people would be able to get a broken tab replaced in an afternoon if they were in a city.

These guys escaped from a camp, Shan.

How do you know? She's pressing icons in the man's data bank, her fingers drawing a parade of numbers and charts, and Shante struggles to make sense of what Grainne is doing. Hey, you're in his data bank, how are you doing that?

It looks like they're illegals. Grainne doesn't look up from the screen. But we must be close to a border if this tab has signal like this.

Now she's got a satellite map open, and she's pinching the screen and turning the tab around in her hands to find their geopoint. Shante half expects Zeb's face to pop up on it, the only way he's existed for her for months now.

If you hacked into his data bank, can you make calls too? she asks. She doesn't expect so, she asks only to be certain that no, she can't talk to Zeb, and yes, they are still in the edgelands far from the real world.

Before Grainne can respond, there's a cry behind her. She's up and running to Locke before she knows it, her throat thick with panic. A part of her knows it was an indignant cry not a frightened one, that part which has been cataloguing the sounds her son makes since he was born, but still her mouth goes dry and her skin prickles.

He's already turning to her, one hand held out to her with a bloody palm facing upwards, his other hand clutching his wrist.

What happened? She takes his hand in hers and pulls him towards her. He hisses. How did you do that?

It was the bike, it's broken, on the metal bit. Shante looks behind him and sees a jagged tear in the rusty frame. I was trying to get the tyre off and I grabbed it by mistake.

He whimpers. It hurts, Mum.

She makes the kinds of noises in her throat that she used to make when he was a baby, those hushing, soothing noises that lie behind language. Behind her, Grainne unzips the suitcase and rummages around inside.

Come on, sit down. Let's get this sorted out. Shante sits on the concrete and pulls Locke into her lap, so that his back is pressed against her stomach and he sits between her legs. Grainne puts a bottle of water and a few bits from her toiletries bag on the ground beside her, then returns to the tab.

It's a shallow but messy gash from the mound of his thumb to the base of his third finger. Shante pours a splash of water on his palm to clean it and blood oozes out again within seconds, trickling into the wet creases. Locke's blood drips onto the concrete with the water she washes his hand in, and for a crazy, fleeting second she imagines that the road is grateful for it, that this was a kind of price that had to be paid, that it was yearning for a drop of blood all along. The forest wanted the blood from her womb and the road wants the blood from her child.

You're being so brave, well done sweetheart. Shante opens Grainne's bag with one hand, full of things they've had no need of here: soap, shampoo, makeup. She takes out a cotton wet wipe and places it over the cut.

It stings! Locke groans.

I know, she says, tearing another wipe to make a bandage. But this will make it better. She gropes in Grainne's bag for antibacterial cream but there isn't any. She tries to remember if she packed any in her own toiletries bag, that day when she stood in her own bathroom and packed the things she thought might be handy for a four-hour train journey.

No, there's no cream in her own suitcase. She remembers that she glanced at it briefly and left it there on the shelf, because it was cheap and available all over the territory, and she wanted to go forward into the future with as little stuff hanging off her as possible.

She wads up the first wet wipe, pink now, and drops it onto the ground. Here, she thinks, have a drop more so you can leave the rest of him alone. She wraps more wipes around and around his palm, pulling tightly.

That's really tight, Mum.

It needs to be tight, it's going to help it stop bleeding. Grainne comes to crouch beside her.

Let's see what happened to you, she says to Locke, and he holds out his bandaged hand with triumph. She circles his wrist with her thumb and forefinger. Ah, you're going to be fine. You're being super brave.

She pushes the dead man's tab in front of Shante's face. There's a geomap there, zoomed right out to show swathes of green, the tessellated grey boxes of a city in the top right-hand corner, and a pulsing red dot in the centre of the screen.

It says we're only three days away from the city, Shan,

Grainne says. We were right about this road, it leads us right to the border.

Shante squints at the tab and lifts her arm over Locke so she can pinch the screen to zoom in. There it is, the faintest of lines through the satellite image of the forest, the old road like a scar, leading up to the concentric rings of the border. This is all those twinkling, straight-line satellites see of this planet as they patrol past us up there, Shante thinks. They know even less than I do about this forest, only that it's green and it claims all the land of the territory that we abandoned.

Three days, Shante repeats. Did you hear that, sweetheart? Two more sleeps and we're going to see Dad!

She pulls him up to standing and gives the tab back to Grainne. She doesn't really want to hold it any longer than she has to, and Grainne holds the thing differently now, more respectfully, like it's an ancient and fragile relic in a museum. There's a difference between using a dead person's things in full view of their corpse to get vital information, and using it just to feel that comfort link, that umbilical cord back to the human world; and they both feel it. Grainne tucks the tab back into the backpack she found it in and scoops up her toiletries bag.

Are we just going to leave them here? Shante asks, although she knows they have to, just like they had to leave the body of the train guard.

What else can we do? Grainne is holding her suitcase again and ready to walk. There's nothing we can do for them now.

Shante swells with a particular, focused guilt. It feels shameful to leave the men's corpses lying in the road for the worms and scavenging birds, but Grainne's right, there is nothing they can do. She wonders who will bury or burn Charlie when the day comes that his corpse is found bloated and maggoty like this. Perhaps it's like a swap, a pay-it-forward kind of obligation. When you stumble across a body with a departed soul you should return it to the earth so that somehow the people who keep count of such things will know, and when the time comes someone else will bury or burn you or your loved ones, and around and around and around until the very last person left alive sits down to gasp her last breath, with nobody left but the trees to watch her cells become ashes.

She pulls Locke by his wrist away from the bodies as they walk past them, and she notices that he is looking at his hand, flexing his fingers as much as he can with the tight bandage instead of gawping at the corpses. They walk quickly until a glance over her shoulder tells her that the bodies are far behind them and out of sight, but they don't slow their pace. Three days, she thinks, over and over again, the rhythm of the words matching her footsteps. Three days, two sleeps, I will be safe soon.

When Shaye wakes up on the next dawn, the sun is already high. The rain has slowed to a drizzle, which cheers many and brings a lightness to the gatherings around the looms, the fires and the places where the skins and furs are hung. She sees the tattooed initiates moving among the forest, marsh and beach folk. Sometimes they stop to talk to an elder, or give their advice to someone who sought it, but mostly they move unmolested through the gathering crowds. Some of the children stare at their inked bodies, trying to trace the pattern with their eyes, until a mother or an older child cuffs them around the head and hisses, don't stare.

Ayla heads out to find meat for the great fire and Brig goes towards the lower beach to fish with her net. Others pass them with birchbark baskets tucked under their arms, ready to gather from the forest. Shaye gives Ludi a new piece of cloth for a wrap, then he leaves with Reo for the place where the children congregate, a section of the forest where there are many dead boughs lying on the forest floor. She feels a pang of worry. There will be lots of children climbing the trees in that small clearing, older children he doesn't know. She wonders if she should get him to stay with Gai Gai, whether he is old enough yet to be among so many children and hold his own place, but before she has fully made up her mind he has left already, and her decision is made for her.

She wraps herself a new skirt from the cloth she brought with her and tries her best to rebraid her hair. It's damp but clean, and it goes some way to making her feel normal again. She calls out that she is going to the beach to wash the dirty things and gathers up the armfuls of cloth Vesti dumps at her feet.

It'll be good to have it clean, says Gai Gai, even if it won't get dry. She tucks Nata into her pouch, the little girl kicking her arms and legs insistently the way that babies do, as if they are itching on the inside.

Are you taking her to the initiates? Shaye catches one of Nata's soft ankles and passes her rough thumb over it. There is nothing so soft in this world as the fresh feet of babies, she thinks, and a longing for Ludi's weight hanging on her front washes over her.

Gai Gai nods. I'm going with Sala, soon. She looks down, sniffs shyly. Shaye knows what she is about to say, and she bends down to gather more of the cloth in her arms so Gai Gai will not see her face.

Then I'm going to find Ker, she says, her voice becoming excited, without a trace of conflict or sadness. I'm going to show him Nata, and then I'm going to take her to his kin, so they can meet her too. She pauses for a moment.

Maybe we should try to find him before we go to the initiates. He would want to come, I think. She turns to Shaye.

If you see him, can you let him know we're here? Can you tell him to find me?

Shaye nods, makes a muffled sound. She's glad that Gai Gai can't see all of her face, because of the dim light and the piled sheets that obscure her vision. If I see him, I'll tell him, she manages, then squeezes Gai Gai's shoulder and leaves the caves.

She wants to go down to the beach to wash because she knows she will have the best chance of meeting Marl there. He loves the sea and he loves to fish, more than he loves to hunt, really. And she wants to take the cloth with her, instead of trotting off happily to find him without a job in hand, to give her something to grip onto in case she does find him. She can't betray her nervousness with writhing, kneading hands.

They had met for the very first time down there on the sand. It was the first frost time after her first bleeding, and he had not long gone on his first hunt too. She had only just become aware that the world was made up of men and women, and the sight of someone bathing or changing their clothes would make her cheeks hot and her chest foggy.

She had been collecting seawort in long drooping strands, looping them over her arms and dragging them along behind her. He had helped her take them back to the great fire, the two of them connected by the fishy-smelling green ropes all the way back along the beach and up the hill, and by the time they got out their flints to cut it and place it in the huge food baskets, she thought he was the best person she had ever met.

He hadn't come back to her plenty-time place that frost time, but the one after. And it was that hunt, his first in her place, that he had shown her that he wanted her. Her heart quickens as she walks past the gathered people around the great fire and she cannot help but quicken her footsteps too. Something is telling her to hurry. Even though she has waited for moons and moons for his touch, now she feels she cannot wait a single moment longer.

Not even this place, the community around the oak grove, has completely escaped the threat of the rising water. The forest, the caves and the sacred grove itself all stand atop high cliffs, the sea crashing far below, but as Shaye walks through the forest and down the other side of the hill they climbed yesterday, away from the river, she sees that the water has risen sharply here. The beach used to be deep; even at high tide there were always flat expanses of sand and the occasional protruding rocks where the crabs would hide, then the soft dunes rolling up to the grasses behind it and the forest line behind them. But now the sea has crept up the beach and made the entire expanse of sand flat. She sees that when the tide comes in, it comes all the way up the grasslands and higher, and the grass at the sand line is withered and shrunken from the salt.

People are out on the beach, wandering along the shallows clutching nets, or squatting and watching for crabs. The gulls soar and screech overhead, landing in large groups on the sand. The terns and the auks that nest on these cliffs are long gone to wherever they go for the frost times.

Shaye stops as her toes reach the sand and stands for a moment, looking out at the long expanse of the beach. It reaches as far as the eye can see, and further still. When she was a girl, she walked and walked and never ran out of sand and ocean. The horizon makes her feel dizzy for a moment. She loses all sense of herself, she cannot tell if she is big or small, or where she ends and the sand or sky or sea begins.

She concentrates her eyes on the heaving sea, green-grey like a toad. There is something malevolent in the expanse of water, like a monster creeping up on her to swallow her whole. The sky is a mottled mess of clouds. Some are brilliant white and some are like charcoal flung up into the air. It is still raining, and it shows no sign of stopping.

She begins to walk down the beach and the sand is welcome on her feet. She digs her soles in deep and rubs them all over to get rid of the dried flakes of mud. The wind is strong coming off the ocean and sending splatters of rain into her face. She doesn't mind. The sensation is clean here, not the foggy feeling that the wet of the forests brings. I will find Marl here, she thinks as she walks. She is sure of it. This is what he likes, this is where his heart lies. She stoops to pick up a piece of cloth dropped from her armful, and carries on walking.

Shaye stares hard at every man with a net, but she knows before she has fully scoped their features that they are not Marl. She knows that she will know him instantly when she sees his frame on the horizon. She knows that his body will call to hers.

She stops to swirl the cloth around in the shallow surf, scrubbing at the mud stains with scoops of sand, wringing the muddy water out and letting it dirty the sea foam. She looks up whenever someone passes by. She spreads the clean lengths out on the flat sand in a long line and weights them with a rock at each end to make an arc when the wind blows, like a colourless rainbow tethered to the earth. She remembers the way she and Gai Gai used to play with the cloth when the wind shaped it like this. She used to run under whole lines of these arcs, and Gai Gai would trot along behind her. Ma and

Sala used to laugh, she remembers, as they lay back resting in the soft, dry sand and watched. A windy day was always a wash day. She sits down in the sand by her arcs of cloth and watches them flutter. There is a film of rainwater over her skin, and she feels a chill brush over her. She lies down in the sand, under the path of the wind across the beach, and feels warmer, even though the sand is damp to touch. She shuts her eyes. She listens to the breath of the sea and drifts on it. It is so noisy here. It is so easy to drown her loud thoughts in the crash and rumble of the water, lying peacefully in the sand, not having to worry anymore.

Later, she walks back along the beach, now bearing an armful of clean and only slightly damp cloth, folded in neat parcels. She feels groggy from falling asleep, and worried about Ludi. She hopes he has eaten, that he has stayed dry-ish, that he has not had too harsh an introduction to the ways of large groups of children. Hunger moistens her mouth. She hurries now, back along the sand towards the cliff, barely looking at the men with nets. Disappointment makes her legs heavy; she has not seen Marl, and she cannot carry on wandering further along the beach to look for him. She stumbles on the sand, almost drops the cloth, rights herself and sighs.

She does not see a shadow, the sun is not strong enough. She feels instead a heat approaching her, feels the air vibrate in a way that she has almost forgotten. She looks up from her feet, surprised, clutching the cloth to her chest. It is all that stops her from falling over.

She blinks. She looks up at him, his head ringed by the moody cloud behind him. A large net is draped over his arm, a scattering of still-twitching fish making it glitter. His hair is long, reaching to his chin, and his beard is clean, shorn short to his face. The sun from the plenty time has toasted his skin like a hazelnut, and salt marks ring his legs. The lines around his eyes are deeper. They fan out towards his temples like sun rays after a storm.

Shaye, he says.

The sound of her name in his mouth makes her shiver, but she cannot say his. Her tongue lies thick on her teeth, and her belly is swooping. She forgets her hunger for a moment. She wants to answer him, she wants to say his name too. She wants to throw her arms around him and press her lip to that hollow on his neck where his jaw reaches his earlobe. She would have, once upon a time. She wonders why she doesn't now. She wonders if he wants her to, if he is feeling as strange as she is. She wonders how she knows not to, when it happened that she crossed over from the territory of his body being an outpost of hers to this barren wasteland of politeness, forbidding her touch.

Silence yawns between them. She could reach out and touch him if she wants to, she is that close. She gropes for some words, any words.

An initiate came, to our plenty-time place, she begins. She cannot breathe very well, as if she's been running. He told us to come, told us that you were here. Her voice is too loud, competing with the wind and the waves. All the men from the hunt, she adds.

He nods. He shows no hint of feeling.

We came too, for the early ceremony. All of us. She pauses.

She is saying stupid things. We got here yesterday.

He nods again. How are your kin? he asks.

Her heart jumps into her mouth. Is he asking about Ludi?

Sala is well. Worried about the river, like everyone. Gai Gai had a baby. She doesn't mention Nata's river mark.

A slight smile curves his lips at the mention of the baby, so Shaye feels bold enough to mention Ludi.

And Ludi is grown, he's a proper little boy now. Gathers hazels and crab apples, climbs the beeches for the best beechnuts like the others. She can see ripples of him in Marl's face. He's a wonderful child.

I'd like to see him.

She clamps her teeth together to stop her heart leaping from her mouth. He'd like to see you. He's been excited about seeing the ocean, can't wait to swim.

In the distance, a slow drumbeat begins. At first, with horror, she thinks it is her heart thumping, betraying her, but when Marl turns away, falling back to gesture to her to walk beside him, she realises it is the signal for the moot to begin. They walk together back towards the cliff.

She cannot think of a single thing to say. This man is the one person she's been longing for since he first laid his hands on her, and now it is as if he is a stranger. Or worse; just someone she invented in her own mind to keep her company. Heat throbs from his body, he feels huge beside her. She is conscious of her hair, her skin, the way she is walking.

How's the fishing been here? she asks, glad of the bundle of cloth to hold onto.

Good, he says. There is a long pause. She dares not look at him for fear she will not understand what she sees. She wonders if he is going to say anything more, or if it is her turn to speak now.

The waters have changed. Different fish.

She nods. It happened to the river too. It turned salty, we had to drink from the rain.

A gull swoops low from inland, cutting in front of them and heading out to sea. Marl ducks back to avoid it, but Shaye keeps walking, her senses dulled. She turns to the sea, to watch the gull curve around and follow the incline of the cliffs. She is disorientated, confused. This isn't how it is supposed to be, talking to Marl.

They leave the beach and begin to climb the hill. The drumbeat gets louder, and they see other people winding their way up from the beach through the forest to the moot place, the clearing in the woods large enough for many people to gather.

Do you like it here with the initiates? Every word is painful. She tries to remember if he was as taciturn before, or if this is something new in him. She remembers them talking for hours, telling stories and laughing at each other, but perhaps she was talking and he listening.

It's different. A long pause. I don't see them very much. I come down here with a net. Fish.

You always liked the sea. She says it with a smile in her voice, she wants to assure him that she likes the sea too, but he doesn't respond.

She thinks maybe there will be gossip when Gai Gai, Sala or Brig see her enter the clearing place with Marl, a thought that fills her with embarrassment. But the clearing place is chaos; babies wailing, children leaping over elders' outstretched legs, voices swelling to try to locate children over the thumping drums, and she cannot see a single face she knows.

A small fire is lit in centre of the clearing, and around that are placed fallen boughs and occasional boulders for the elders and the most learned initiates to sit. Everyone else places themselves on the outside, between the elders' circle and the trees, and it is this arrangement causing all the upset.

Marl touches a finger to her elbow, and she turns to him.

I'm going to find a place to sit for the moot, he says. The place on her arm where he touched her is burning. I'll see you.

She wants to call out to him to wait, to sit with her, to help her find Ludi. Don't you want to see him? she wants to shout at his retreating back, but the words stopper her throat and he has already disappeared into the crowd of people.

The drumbeat is echoing in her chest. She looks around, tries to find Ludi, but she can only see the dark heads of children moving like midges, too fast to see any particular one. Panic swoops across her body. He has never been lost to her like this before.

Some tattooed initiates are standing silently by the fire, watching with still eyes. Shaye sees the same repressed impatience for the flurries of people finding a place to sit as she found in the guest who came to their plenty-time place.

She sees Sala sitting on a scarred bough near the fire, her head bent towards another elder in conversation and the firelight flickering on her hair. Just behind her, she sees Ker standing with his meaty arms crossed over his chest, his face covered in a dense black beard and looking twice his age for it. She begins to make her way over to them, stepping over the extended legs of people already sitting down, meandering around women hitching babies onto their hips and children wriggling to be free. She keeps her eyes on Ker's tall frame, and as she comes closer she sees Gai Gai standing beside him, rocking Nata from side to side and gazing intently at the initiates. She looks calm, content. She stands close to Ker, but she is not touching him or looking at him. She does not need to, she knows he is there. The three of them form the perfect shape of a family.

Shaye is so close she could try to shout over the drumbeats to catch Gai Gai's attention, but she is stuck in a press of bodies. The smell of people she doesn't know assaults her, fish and sweat and smoke in the hair of the woman standing in front of her. She pushes slightly, only enough to clear a space in front of her to move forward, but it makes the people around her hiss. She doesn't care, she has to get to Gai Gai and make sure Ludi is with her.

Ker sees her first, and he opens his arms wide to receive her, his face breaking into a broad, white-toothed smile. Ludi is standing next to him, and he turns to her as well.

She trips over someone's dangling foot and lurches into Ker's outstretched arms, one hand catching Ludi and dragging him into the embrace.

Good to see you Shaye, Ker says in her ear. His deep voice is like the drum; it cuts under every other to be heard first. He pulls her away, takes her by the shoulders and gives her a serious look.

I have to thank you for bringing my daughter into this world. Shaye smiles slightly, embarrassed, one hand resting on Ludi's head to assure herself he is still there. Ker bows his head the way he would to Sala or Brig, and Shaye is surprised to feel tears spring to her eyes. This is something like the way she has dreamed of being greeting by Marl, but here it is coming from this kindly, brotherly man.

Ker gestures behind him, to where Gai Gai stands with Nata suckling.

And you know, you brought a sacred child into the world. He puffs up with pride, like a pigeon about to coo for its mate, and the bubble of worry Shaye has been carrying for the little baby dissolves.

The initiates have said they want her, in a few frosts' time when she's grown. They think the mark on her back is a sign of great power. He says this as if telling a secret, leaning into Shaye and lowering his voice to a whisper.

Thank the spirits, Shaye thinks. It will not be Nata, not today. She will not have a normal life, but she will at least have one.

He places his large hand on Ludi's bony shoulder. Your boy here is a good one, Shaye. Ker laughs, and Ludi looks up at Ker as though he is a spirit incarnate, the sun descended to earth and taken the form of a man. We've been out having adventures today, haven't we little man? Ludi nods fiercely, turning to his mother with a smile that has a benign, loving secret. Something cracks in Shaye like a rotten bough falling off a tree. Marl should be here for Ludi to look up to like that, she thinks.

She nods to Brig and the others, settling themselves behind Gai Gai, and sits down herself. She pulls Ludi down beside her and rests her elbows on the almost forgotten pile of dampish cloth in her lap.

Ma, I did such great playing today. You should have seen me. He talks breathlessly, the way he does when he's missed her. I was with Reo, and we went to where the children play, and we jumped off the logs, and then Reo hurt his leg and had to go back but I was alright, and then Gai Gai came to get me with Nata and we sung her some songs and then Ker came and we all went walking in the woods and he showed me tricks with his bendy twigs and it was great, Ma, and can we play more with Ker tomorrow? And Nata? And you can come too, Ma, I want to show you want I can do with my twigs.

She wipes away a drop of moisture at her nose and sniffs.

I will come tomorrow, we'll do lots of playing, don't worry. She pulls him towards her and presses her face into the top of his head. She sniffs deeply of his damp hair, the sweet scent of childish sweat, the sea and mud. She feels her heart settle into its usual rhythm. She doesn't want to move her head away from her son to look for Marl around the fire. A vague anger begins to rise. He doesn't deserve her, or Ludi.

The drums fall silent. Anyone who is standing sits down abruptly, and there is a frantic rustling and snapping of the leaf mulch and twigs. Shaye drags her attention away from her son and towards the initiates by the fire, but she keeps one hand resting at the small of Ludi's back. Through the gap between Sala's back and the folded arm of the elder sitting next to her, she can see an initiate raise his hands to the sky. She sees that it is their leader, the high initiate, the person who is closest to the great spirit of them all. They say that this man can see far into the past and the future in his dreams. They say he can take the form of any animal he wishes, and travel over the land and sea like a wolf or a seal. They say he knows every story the ancestors ever told.

The trees rustle with the wind, as if they are whispering secrets and wish to be heard, and the rain goes drip drip drip on the leaves.

Kindred, the initiate shouts. His voice is sucked up by all the listening ears of the clearing, and Shaye can only just hear him. She tries to tune out the wind and the rain, frowning to concentrate on only the man's voice. I thank you all for gathering.

He pauses, swallows, takes a breath.

You know why we are here. You know why you have come. For many of you, our moot and the sacred oak grove is the only place you are safe. Others of you have come because you know you will soon no longer be safe in your plenty-time places. No matter why you have come, you are welcome. And you are safe.

He licks his lips. Shaye looks around the other tattooed men and women standing by him. Their faces are still, expressionless. They look to the ground instead of at the speaker, their hands tidily clasped at their waists.

We come together to discuss the threat that we all face, and what we can do to save our world and our kin. He turns around to address the people on the other side of the clearing, and now Shaye can only hear his words as echoes off the trees. He opens his arms wide to indicate the elders seated around him. The other initiates sit down as one, placing themselves at the foot of the circle of elders.

Here are elders representing the peoples of the forest, the marshes and the beaches, he shouts. They are leaders, healers, the holders of our stories; they represent you all. We will listen to their thoughts on the water spirit.

The clearing is still silent. Not even the babies at their

mothers' breasts make a sound. The initiate gestures to an elder near to him, a stooped, white-haired old man who reminds Shaye of Cherl. He gets to his feet, leaning on a gnarled stick. He is dressed only in his wrap, and he shivers slightly. Shaye wonders if his furs and skins are drying, somewhere back in the caves, like hers.

There is a sadness in us elders, the man says. He looks around him and raises his voice, and it sounds weak, as if he has been crying. We do not know what to do. These are the lands where we hunt, where we gather, where our ancestors lie in the earth and offer us wisdom. He stops, wipes his eyes.

I speak for my kin when I say that we will do whatever the sages of this sacred place think is best to save us. I offer my prayers to all the spirits that it will shift the waters.

The man sits down, and the initiate nods to him. He turns around, and gestures to someone Shaye can't yet see. A tall woman stands, proudly, without the aid of a stick. Her hair is wrapped in green cloth and piled on top of her head. She wears a skin made of grey hare fur, and before she starts talking she revolves slowly on the spot, to look at everyone around the clearing.

There are many among us who would rather die than leave, she begins, and immediately Shaye knows she is an elder who is accustomed to being obeyed.

There are many among us who have already died rather than leave, Shaye thinks. She thinks of Cherl, and of the couple lying with their faces turned to the muddy water of the flooded river.

But we cannot be afraid! We should leave. We should seek what is beyond the horizon. Everything changes, this is what we praise the spirits for.

The woman raises her arms. There is something tense in this meeting, something stirring that is important. The effort of listening forces all thoughts of Marl from her mind.

Just as the plenty time gives way to the falling season, perhaps this is merely the land's natural cycle, one we cannot understand. The woman looks around the gathering to the other elders, holds her hands out to them.

Have you never wondered what is further on from our great forests? Have you never climbed to high ground on a hunt and looked in all directions around you and thought of what lands there might be elsewhere? Perhaps there will be no ocean there, perhaps there will be trees we do not know, bearing spirits we do not recognise, but maybe, think of it, there will be food and prey and a river that does not run salty. If we walk in the direction of the setting sun, away from the flood waters and all that has made our blood quiver with fear these past frost times, perhaps we will find another land, one where we can live well and be easy again. Our land is dying, wise men and women of the oak grove. That is what my heart tells me. That is what my eyes tell me. I see forests of dead oaks, submerged in what is now marsh, poisoned by the salt. I see fish I do not recognise in my net. I sweat during the moons I am accustomed to shivering in. I see that our world here is ending. And I might only speak for myself, for I cannot pretend to speak for all my kindred gathered here, but I know that if I stay here, despite the power of our ceremony, I will die as the land does, slowly and desperately.

The initiate by the fire narrows his eyes, and Shaye has the impression it is because he is moved. He bows to her and keeps his eyes on the ground for a long moment. Then he raises his head and looks at her, but there is a smudge of contempt on his face.

It is not our concern if you die, he says, and although he is shouting so that everyone can hear him, there seems to Shaye to be a quiet malice in his words. There is a soft intake of breath from the elders closest to him. He turns around to face the other side of the clearing and raises his voice still further.

It is our concern to save those who do not yet wish to give up on their land. If you are one of those, elder, speak now. If you are not, you are free to leave and take whichever people wish to follow you into the unknown lands you speak of so freely. There are no stories about lands beyond the forest. If there was somewhere else for us to go to, our ancestors would have spoken of it.

The woman stares at the initiate for a long time. Shaye can see them both, facing each other across the fire like rutting stags in the falling season, the firelight flickering sinisterly across their faces. Shaye thinks for a moment that the woman in the grey fur will speak again, but she does not. She sits down slowly. Shaye cannot see her face, but she thinks there is something victorious in the way the high initiate turns away, and gestures to the next elder to stand.

Some more elders speak. They talk of the way the river has crept up on them, the incessant rains of the past few days. Some talk of the flooded marshes, others of the difficulties of hunting. The initiate listens to them all, patiently. He doesn't interrupt any of them. As long as they agree with him, Shaye thinks, and agree to do whatever the initiates suggest, he doesn't seem to challenge them. She begins to feel suspicious of him.

When it is Sala's turn to speak, she does so quickly, and does not say anything that has not already been said. Shaye thinks of the mark on Nata's back, and glances quickly at Gai Gai. Is Sala thinking of the baby now, as she speaks, as she looks at the high initiate and the sweet smoke of the fire?

Sala sits down, and the next elder stands up. He looks old. He is perhaps older than anyone else in the clearing. His hair is white like some of the others, but his face is a web of wrinkles and his shoulders are hunched right over.

There have been signs, the elder says. His voice is soft, but it still carries across the silent clearing. The animals have known, the trees have suffered. Each spring has been warmer than the last, this is not happening suddenly. I remember my mother talking about the hot days of plenty times, of the deer not breeding in the same places.

Some of the other elders nod their heads. The man looks at them, and erupts into a passion.

We should have done something before now, it is too late! he cries. There were warnings, we should have heeded them. His voice chills Shaye, the desperation and the grief of it. We have all trusted you, we have done as you told us. Why should we trust you further? Tell us this, answer our people this question before we go any further.

The initiate narrows his eyes and cocks his head to one side. Do you think you're the only one with this knowledge, elder? Do you think we haven't seen for ourselves? Do you think we have not visioned and quested and talked to the highest of spirits about the changes we have seen in our land?

The initiate's voice is like a spark from two flints struck together and the elder shrinks away from it. He seems diminished by the sound of the initiate's harsh voice and his shoulders hunch even further.

No, I—

We know. We have seen. The initiate seems taller now. He clasps his hands together in that tidy way and raises his chin.

But our land is like a beast, elder, like a wolf in hungry times. She's fickle and sly and cruel, and she can change any time she wishes. She does not have to host us. She does not have to host the hawk either, nor the fox, nor the oak nor the sloe. If she chooses not to have us here, we will cease to be.

The elder sits down, and the initiate turns away from him and addresses everyone in the clearing, those sitting behind the circle of elders, those who are listening to his words with stones passing through their throats.

We complete our ceremony every frost time to thank her for her generosity, for what she provides. She sacrifices her creatures, her leaves, her nuts and her berries for us, and we give her something in return. This is the way of life. This is the balance.

But our land asks more of us. She has given too much, and we have not repaid her.

The initiate pauses, narrows his eyes. But we must! he shouts, and Shaye jumps. Her mouth is dry with fear. She thinks of Nata again, lying on top of the stone pillars, but she dare not move her head to shake the vision out. She tries to swallow, but her throat feels like she has poured ash in her mouth and she gags on a cough.

We will give the land what she asks for, and then we will see if she wishes to give us what we ask. We do not control her. We beg her to let us continue our lives upon her soil, and that is what we shall do on the night of the ancestors.

He is silent for a long moment. Shaye frowns. There is something he is not saying. The people sitting around her start to shift. They know they will do the ceremony early, that is why they have come. A murmur ripples through the crowd.

The initiate raises his arms for silence.

Each frost time we give one man to the great mother spirit who nourishes us. We do this in the darkest moon, near the longest night, to ensure the light comes back to us.

He looks around the clearing again. Shaye has a feeling he is enjoying his power over them, as though he is in charge of drawing back the clouds to reveal the sun after a storm, or drawing a rainbow in the sky.

But now, with our world in shambles, we must give more. As the full ancestor moon approaches, we will give our mother spirit more of us. We will pour the blood of the best of us into the most sacred of our soils and we will dance for her, to ask her to take away the waters and bring us peace again.

There is a long silence. Everyone in the clearing, observers, elders and the other initiates, holds their breath. A gull screeches above, and the high initiate waits for it to pass.

We will give the great spirit one body for every moon. We will perform a ceremony the like of which has never been seen before, and we will save our world with their sacrifice.

Shaye's heart begins to pound uncontrollably. Perhaps they lied that they wouldn't take the baby. She cannot look at Gai Gai, she cannot bear to see the torment on her face. The solid block of Ker's body is between them, but she feels Nata stir in Gai Gai's arms and make suckling noises. She turns her face away from them, rubbing her fingers on the small of Ludi's warm back. There is nothing she can do. Better she start to grieve now and be over the worst shock of it, so that she does not interrupt Gai Gai's tears with her own.

The high initiate is leaning over into the huddle where the other initiates sit. He is holding out both his arms to someone sitting on the floor, and Shaye watches, craning her neck to try and see through the gap between Sala and the elder sitting next to her.

A woman stands next to the high initiate, bearing the same tattooed lines and swirls. Shaye leans forward to look past Ker and dares a glance at Gai Gai. She rocks her suckling baby, her shadowed face blank.

The high initiate takes the woman's hands and begins to walk backwards, leading her out of the circle of elders and into the spaces where the people are sitting. The woman does not look like the rest of the initiates, despite her tattoos. Her black hair is unbraided, falling to her knees, and it undulates as she walks. Her eyes are closed, and Shaye watches with bafflement for a moment until she realises that this is Duana, the blind prophetess who chooses who will be given to the great spirit in the ceremony.

A shiver of fear runs through those assembled on the forest floor to see the woman, and it seems to catch in the oaks that ring the clearing, making their leaves rustle. There is a light shower of leaves. Shaye feels one of them stick to her back, still damp from the rain that she has almost got used to now.

It is supposed to be an honour, to be kin in some way to a man chosen for the ceremony. Once, when Shaye was a little girl, it was a woman chosen. She had been distant kin to Cherl, and he had bowed his head graciously whenever someone congratulated him on it. But Shaye remembers that as the knife sliced into her flesh and the blood began to run, he had shut his eyes tightly. She had been staring at him, looking up at his head ringed by the cloudless glow of the moonlight, and she saw him screw up his eyes until the singing had stopped and the drums and the dancing began again.

Duana the blind is moving among the people, led by the high initiate stepping backwards. Everyone pulls their feet, their children, the stray ends of their cloaks out of the way as they pass. As they come close to Shaye, they bring a coldness with them, a chilling of the air. Ludi presses himself close to her as the woman stops, sniffs. Shaye hears a roaring in her ears.

The woman lets go of one of the high initiate's hands and flings her arm out. With one finger that is missing its top knuckle, she points towards someone Shaye cannot see.

Him, for the wolf moon, she says quietly. Those on the other side of the fire would not be able to hear it, but then the high initiate shouts in his booming voice.

Stand up, kindred, stand up! Show yourself to your people and accept your honour.

A young man stands, tall and gawky. He has probably only just gone on his first hunt, this springtime or the last. His face is pale, like the approaching full moon, and he stares at Duana the blind. He is thin, perhaps from the difficulties of the plenty time, and Shaye can see his ribs shaking as he drags his breath in.

The initiate beckons to him, and the young man steps over the legs and children and cloaks. Now Shaye cannot see his face, but she hears a muffled sob, and the sounds of hurried, soothing shushes. Shaye recognises the sound. It is a mother's cry.

The young man goes to stand by the fire, next to the initiates, who are now standing in a line, their hands obediently clasped as usual.

For the wolf moon! the high initiate shouts, but nobody moves. There will be one body for each moon, he said. Duana the blind has so much more seeing to do.

He takes the woman by the hands again and leads her around the circle. Shaye holds her breath as they pass near to her, but she does not stop to fling her stunted finger in Nata's direction. They keep shuffling their crab dance.

On the other side of the fire, Duana the blind stops again. Shaye cannot hear what she says, but after a pause she sees another man, this one shorter and wearing the sealskin cloak of the sea fishing peoples, make his way to the line of initiates by the fire.

For the hungry moon! the high initiate shouts, and still there is no reaction.

They walk for a long time, taking a different path around the clearing each time they circle it, weaving in and out of the groups of people on the ground. Shaye wonders how the woman chooses, how the spirits tell her. What kind of powers will Nata have, if she is not called for the ceremony? She'll grow up here at the oak grove, gaining a new tattoo each springtime until her moonblood begins and she becomes one of these quiet, watchful people who stand so still by the fire, receiving those who are about to die calmly, without a single murmur of surprise or dismay.

Shaye is not listening. She misses it when Duana the blind

announces the next two men, both wrapped in deer hides.

For the melt moon and the hunter's moon! the high initiate calls, and the two men join their kin by the fire. Shaye wonders what it feels like to stand there with everyone staring at them, feeling the heat of the flames on their skin. Do they feel afraid now, or will their fear only punch at the moment when the drums begin? Maybe it won't start until the moment when the knife presses into their neck.

The next person chosen, for the flower moon, is a woman. Her hair is elaborately braided and she's wearing neither fur nor hide. Her skin is slick with drizzle, and she walks proudly to join the men.

Duana the blind chooses a young boy next, for the oak moon, and she feels Ludi press himself to her as if to hide from that roving finger. She squeezes his thigh, draws him under her arm. They are on the other side of the clearing now. They cannot come for Nata, not yet.

A fisherman from the beach people is chosen for the green moon, and as he stands up he hands his net solemnly to someone sitting next to him. An elder from the circle closest to the fire is chosen for the singing moon, and a youth who looks only a frost away from his first hunt for the thunder moon. Shaye shuts her eyes as the high initiate calls them forward. It is almost done, they have almost chosen all the bodies. She listens to the gulls call in the silence while Duana the blind is led through the clearing. They sound as if they are mourning already.

She chooses another woman, an elder but one who did not sit in the circle near the fire for the fruit moon. The woman takes her place by the initiates with her head bowed. None of the other chosen look at her. Perhaps they are trying to recall the sensations of all the blessings of this world before they leave it. The hawthorn bushes bathed in white blossom, a rainbow after a storm, the feeling of floating in the sea on your back and listening to the yawning waves, watching the clouds laze in the sky.

It is a while before Duana the blind chooses for the ancestors' moon. She shuffles around the clearing, the high initiate patiently walking backwards to guide her, and there begins to be a threat of restlessness. The people want this choosing to be over. The tension has become so tight it will snap if not released.

Finally, Duana stops. She points, and a man stands up. Shaye looks in his direction, then narrows her eyes and looks harder. She knows the man. She knows the shape his matted hair makes against the grey sky, the shape of his slightly curved back, his thick shoulders. She knows his face, the set of his eyes, the particular slope of his nose, the sweep of his lips. She watches him walk through the clearing, past the elders' circle and towards the initiate. She is cold, stuck to the spot. Perhaps she is breathing, perhaps she is not, she can't tell. She is staring at the man, she cannot take her eyes from his face, she has never been able to take her eyes from his face.

She doesn't hear or see who is chosen for the snow moon or the darkest moon. She doesn't care. She stares at Marl, standing in line next to the young boy, his silhouette outlined by the fire behind him. She lets go of Ludi, lets his body fall away from hers as she floats away, untethered.

The great spirit has chosen the bodies of our kindred! the high initiate calls. Duana the blind goes to stand with the other tattooed initiates, now there is nothing remarkable about her at all. The night of the ancestors will be held tomorrow tomorrow, he shouts while the silence in the clearing holds. Be ready.

Then the moot is over and the eating can begin. A bubble of noise swells and bursts. People begin to talk first in whispers, then a hum, and then a babble. The difficult, uncertain part of the ceremony is done, now the wild part is about to begin. Everyone stirs, stands to stretch their legs and walks back through the forest towards the great fires where hare meat will be roasted, and large baskets of berries will pass from hand to hand for everyone to take as many handfuls as they like.

Shaye doesn't move. Her legs have become heavy, they are roots sinking into the earth and claiming her for this one place, this spot in this clearing where she can still see Marl. He is standing with the initiates and the other chosen ones. He does not look panicked like some of the others. The high initiate is talking to them and he is watching with a blank expression on his face, the same blank expression he wore when he spoke to her earlier.

Ma, get up. Ludi is pulling at her lifeless arm, entwining his fingers in hers. Ma! Come on, let's go to the fire. I'm hungry.

Shaye turns to face her son. For a crazed moment she doesn't recognise the little boy dragging at her and she makes to fling him off, like she is swatting a fly. But then she sees something about the arrangement of his eyes and lips that reminds her that she carried this boy inside her all those moons, then carried him at her breast for many more.

She sees, as though she is someone else entirely, that Ludi is becoming frightened. With that wordless intuition children have, he knows she is far away from him but he doesn't know how to bring her back.

Ma! Let's go, he says again, and his voice is louder this time. He takes the cloth from her lap and tucks it under his free arm. A gull squawks overhead. Shaye wonders if there are any other sea birds left apart from those gulls, or if they are the only ones who can take the kind of destruction that the water is wreaking. They're like us, Shaye thinks dimly, as she lets Ludi pull on her arm and stands up. Her legs are weak. She looks down at them, wondering who they belong to. Gulls can live anywhere, eat anything, they'll survive every disaster the great spirit can devise. She begins to hate the sound. It reminds her of walking towards this place, of feeling that aching relief of arriving here, of seeing Marl so close she could have held him, back there on the beach, back when she thought she would get to hold him again.

They begin walking out of the clearing and towards the great fire. Ludi holds onto her hand and leads her.

As they pass into the trees and under the canopy again, Shaye passes people who turn to her and bow their heads. She doesn't turn to look at a single one of them. She does not care if or how she recognises them, she only wants to not see the people who honour her loss as if it is a thing she should be proud of. She wonders if Ludi knows that they are also bowing to him.

Ludi leads her over to where Gai Gai and Ker sit with the rest of their kin, a basket of mushrooms perched between them.

Don't you dare bow to me, Shaye thinks as she kneels in front of them. Don't you dare show me the top of your head, I'll scream.

She doesn't want to scream. She doesn't want people to know she is grieving the choices of Duana the blind. Nobody can grieve the choices of Duana the blind.

None of her kin bow to her. But they will not look her in the eye. Not Gai Gai, sat next to Ker with Nata cradled on her lap, nor Sala, crouched over Rilk who has a gash on her shin. Even Brig, usually so outspoken and critical of the initiates, avoids looking at her.

She knows they are letting their eyes slide past her because to look at her openly, without bowing, would be to tell her that they understand her horror. And that would mean questioning the right of the tattooed initiates to give anyone's life to the great spirit. No one belongs to their body. They belong, all of them, to the great spirit.

A hot, choking sense of powerlessness rises up her throat as Gai Gai offers her the basket of mushrooms. Because she knows this, she has always known this, each frost time as she has sat around the fire and listened to Duana the blind announce who would die for the great spirit.

She shakes her head, waves the basket away from her. There is an empty gnawing where her stomach used to be. It cannot be. Not him, not Marl. It should be someone else, she thinks, and even in the confines of her own mind her thoughts sound whiny. Take another, choose someone else, what does it matter. We've all got the same blood.

She sits and listens to the sounds of eating and the shrieks of the gulls. She hears the chatter but she cannot make out any words, not even those coming from Ludi's mouth. She feels as though she is underwater, as if she is diving for mussels and there is nothing important to hear but the roar of the endless ocean. She does not speak and no one asks her to. She isn't sure if she can anymore. She ignores the people who come to bow to her, both those she knows and those she doesn't. She sits on the cold, damp earth, letting her fingers work into the mulch and crumble tiny fragments of old leaves between her fingertips, and she listens to the gulls, those harbingers of death, and she curses each screeching one of them with a fury she did not know she had.

At some point, Ker takes Ludi off somewhere. He kisses her on the cheek when he goes, and for a long time she feels a chill on the damp place he left, the colder for having been, briefly, warmed by his lips.

When it becomes dark, Gai Gai takes her by the same hand Ludi led her by and walks her back to their place in the cave system. Ludi is already there, lying half asleep on his mat. Shaye looks at the things she spread out there yesterday: her waterskin, the large skein of thread she wove while walking on the path, the drying hides releasing a pungent smell as if the animals they used to belong to are dying all over again. She doesn't recognise any of it. It belongs to another woman, someone she does not know now, and she doesn't care about any of it. She lies down on her mat, curling herself around Ludi's warm body. His chest rises and falls with his breath and she listens to it, tries to match it. She is not sure if she is breathing anymore, there is something stuck and rotten dragging on her chest. Gai Gai says something, but she cannot hear exactly what she said because her ears are tricked by the way that voices inside the caves slither and distort. She shuts her eyes and is pleased with the absolute darkness. She doesn't ask Gai Gai to repeat what she said. She doesn't care.

She dreams that she is an earthworm, chewing on dead things and shitting them out as acorns. She meets Marl, and she wriggles all over him, sipping at each of his hairs with devotion until she comes to his face and sees that it is alive again, animated with life like it used to be. She tries to ask him if he is happy about Duana the blind choosing him for the ceremony, and if he will just tell her that he loves her before the knife hits his throat, but he cannot hear her, for she is just a worm and her mouth is good for nothing but cleaning the rotten things from the world.

They walk for the rest of the day. The light shimmers off the concrete on the horizon, reflecting onto the trees on either side and making them sparkle. The air is still again, the pressure high, and Grainne says she thinks there'll be another storm soon. They stop every so often and drink from the bottles in their suitcases. The water is warm and has sediment floating in it. Shante scrapes it off her tongue with her top teeth and spits it out. It has a vaguely metallic taste that makes her feel uneasy.

Why does it taste so bad? Grainne asks, coughing as she swallows.

Shante shrugs. I put the tablets in them, I don't know what else you want me to do. She had imagined that rainwater would taste like dark underground caves, but what's in these bottles is more like dropping a cup into the river at home and gulping it down. Grainne makes a face and has another sip.

They don't talk much. Locke complains about his hand hurting a few times, and Shante strokes his head and coos that it'll start to feel better soon. It's hot, perhaps hotter than it was before the night of the rain when they filled up the bottles, and they stick to the shaded side of the road, drifting across towards the trees as the shade gets shallow and then back towards the centre after midday when the trees' shadows lengthen. Shante finds herself longing for the coolness of being among the trees. She thinks of the way the sun fractures as it finds any tiny gap between the leaves to make puddles of light on the floor. She keeps licking away the sweat from her upper lip, and her back is damp from the lute pressing against her T-shirt there.

Grainne asks her what she's looking forward to most about getting inside the border, and for a long moment Shante can't think of anything beyond the trees and the road. Showers, normal food, their tabs back on. Sleeping in a bed, fridges, music, screencasts: these are the things she wanted most when they first began to walk.

I'm looking forward to having chocolate again, says Locke, fiddling with the bandage on his hand.

Zeb, Shante says at last. I'm looking forward to seeing Zeb. And this is true, perhaps truer now than it has been all journey, because she has stopped thinking about him and the way his mouth feels on hers and this scares her. She needs to see him again to assure herself this has all been worth it, that she still loves the man she calls her husband.

That night they go to sleep without talking any more about what will happen when they get to the city. She hears Grainne start to snore, and Locke's deep, slow breaths, and she tries to remember the feeling of Zeb's weight on top of her, the hunger in his eyes when he reached for her, the sight of their thighs lying slack and sweaty next to each other in the bed. She closes her eyes and tries to conjure the smell of him, the sleep-dank mustiness of him when the alarm would go in the morning and he'd turn over to press his face into her warm neck. She can't. All that fills her nostrils is the damp earth and the dusty wind. She rolls over and presses her face into the T-shirt she's lying on. Two more days now. Only two.

The next day they start walking as early as they can. The sky billows with fluffy white clouds, and Grainne says, That'll be the beginning of the storm. You're right, Shante murmurs, and they walk a bit faster. There's a whisper of wind now, after so many days of still, hot air, and she thinks she can feel something changing. The trees are telling her so.

Now she can say that tomorrow they'll reach the city. Now she can tell Locke they'll see Dad in only one sleep, and she tells him confidently that he'll be waiting for them just on the other side of the border with a big plate of pasta for dinner and a chocolate bar, even though she knows she shouldn't promise anything of the kind.

There's no sign that they're coming up to any border, the road is the same as it has been for many miles, sloping gently upwards. Shante tries to think of the practical things that will be important when they get to the border: the time and date of the train they were on, Zeb's information, their visas, passports and certificates. Their tab information will be out of date of course, but there's nothing she can do about that. She tries to work out the date, but she's completely lost track. She counts from the day they got on the train but she gets a different answer every time, because after that night when the rain fell she stopped counting the bottles so obsessively.

Grainne, what's the date today?

Grainne pauses, then says, It's the tenth of October.

Right. She's surprised. She hadn't thought they'd been out here for that long.

Here, do you think the border guards will hold it against us that we've got this gap in our tab data? Shante asks. She doesn't want to think of that, not yet, not while there are still trees around her.

Grainne sighs. I don't see how they can. They must know there's no signal out here.

She's not crossed an intercity border since she was a child, she doesn't know what the officials will do. Her hand flies to the handbag with the passports again. She thinks of her mother. She didn't have a passport, a health certificate or a visa; only a fistful of cash for the smuggler and a pair of armbands her grandmother gave her in case the boat capsized.

Their mother never used to talk about her flight from her home much. Only in abstract terms, like a history lesson. She told them in a calm voice how people had been fleeing drought and famine and war for seventy years or more and millions didn't make it, their bodies sunk to the depths of that ancient sea that was once thought to be the only one in the world. She told them that there was nothing but dust in her territory now, how the desert had crept up behind their cities and swallowed everything the sea couldn't reach. She'd been nineteen when she got on that boat, she told them. Everything was collapsing in upon itself. Later, when she was dying, she spoke more about those times, and Shante finally heard something of the terror and chaos in her mother's memories. It was like witnessing a breech birth of the new world, her mother whispered as she lay in bed in her final days, staring at the world map of pictures Charlie had made for her, clouded with private memories. Painful and bloody and a howling mess.

My hand's really hurting, Mum, Locke says, and he holds it up to her.

We're so nearly there sweetheart, honestly. We're going to see Dad tomorrow.

She stops to unzip the suitcase and gropes for the bottle of child paracetamol. The lid is sticky, with crusty pink remnants of the dried syrup hanging around the mouth. She pours some out into the lid and passes it to him. She notices that his skin is paler than usual and there are two points of pink under his cheekbones. She presses the back of her hand to his forehead. He's hot, but they all are. It's probably the hottest day they've spent walking yet.

The wind picks up as the sun climbs and there is a great show of clouds across the sky. Locke points out all the different shapes he can see, and they all join in the game because it's useful to occupy their minds.

Look, Mum, I can see a tiger in that cloud there. Shante follows Locke's pointing finger and says, Oh yes, I can see, there's its claws. She wonders if Grainne meant that it's a three-day walk to the city from where those bodies were in the sense that they would arrive on the third day, or if she meant that they had to be walking for three solid days before they would get there.

And that one looks like a tram, Locke says, pointing in the opposite direction. It's even got electric lines above it, can you see?

And how fast should they walk to make it in three days? Was that the time it took for adults walking fast, or was that a kind of average? Perhaps Grainne had put the correct data into the tab and it had adjusted the estimate to take into account the fact that they were walking with a child.

Perhaps they wouldn't arrive at the border tomorrow, it would be the day after. She begins to feel anxious. Rain is coming, and it looks as though it'll be the kind of rain that no one wants to be out in. She imagines them walking down this old road, unable to see more than a metre in front of their faces, soaked to their skin, and she wants to scream.

By late afternoon the clouds are heavy and dark, the colour of steel, and Shante has a headache. They stop for some food and water, and they watch the sky, trying to read the omens of what it's going to do. She unwraps the bandage from Locke's hand and sees that the cut is seeping with yellowish pus. She hesitates before she pours more water onto it, but it seems to be the right thing to do. She rewraps it with another of Grainne's wet wipes and Locke tells her that his whole arm aches.

It'll be alright, she tells him. It's healing. She gives him another lidful of the liquid paracetamol.

It starts raining just before sunset. They find one of those spreading root trees to shelter under and watch the rain tumble in sheets on the concrete. It's like the night of the rain when they filled up the bottles, but with no laughing, disbelieving relief, and a lot more water. They open up the suitcases and put on jumpers and raincoats, but their feet are already wet. The air is cold this time and the three of them shiver by the trunk of the tree as they watch the water bounce off the ground in glittering pellets.

Can I take my jumper off? Locke is tugging at the collar, rubbing his neck as though it irritates him. I'm too hot.

No, keep it on, she replies, pulling the hood over his head. It's going to get dark soon and you'll get cold.

We should just sleep here for the night, Grainne says.

Shante nods and bites her lip. She's been considering how they'll manage to sleep when there's this much water falling with no prospect of it stopping. If they lie on the ground they'll wake up floating in a lagoon of mud in the morning, but there's nowhere else to go.

They listen to the thunder and the splatter of rain on the canopy as the darkness draws around them. The water is beginning to slide off the leaf litter and down any little slope it can find, making deltas out of each track. Shante watches the puddles spread with panic shortening her breath. There's nowhere safe on this whole earth anymore, she thinks, the water is coming for us no matter where we are.

She looks up into the tree they're standing under and thinks of how she might climb it. Raindrops tumble from her hood into her eyes, and she wipes them away to squint into the gloom. Its lowest branches are too high for her to reach, but with the last of the light she can see another spreading root tree only a few metres away with branches reaching downwards, the way she used to reach towards Locke when he was a baby and toddling towards her with his arms held out.

We're going to have to get up a tree, she calls to Grainne as she walks over to the other tree. She wonders how they'll manage this. She has never felt more human and vulnerable, out here with only some leaves between her and the plunging sky. The wind starts to pick up and the higher, thin branches groan.

She takes a couple of long T-shirts from her suitcase and ties the lute onto one of the lower branches, arranging it so that it's hanging underneath the wood and close to the trunk. She thinks it'll be drier that way. Then she leans the suitcases against the trunk of the tree and hoists Locke onto one of them. Grainne steadies the suitcase under his feet. He clutches at the main trunk of the tree and swings his feet onto one of the branches, crouching gingerly until he's straddling it. He looks down at her but all she can see is a pale face hooded by blackness.

It's like the whole world's going to wash away, he says, and it seems as though there's something else talking through him, the tree perhaps, or one of the bedraggled birds who must be nearby, taking shelter under one of the broader leaves.

Budge over, she says, forcing her voice to be calm. We're coming up there too.

She pulls herself into the tree, and straddles the same branch as Locke. She rests her back against the trunk and shifts her back to find a comfortable groove in the bark to settle her spine into. Below her, Grainne shifts one of the suitcases around the trunk and climbs up the other side. She climbs into a higher branch and lets her legs dangle down almost to Shante's head height.

You alright up there?

Shante hears the scrape of Grainne's plastic raincoat on the bark as she tries to get comfortable.

I'm alright, Grainne says. Can't wait for morning.

Shante doesn't sleep at all. She holds onto Locke with her arms wrapped around his waist as the rain pummels her hood. Her feet are wet, her jeans are wet, and her face is wet with spray and it is only the warmth from Locke's sleeping body keeping her teeth from chattering so hard that they wake him up. Water drips from every leaf tip and between each bark seam, from Grainne's shoes above her, from her hood onto her nose, from her nose onto Locke's hood nestled under her chin. The rain is constant, and as she listens her eyes get droopy and start to close until a huge gust of wind startles her awake. They are protected from the worst of it by the trees huddled close together, but when it roars like that she can hear it howling along the road as if it's funnelling along a corridor, whistling through the leaves so fiercely she trembles.

Her eyes get gritty and so she shuts them for a bit, biting her lip when she feels the bough beneath them shift. She whispers a thank you to the tree, taking one hand away from Locke to press it to the bark by her hip. Just until the morning, she says under her breath, we'll get going when the light comes. She repeats it and repeats it until the words lose all sense, and when the sky finally begins to lighten and her vision of the green world returns, she leans her head back against the bark and yawns. One more day, that's what the dead man's tab said. They should come to the border today, and then they'll be inside a city again, safe, and everything about this strange walk along this ghost road, even the joy, will fade away back to the place where dreams go when the morning comes.

She knows where Marl is. Everyone knows where the men chosen by Duana the blind are kept the day before the ceremony, but no one goes there. No one has ever told Shaye that she shouldn't go, just as she has never told Ludi to stay away. No one has ever told her that she shouldn't eat the same carrion as delights the buzzards either, but it would make her stomach twist with revulsion to think of it.

But she is hungry now, starving for the sight of Marl, and she has heard that people will eat anything if they are hungry.

She pretends to be asleep until everyone has woken and left the caves. She feels Gai Gai lift her arm, whisper to Ludi to come with her, and then gently place Shaye's arm back on the mat.

She does not greet anyone as she wanders past the fires, plunging a hand into the nut basket and cramming a fistful of fire-smoked hazels in her mouth. She is not hungry, but there is a distance between her head and her eyes that she recognises as a feeling somewhere past hunger, when the body seems to float through the air as if in water. She wears the skin again, drier now but smelling like a grave. It doesn't seem like hers anymore. She does not recognise the person she was when she skinned the deer it is made from and stitched their hides patiently together. She is someone else now. She pulls the hood up over her head and she is glad of the barrier it makes between her and the world as she walks into the forest, towards the sacred oaks.

There is a dwelling hidden by the ancient trees that she has always pretended not to notice. It is made of the fallen branches of the oaks, stacked together higher than a man's height, with more branches draped at the top to make a roof.

She does not go through the clearing with the sacred stones, she cannot bear to see them. Even the imagining of them is enough; visions of their carvings chase her as she walks the long way through the oaks, the power that whirls between them humming just too low-pitched for her to hear. She tries not to touch any of the bark or let any dangling acorns brush her hood. She is trying to walk softly, without alerting anyone to her presence.

She can hear voices before she can see the stacks of branches. She pauses, listens for words, but she cannot make them out. She creeps forward, her eyes scanning the thick trunks for the movement of people. There is some shelter from the rain here. The dense canopy slows the water and blocks out so much light she might as well be inside the caves.

She sees a group of men sitting outside the dwelling. She walks towards them slowly, taking care with each footstep. Now she sees the chosen women and children. One of the women is unbraiding her hair, but lazily, moving so slowly that she is really just moving it around her shoulders, one tendril at a time. Shaye is very close now, close enough to see their faces and for them to have noticed her presence, but not one of them looks at her. There is a dazed look on all the people she can see, a sense of their eyes and lips falling from their faces.

She stops, her feet now silent on the dead leaves. She realises the ceremony has begun for them. They must have already eaten the dried spirit flesh mushrooms from the initiates' baskets. She walks forward, not looking where her feet land, and the twig snapping under her step draws slow glances from the group.

Marl looks up, squinting towards the trees. She watches his face change as he recognises her, from curious to confused to joyful. His reaction is so different to that on the beach that she steps towards him, emboldened.

Shaye. He stands up awkwardly, swaying a little, before moving towards her with his hands flailing. She is not sure if he is waving in welcome or trying to tell her to stop. He smiles gently, then a fleeting frown passes across his eyes. Something twinges in her belly to feel the warmth of this greeting. She wonders what has changed from when they met before.

You shouldn't be here, you can't see me, you know that. His words are thick as though his tongue is hurting him, his voice distorted. The initiates might catch you.

He looks over his shoulder, back at the others, sitting in their huddle next to the dwelling. They don't look back at him, they are each staring into nothing, some at the ground and some at the sky, none of them seeing a single thing. He turns back to her and as he comes closer Shaye can see that although he thinks he is moving quickly, to her he is maddeningly slow.

They gave you the spirit flesh already, she says. She wants to reach out to touch him, to brush her fingers across the dark beard shadowing his face, to take a gentle fistful of his hair and run her thumb over the strands. Tomorrow, the initiates will take a sharp flint to his skull and shear all the hair off. They'll leave it lying where it falls on the earth, another offering to the great spirit.

He smiles, a slow sunbeam yawning across the sky. This is the sight she has missed, the thing she's been longing for this whole journey. But there is something stupid in his smile, something dumb that reminds her of a baby.

I know, he replies. They have to. We'd be too scared otherwise.

She has nothing to say to that, for it is nakedly honest in the way that no one can be unless they have nothing left to protect.

They're going to kill me tomorrow, Shaye. Did you know that?

She nods, her throat too thick with sadness to speak.

But listen, Shaye. I'm glad. He takes more steps towards her, lurching as his legs buckle under him. He comes so close she can feel his warm breath on her mouth. She feels her stomach swoop the way it used to when he came this close to her. She sways forward onto her toes to meet him, her skin becoming taut and tingly at his nearness. She breathes in his scent, her eyes heavy lidded. Damp animal skins and smoke, sweat and roasted fish, and then underneath it all, a sniff of what drives her mad about him, something she has never even caught a hint of in any other man. A musky promise, a secret world. She inhales it deeply.

How can you say you're glad? She lifts one hand and lays it on his cheek. He nuzzles into it.

It all made me too sad, Shaye. You didn't see it in that safe old plenty-time place, far away upriver, tucked in that curve with the steep banks. It took you and your kin so long to get properly worried, the way you are now. But I've seen it. I've been seeing it for so long.

She lifts her other hand to his cheek and cradles his face. Her head is tipped right back, to look into his eyes. Their bodies are drawing together as helplessly as the high tide draws up the beach, and it feels so perfect that Shaye hardly notices when their bodies bump gently, and stay pressed to each other. It only feels right, like two firesticks when they finally catch and a sparkling coal is born.

I know it made you sad, I saw it. I grieved twice, Marl. Once for our world and once for you.

He brings his hands to her waist and runs them over her buttocks. He is silent as he fills his hands with her flesh, and then draws his fingers up again, under her deerskin cloak, to trace seams up and down her sides. Shaye's thoughts blur with his hands. He cups her breasts, runs his thumbs over her nipples as if in a trance.

I loved you, Shaye, he whispers. She can see that his face is sweating, there is a shiny film on his skin that gives an eerie glow to the pale colour beneath. I loved you and I loved the river but I couldn't do anything about it. Everything was wrong, on each hunting trip it got worse and worse.

He traces patterns on her skin, letting his hands roam all over her as though he cannot control them. His hands know exactly where to go, which secret parts of her delight in exactly how much pressure, but the smile on his face is dreamy as if he is discovering her for the very first time.

You left me though. Her tongue is sluggish too, as though she has already chewed on the spirit flesh mushroom.

Everything was dying, Shaye. He is speaking with effort, stumbling over each word. Now I can put it right.

She lets her forehead fall to his, and feels tears spiking behind her nose. He will die, and she will live on without him, and there will be nothing left in the world that can make her feel alive again.

Then his lips are pressed to hers and his tongue is in her mouth and she can taste that pungent mulch of the spirit flesh mushroom. Now she can feel him rising, the bulge under his wrap pressing against her and she presses back, grinding her hips against his as though she could make fire there. A sound between a growl and a moan rises from his belly and escapes into her mouth, where it is met with her heaving breath. He pushes her back, keeping hold of her hips, and she steps backwards as he steps forward, like their ankles are tied together.

He presses her against the bark of an ancient, sacred oak and tugs at her skirt, grabbing fistfuls of it to pull it up to her waist. His mouth gulps at hers greedily and she cannot think, she cannot speak, she cannot breathe deep enough until he enters her with a sharp thrust that reminds her of a knife in the guts of caught prey, and she presses her open mouth to his shoulder to swallow her howl.

He moves urgently inside her, holding her hips with both hands. They have both forgotten the other chosen ones sitting only a few steps away. His face is bowed low, pressed into her shoulder, and Shaye lets her tears run into the mass of dark hair that will fall, sacred, to the ground. She holds his head, digs her fingers into his back and as he shudders to a climax a huge sob escapes her mouth.

She notices the forest sounds again, the pitter-patter of rain on the highest canopy, the whispers of one tree's leaves to another's as the wind gives them voice. Their ragged breathing, dragging at the humid air.

He draws his body away from her, letting her skirt fall to her knees again, but he keeps his forehead pressed to hers. He kisses her with that earthy taste of the sacred mushroom again, and she clings onto his lips for as long as she can, for she knows it will be her last taste of him in this world.

Will you do the burial rites and sing for me, Shaye? he whispers. He takes her face between his palms and stares at her. The inner black circles of his eyes are wide, leaving only a tiny rim of green ringed around them and it makes him look feral. There'll be no one else to do it.

She nods, and he pulls away from her. He lets his hands drift down her neck, her shoulders, her arms, coming to rest when he entwines his fingers with hers.

They'll be back soon, he says dully, although he does not take his hands away. You should go before they come.

She doesn't move. Mucus drips from her nose like his seed spills from between her legs.

They stand for a long time, listening to the wrens and the blackbirds twittering in the canopy. They sway with the same winds that brush the oak leaves over each other and hurl ripe acorns onto their heads. She looks at each part of his face, over and over again, trying to memorise it. She wants to brand him onto her brain, to be able to shut her eyes at any moment of the night or day for the rest of her life and call him to mind instantly.

He hears the footsteps before she does, his senses sharpened by the spirit flesh. He cocks his head, lets go of her hands and she feels a pounding of fear grip her heart.

They're coming back, he breathes, turning around to look desperately into the trees. You have to go, Shaye.

She steps back, weaving around the trees when she senses them looming behind her, not daring to take her eyes off him. He melts away too, back to the huddled group of his fellow chosen ones sitting outside the little dwelling made of dead oak wood. Now she's shrouded by the thickening trees and the gloom, she can barely see him except as a smudge of movement back there in the forest. She hears voices, loud and commanding in the dank silence of the oak grove, and she knows the initiates have come to do whatever it is that the great spirit demands they do to those she requires blood from.

When the voices have faded and she can no longer feel Marl's heartbeat pulsing through the twisted roots beneath her feet, she turns and runs. Not back to the caves, but all the way through the forest towards the cliff. When the trees thin and the ground starts to slope downhill towards the beach, she finds she starts to trip over her feet, stumbling as her body picks up pace, even as her lungs burn and she pants like a trapped boar. She comes to a stop when her feet kick up dry sand and she leans over, her hands on her knees, to catch her breath. The gulls harmonise with the ocean, singing their songs, reciting the names of everything they know.

She walks to the edge of the water and wades into the waves. The rain is heavy again, and the line where the grey ocean meets the smoky sky is blurred. There are a few people on the beach, fishing or teasing long strands of kelp from the rocks, but she ignores them. She stares out at the water, watching the arcing of the gulls' wings as they soar. Her feet become numb but she doesn't move. The cold water is helping her not to feel. She wants to plunge in and swim away, as far as she can, until the waves drag her under the water and drown her. She wants the sun, hidden by the thunderclouds, to stay still. For tomorrow never to come, for Marl's blood to stay under his skin, for the water to stay exactly where it is and stop its endless, heartless wandering.

The suitcases are covered in mud and the forest floor has become thick with churned sludge. The wind is still now, but the rain is only a bit lighter than during the night. Shante doesn't know if the worst of the storm is done or if there's another concerto of wind coming, but now that it's light enough to see where they're going, she wants to start walking and warm up. Her eyes are gritty and her legs weak, but things won't get any better unless they start to move. Only one more day to go. Her hand flits to her handbag. She kept it on her all night, feeling for it every so often to make sure it hadn't fallen into the mud. The documents are back to being magic talismans again, glowing in their dark pouch. They'll get to the border today and she'll wave those pieces of paper and they'll never have to deal with anything like this again.

Shante jumps down from the bough, landing with a splash of dirty water, and stumbles against the tree. A wave of mud pours into her shoes.

She turns around and holds her hands up to Locke. Grainne jumps down on the other side of the tree. Fuck! she hisses as her feet are sucked into the mud too, and Shante can't help but feel glad that she's not the only one who feels awful.

I don't feel well, Mum, Locke says as she lifts him down. She places him as gently as she can onto a patch of dirt that looks as though it's solid, and draws his hood back from his head.

Tiny bubbles of sweat have erupted on his forehead and there's a feverish, detached look in his eyes. She presses her hand to his forehead. She doesn't know what she thinks she'll learn by doing that, it's just something a mother should do, something she remembers her mother doing whenever one of them came to her listlessly, complaining of a pain in their bellies or an ache in their chests. Locke shivers, but his skin is warm.

My hand's really hurting me. He holds it up to her, the wet bandage loose and soaked through. She unties the wipe and lets it drop to the mud. The cut along his palm is puckered and wrinkled as though he's been in the bath, and there is yellow slime seeping from it. As soon as it is uncovered to the air she can smell the infection, like a hunk of rotting, mauled meat.

Shante feels her vision narrow to a tiny pinprick of light in which she can only see Locke's hand, far away, as if she's looking at it from the wrong end of a telescope. The earth heaves under her feet and she sways a little. She's used to this feeling now, this gaping horror that grips her stomach whenever she senses a threatening darkness lurking to take him away from her. The moments when she's in the supermarket and she looks up from checking a label and can't see him; the times when he falls off the climbing frame in the park and lies motionless on the rubber for a second; the times when he spends the whole night spluttering with phlegm and she lies awake on the other side of the room, counting his breaths. She doesn't know where this feeling lives when Locke is healthy and happy and right by her side, but it must be somewhere close because it only takes a fraction of a second to smother her and clamp her guts. Most of the time it proves to be a false alarm. He has only wandered into the next aisle to look at the sweets, he rolls over onto his stomach and giggles at his fall, he wakes up in the morning and shuffles over to her bed to demand a story.

She swallows. She wipes her thumb across his damp forehead, leans forward and presses her lips to his skin.

Let's get you something to eat. You'll feel better after a bit of breakfast. She glances up at Grainne over Locke's head and she wants to scream at her sister for the stricken expression she sees there. Fuck off, she wants to shout, but she bites her lip. Don't you dare look at him with that long face, it's just a cut on his hand.

Grainne slides her eyes away and reaches into her suitcase. She takes out one foil packet and pops it open.

That's it, Grainne says, taking one cracker and passing the packet to Shante. That's the last of our food. Shante closes her eyes. She doesn't feel hungry, but she takes one cracker from the packet and passes the rest to Locke. They'll reach the border today. They have to reach the border today.

She gives him another glug of the liquid paracetamol, although she doesn't think it will do much good. She wonders if she should bandage up his hand again or if it's better left exposed to the air. She should know this kind of thing. Why doesn't she know this kind of thing? He's holding the crackers awkwardly in his hurt left hand, the flesh on his palm too swollen to grip properly.

We're not going to put another bandage on it, I think it needs a bit of air, she says. Locke nods. Perhaps he can hear the shrill note in her voice. Perhaps he is more frightened by her fear than by his own pain.

Come on, we can eat while we walk. She holds out his bag to Grainne and starts to undo the knot in the shirt that holds the lute to the tree.

It looks wrong. The long neck of the bag lists to one side and the ears that slope backwards twist at a strange angle. Shante draws the instrument out of the bag and sees that the neck is cracked along a fret, the strings hanging loose. There is a constriction around her chest, a hopeless kind of sick feeling.

We can get it fixed when we get there, Grainne says in the kind of conciliatory tone she uses when Locke whines about a toy he's lost. Or you can get a better one!

Shante does not reply. She blinks away the tears and zips the bag again. She should not be crying about an object when her son is ill and they have no home and no food and dirty water.

She shrugs the broken lute onto her back and tries not to flinch at the discordant sounds from the loosened strings. She takes the suitcase by the handle to drag it through the mud towards the road. Locke walks beside her, trying to keep his crackers under the shelter of his coat. Grainne follows them, cursing softly with every step.

The concrete is sodden, the water running down the camber towards the shallow channels where the road meets the forest. Those channels have become a river now, brown water flowing fast in the opposite direction to the one they're walking in, and they jump over it one by one to stand on the road. The water is a moat separating the world of people from the world of trees.

They walk in single file, in the narrow strip of concrete that is under the trees but not in the river. Shante goes first, trying to walk with a gap between her legs as her wet jeans are chafing her thighs. She hears Locke crunching the last of the crackers behind her, and she tries not to think about what he'll eat next. There's nothing to eat, not even the purple berries or those tiny leaves with the white flowers. The rain has drowned everything.

When the road slopes uphill and there's more space to walk abreast, they resume their old walking formation, with Locke in the middle. Grainne carries his backpack. She hasn't said a word, but there's a trench between her eyebrows that Shante cannot look at.

She walks with her gaze fixed on the hazy horizon, her eyes screwed up against the rain. She doesn't know what the border will look like above ground. She's seen footage on the newscasts before, guards patrolling just outside the perimeter cradling machine guns. She rehearses what she'll say. We were on a hijacked train, please can you help my son I think he's got some kind of infection, I've got all the relevant paperwork, do you need my husband's name and tab number, please just get him to a hospital first, of course there's a gap in our data, there's no network out in the edgelands. She practises explaining it all clearly in case an immigration officer finds them first. No, we didn't meet anyone else, we drank the rain from the storms, we brought a lot of food with us.

The rain falls stubbornly, and they hardly stop walking all day. She holds Locke's good hand and strokes it with her thumb. When tears pool in the corners of her eyes she lets them fall down her face and mingle with the rain. She concentrates on the rhythm of their feet on the road, the slap of their soles on the water and the squelch of their toes inside their shoes. She puts one foot in front of another, and she looks to the point on the horizon where the road meets the sky. Locke's steps are uneven, he stumbles now and then and she tightens her grip on his hand to steady him. She turns every so often to press her wet fingers to his forehead and ask him how he's feeling. He shrugs, shakes his head to make the droplets on the edge of his hood fall away. Alright, he always replies. It still hurts. Each time she bends down to look at him and sees that his skin is still grey and blotchy the fear gripping her stomach clenches tighter. Almost there, she tells him. We're nearly there now.

The sun is hidden by a thick layer of smoggy cloud, so she doesn't know what time it is when they get to the place where the trees end, abruptly, as though a giant has drawn a line across the forest and swept everything from the land on one side of it. They stop walking as they come to that line, looking ahead to the vast grey buildings that border the road. Shante takes a breath, nervous. The buildings look like factories but they are unbranded. They're spooky, nuggets of the city world out here in the forest. Someone came once to cut down these trees and build these factories, warehouses, whatever they are, but now they are gone. She wonders if this is trespassing. Perhaps there is a camera on them right now, recording their hesitation.

Is this it? Locke sounds tired. Is this where Dad lives?

Almost, Shante says. We're almost there now. Just a bit more walking my love, only a little bit more.

They walk between the giant buildings and greyness closes over them. The road is better kept here, there are no weeds spilling out of the cracks in the concrete, no wild purple bushes weaving around the central barrier. Shante wonders who comes out here to pull those plants out, and why they would bother. There are no sounds coming from within the buildings, not even the hum of a generator or the whizz of robotic makers. The rain drums on their roofs and the sound of it tumbling into gutters and splashing through drainpipes into muddy pools by the walls makes her homesick.

She expects to be caught at any moment, maybe by a swarm of border guards dressed in their black body armour, the circle of a gun barrel pointing directly at her face. She looks quickly from one side to the other as they creep along, her fingers skittish on Locke's, ready to stop and throw her hands into the air if she hears a shout, ready to cry out that they're claiming asylum and they already have their visas.

She steps into the shadow of the border wall that rises almost to the light place in the overcast sky where the sun burns, and the sky becomes darker and darker the closer they come. They are walking very slowly now. Shante places her feet deliberately on the road and makes her breathing shallow so she can hear every pulse of the silence. The wall is a solid block of beige concrete like the riverbank defenders at home, darkened with rain dripping down its length like paint. It was made to keep people like her out, its featureless menace its only purpose. Shante blinks every few steps to adjust to the dimness. They are leaving the light behind. She will get food and clean water and antibiotics back, and she will lose the light and the trees.

Now they are so close to the wall Shante can hardly see sky, and as they come closer she sees a door cut into it, wide enough for only one person to pass through, leading into a black space blinking with green neon lights. There is a row of swivelling cameras over the doorway, rotating in all directions. They look like the gargoyles perched protectively on the top of old churches. Or dragons sitting atop a hoard of treasure, ready to wake up and breathe fire on any trespassers. The visas burn with their special magic.

They stop in front of the cameras, watching them uneasily, trying to shrink themselves into their sodden clothes. Locke grips at her hand and presses himself to her side. She wishes she could pick him up and wrap him in the sling like she used to. Carry him close to her heart, where she can feel his chest rising with hers, her body teaching him to breathe. She should not have left him near that bike. She told him to get the tyre off it, she's a moron.

What do we do, just walk through? Grainne leans to one side to try to see into the tunnel.

Shante shrugs. I guess so. There's probably a load of guards in there somewhere.

Grainne looks at her. Shall we go?

Shante peers into the black space. She can't tell how far it extends or how big it is.

I think it's the only option. She nods to the cameras. They'll know we're coming by now.

She lets go of Locke's hand to step into the tunnel and walks slowly, one hand feeling in front of her along the cold, damp wall. The neon lights are set into the ceiling but they don't illuminate far ahead. She hears Locke's shuffling tread behind her, and she wants to stop and grab hold of some part of him, tell him not to be afraid, but the only way out is through, so she keeps walking. The sound of the suitcase wheels is amplified until it is a roaring that hurts her head.

The tunnel opens into a room with walls made of the same damp concrete as the border wall. Four border guards stand in front of a glass-fronted office booth, dressed in full patrol uniform. Black boots laced up to the knees, heavy weapons belts, black balaclavas wrapped tightly around their faces, helmets with lights fixed onto them like a snail's antennae. Imagine standing here all day with only a death machine for company and waiting for straggling immigrants, Shante thinks. What a terrible job.

Stop! one of the guards shouts. Shante can't see who's speaking, she can only see the slits of their eyes. You're trespassing on sovereign lands and must turn around.

Shante's seen this on a newscast, she knows what she has to say. She lets go of her suitcase handle and edges sideways so that Locke and Grainne can follow her out of the tunnel, holding her hands up. She has a strange urge to laugh. It's all so ridiculous, so dramatic. She feels as though she's playing a part in a play, reading off a long written script and soon the curtain will come down, the audience will clap and she can go back to her life.

I claim asylum from the rising seas, as per the Refugee Act, for me, my son and my sister. She gestures slowly to the handbag dangling at her hip. Rain drips off her coat and pools on the floor. The guards are so silent that she can hear the water dripping from Grainne's and Locke's coats too. I have our passports and visas just here.

One of the guards lifts up his helmet and drags the balaclava off his face with it. He's many years older than her, his beard studded with silver. His eyes are bloodshot and he looks as though he's been on duty for many hours. He drops his helmet on the floor behind him and steps towards her.

Present your documents, please. He has the gun balanced in one hand and the other hand outstretched. The drama has faded, now it just seems like a routine transaction.

She takes the folder from her handbag and places it in his hand. The room is silent. Locke comes and leans his weight into her.

What's wrong with the boy? the guard asks, nodding at Locke.

He hurt himself on the road, Shante explains. She wants to say more, she wants to ask him to take Locke to a doctor right away, but she needs to focus on one thing at a time.

We'll get this done as quickly as we can. He takes the folder and walks out of the room, past his colleagues who keep their guns aimed at Shante's face. He reappears on the other side of the glass enclosing the booth, puts his gun behind him and sits down with a heavy thud. She watches as he takes off his gloves and taps a screen. His face lights up with that familiar blue computer light, and it makes him look even more tired.

She turns to glance at Grainne, who is watching the guard in the booth carefully. That man has the only proof that they exist behind that glass. Grainne's eyes are narrowed, her chin raised. Shante wonders what her sister will do if this man does something to those pieces of paper. She imagines Grainne's screams and the hail of bullets, and she blinks quickly to erase the image from her eyes. The guard is alternately tapping at the screen and glancing down at one of their passports. He's checking they are who they say they are. He's not a man of violence this one, despite his costume; he's just a man trying to do his job. This city is a civilised place, that kind of corruption wouldn't happen here. She thinks of Zeb's frustration with the queues and the tab surveillance and the looting back in her city. She was proud of its lawlessness once, mainly because Charlie seemed to be. He'd complain with a rueful pride, as though his home was a charming, brilliant prodigal that could never be blamed for its faults and always forgiven its insults. She wonders what it's like trying to cross the border there. Nobody would want to. Her home is a sinking place people are trying to flee, it has no reason to watch its border guards for signs of the madness wrought by petty power.

The guard knocks on the window and beckons for Shante to come forward. She shifts Locke so that he's standing upright and walks calmly past the line of guards, whose eyes do not follow her as she passes.

There's train tickets here, he says. Why didn't you just get on a train?

We did, it was hijacked.

So you walked?

Shante nods. Her shoulders tense, she opens her mouth to give him the speech she's prepared about how they are law abiding really but they were trapped and desperate, but the guard turns back to his screen, disinterested. Shante realises that it's common for him to hear about trains that stop and lose their cargo and passengers, he's not shocked at all. It's as if a window has opened on the edge of her vision where she can see all the ugly mechanics of the world. The border guards know, she thinks. They know there are people roaming out there in the edgelands, they know and they don't care.

I've run your IDs, everything's looking good. He gathers all their documents together and shoves them back into her folder. Luckily, your sponsor has registered you all as missing persons, so you won't face criminal charges for trespassing in Unauthorised Areas of the Territory.

Does Zeb know these things too? Shante wonders. Did he guess their train had been hijacked? How does everyone else seem to know how this rotten world works apart from her? She's just been hiding behind her lute for too long, pretending to live in a past that never really existed.

So, now we have some procedures to follow. The guard is businesslike now, repeating words he's said a thousand times before. You'll stay here until you're collected by your sponsor, and in the meantime we've got your medical checks, your entrance interviews and your Biosecure account setups. Can I check your sponsor's tab number, please?

He reads Zeb's details off his screen, and Shante nods.

Yes, that's right.

The guard stands. He leaves his gun and gloves on the table behind him.

Follow me, please.

The folder doesn't seem important anymore, it's done its only job. She grabs her lute and her suitcase and follows the guard. He presses six numbers into a pad on a glass door to one side of the booth, and it swishes open. Another dark corridor, but this one isn't encased in concrete, the walls are painted a drab, municipal grey and the floor linoleum is scuffed. This is what all cities look like in their bowels. She forgot about the ugly bits.

Grainne goes first, following the guard, then Locke walks after her. Shante watches his feet move one in front of the other, the heel of his left trainer flapping every time he lifts it from the floor. He needs new shoes. He's moving slowly, listing slightly to his injured left side. She feels that tightness in her stomach again. She'll ask if Locke can go first for the medical check. She catches a whiff of that infection smell drifting from Locke's hand. To come this far and have her child enter his new home sick; it doesn't seem fair.

The corridor is never-ending. The strip lights set into the ceiling flicker and hum and the linoleum squeaks with their wet shoes. Her feet feel heavy, all the water hiding in the seams of her clothes feels like it's dragging her to the bottom of a river and trying to drown her.

And then, another glass door. This time the guard presses his palm to a key panel and it opens with that same swish. Another windowless, drab room. This time with six plastic chairs bolted to each other and to the floor, facing a large screen and a vending machine.

Are you hungry? the guard asks.

Shante nods, but she isn't. She feels nauseous, and the smoky taste of the water is repeating in the back of her throat. The guard digs into his pocket and draws out some tokens for the machine.

Have these, get yourselves something. The medical team will be here soon. Something flickers in his eyes, something that Shante can't quite decipher. Annoyance, perhaps; or maybe even pity.

Good luck, he says over his shoulder as he turns away, and disappears back through the glass door towards the dark little room where his gun awaits him, ready to shoot the next stragglers who wander into his home.

They take off their sodden raincoats and drape them over the suitcases, where they keep dripping and make puddles grey with the dirt flaking off the suitcase wheels. Shante's jeans are starting to dry tight on her skin and she tries to pull the denim away from her seat to stretch it out.

She tips the tokens into Grainne's hand and sits down on one of the plastic chairs, pulling Locke onto her lap. He doesn't protest, just rests his feet on the seat next to her and lets his head loll onto her shoulder. For a moment, she enjoys feeling the weight of his trust against her body, the knowledge that she is the person he needs most in the world. She holds him tighter to dispel the thought. Shameful, to look for such proof of a child's love.

The vending machine spits out packets of food, branded with logos Shante doesn't recognise, and Grainne gathers them up and deposits them on the seats. Crackers and banana chips and fruit bars. Exactly what they've been eating these past fourteen days. She holds back a scream and picks up one of the packets she doesn't recognise to examine it.

Let's have some chocolate, that'll make you feel better. She unwraps the bar and holds it out to Locke. He shakes his head.

Come on sweetheart, you haven't eaten much, you need to keep your strength up. She breaks off a square and holds it up to his mouth. He turns his face away, pressing his lips together. That clutch of fear in her stomach again.

I'm going to have some. She puts the piece of chocolate in her mouth and chews. It's almost tasteless, and within seconds has disintegrated into a soggy, sugary mess. She swallows it and instantly feels more nauseous.

They wait in the concrete room, listening only to the drips of their coats and the rustle of the fruit bar wrappers. Shante twists the lid of a clear bottle of water and holds it to Locke's mouth. Come on, love, have some of this. It's good for you.

He gulps at the water until he's drained the whole bottle, and she presses her hands to his head again. He is hotter now. She tugs his jumper over his head and wipes her palm across the sweat on the back of his neck.

It's alright, you're alright. The doctors are coming and they're going to make you feel better.

Grainne passes her another bottle and she takes a swig herself. It tastes clean. Her eyes prickle at the thought of the grey water festering in the bottles in their suitcases. I've been giving that shit to my son to drink and now he's ill, she thinks. This is what water tastes like, I've become so savage I can't tell the difference anymore.

Shall we sing a song? she says. Shall we sing the one about the monkey and the elephant?

Locke's breathing is shallow and quick. No, Mum. No singing. My head hurts.

Shante wraps her arms around him and rocks a bit. She can feel Grainne trying to look at her from where she sits on the plastic orange seats, munching through a packet of some almost-cardboard snack, but she ignores her.

The doctor's coming soon, she whispers. They're going to give you medicine to make you feel better.

She rocks him gently in the silence, listening to his wet panting, swallowing her panic each time it claws at her throat wanting out in a scream. He is heavy and warm in her arms, his legs swinging against hers. She remembers when she first held him, reaching out her hands as the green-masked doctors lifted him, squalling, over the sheet that hid her flayed stomach from her. He was slippery, streaked with pale fluid and blood, the blue cord pulsing at his belly. She had pulled his hot little body towards her chest and laid him there, the animal scent of her womb drifting from his hair. Zeb placed his large hand on his son's naked back, pressed his face into the operating table and sobbed. His tears mingled with the sweat of labour in her hair.

Grainne hears the footsteps first, and she jumps from the chair to greet the pair in white lab coats, latex gloves and surgical masks tied over their mouths. The man wheels a trolley rattling with pills and needles, and the woman moves towards Grainne with her hands held out. Shante can't tell if she is moving to hug her or to stop her from coming any closer.

Welcome, she says, and her accent is sing-song like Zeb's. We just have to do a few tests and then you'll be on your way.

Can you look at my nephew first, Grainne says. He's cut himself, he's not feeling well.

The doctor kneels in front of Shante and takes Locke's hand. He doesn't protest, but he buries his face in Shante's shoulder as she peels the yellow wipe away from his palm. The skin around the cut is puffy and red and there are patches of black at the base of his thumb.

Shante feels bile rise in her chest but she cannot drag her eyes away from that hand, as if by staring at it she can burn away the infection. She smooths Locke's hair over his neck. The doctor's here now, sweetheart, she says. She's going to make you feel better.

The woman prods at the cut and it oozes more thick yellow pus. She runs her fingers up Locke's arm and squeezes his shoulder. He hisses and burrows into Shante's body. She clutches him closer. There is a new coldness in the room; this woman dressed in ice has a new kind of clinical chill in her uncovered eyes and it is making her shiver.

The doctor says something quietly to the man with the trolley. Shante strains to hear it but there is a roaring in her ears. She told him to get the tyre off that bike. Why? What good would a tyre do her, a woman who cannot even recognise dirty water when it falls from the sky?

The man is kneeling by her side, unwrapping a swab.

She should have sent him off into the trees, Shante thinks. She should have told him to look for the leaves of that star tree, she should have told him to count the petals of one of those wild purple brush things.

This might hurt, the doctor is saying, and she touches the swab to Locke's cut. He moans again.

The skin is like the city; it holds all of life. She's watched documentaries about border walls going up around the world, how they decided on the boundaries, how they built the defences. Nobody has to make such a decision about their own skin, they just have to keep it whole to stop the savage edgelanders getting in.

The man takes the swab and dips it into a tube with a pink solution in it, lays it gently on a tray next to him. He unwraps another swab, hands it to the doctor to plunge into Locke's blood, waits for it to be handed back.

Shante realises they're not cleaning the wound. They're testing it.

The woman keeps scraping the swabs against Locke's skin and the man keeps putting them in tubes. They only stop when one of the tubes turns from a light pink to green.

It happens as soon as the swab hits the liquid, Shante's watching it. There is no doubt Locke has whatever that is.

The man holds it out to the doctor without a word, and she blinks. She gives him the last swab and he puts it quickly into a tube and seals it with a flick of his wrist.

How did your son cut his hand? the doctor asks, standing slowly. Shante only notices she has backed away when she sees she is on the other side of the room. The man has scooped up the tray with the swabs and is back at his trolley. He's tipping the collection of swabs into the yellow box marked with a skull and crossbones.

On a bicycle, out in the edgelands.

Our train was hijacked, Grainne cuts in. We had to walk.

How long ago was this?

Shante pauses. Three days. I think? She turns to Grainne and her sister nods.

Does he have a fever? Lethargic and sweaty?

Shante nods.

The doctor sighs. I'm afraid it's bad news. Your son has contracted an infection of a necrotising bacteria that travels along the bloodstream to attack the main organs of the body.

What's the treatment? says Grainne, too loudly for the small room.

The doctor acknowledges Grainne but keeps her eyes on Shante. It is this, more than the mournful look in her eyes, that tells her what she's going to say next.

I'm afraid there is no treatment. The bacteria keeps mutating before we can develop an effective antibiotic.

So he'll die?

The doctor takes a long breath and drops her eyes to Locke, before squaring her jaw and looking clearly at Shante. Yes.

The infection has spread far enough that an amputation is no longer viable.

Their mother died only weeks before Locke was born. She refused to go to the hospital, refused any treatment other than the syringes of black-market morphine. Shante sat on the floor listening to her mother's rasping breath and watching Locke's limbs stretch the bubble of her belly. Sometimes, they would breathe and kick in perfect harmony, and Shante would feel frightened. It was like the unborn baby and his dying grandmother were communicating from the border place Shante couldn't go to.

Can you give him something for the pain? Grainne asks. Can you take him to the hospital, make him comfortable?

The doctor exchanges a look with the man with the trolley, and her eyes are even chillier when she turns back to Grainne. I'm afraid we don't have quarantine facilities for this bacteria. City-wide guidelines are that any migrants found infected are refused entry.

Refused entry? Grainne makes a keening sound in her throat that sounds like a scream to Shante. She's hearing everything muffled and slow, like she's underwater. You can't do that, she's got all the paperwork. Locke's been a citizen since he was born!

The law applies to everyone. We have ten million people to protect.

Where will she go? Grainne whispers.

The doctor doesn't answer. She's a state employee, she's not supposed to acknowledge the existence of the edgelands, but her silence whistles through trees and caws like those huge black birds that sit on the uppermost branches.

Will you let her back in? Grainne says quietly, with a

quick glance at the black dome of the camera on the ceiling.

If she's not infected and has the proper paperwork, it's a possibility. But I have to warn you that this is a very contagious bacteria we're dealing with.

Grainne doesn't stop to imagine that she might have caught the infection too. Perhaps that knowledge is festering at the back of her mind and she's trying to scrape it out. She kneels and fumbles with Shante's suitcase, pulling clothes out and dumping them on the linoleum. Her hands are shaking and her fingers will not grip anything.

They'll let you back in, Shan, there's nothing wrong with you! I'll tell Zeb, he'll sort it out, he'll get you back in.

Shante moves her knees from side to side to rock her son. He is limp and heavy, his breathing shallow. He shows no sign of having heard what the doctor said. She leans to see his face and sees that his eyes are closed, fluttering a little. He's got worse even in the past half an hour. She wants to ask the doctor how long it will be until he dies, but her throat is too blocked. The doctor will think her a monster if she asks. Maybe she is a monster even to wonder.

I'll get more water, you shouldn't drink that stuff from the rain. Grainne pulls out a pair of Shante's jeans and replaces them with the food she got from the vending machine. Then she pulls the folder out of Shante's handbag, sorts through the papers to make two piles, makes a show of putting one pile back in the bag. She wants me to know she's got hope, Shante thinks. She wants me to have hope too.

I'll take the lute, Grainne says, placing it tenderly on her own suitcase.

Shante looks at it, lying against the plastic chair. Why did she even bring it? She should have left it behind to drown like all the other artefacts from dead lives. What did music matter now?

She nods.

I'll get it fixed for you, she says. I'll keep it safe for when you come back.

Madam? the doctor says, carefully avoiding looking at Shante. You need to let your family leave now and have your own examination.

Wait! Grainne grabs the three tokens lying on the plastic and darts to the vending machine, drawing bottles of water with heavy thuds. She puts them into Shante's suitcase and zips it closed.

I'll see you soon, Shan, Grainne says. She doesn't come to kiss her, Shante doesn't want her to. She is white, her teeth chattering with fright. I'll find Zeb and tell him, we won't leave you out there.

Shante looks at her sister and now, for the first time, feels her eyes well up with tears. She opens her mouth, but before she can force anything out, the doctor has wrapped her gloved hand around Grainne's arm and led her out of the door following the rattle of the trolley. In a second, she is alone, the only sound the whistling of air through Locke's labouring throat.

Her son is wrapped in pain that tightens around him each minute, she can feel the tiny convulsions in his back and the twitching of his limbs. She could lift his T-shirt, press the cotton against his face. He's probably too ill to struggle. She could lay him out on this cold floor and wait until someone watching the cameras notices that the child is dead. They'll burn him, rid his body of this parasite and leave only the pure memory of him.

There is a hiss of a sound system and a voice crackles from somewhere on the ceiling.

Your entry has been rejected on medical grounds, you have five minutes to clear the room.

What if she just stays? They'll come with their guns and their hazard masks but will they really shoot her? Would they risk all that infected blood spraying all over this place when there's nothing on earth that will clean it behind her?

She could stay, but then Locke will die on a plastic chair in the bowels of his father's city, and she will be shot a second later.

She slips her arm under Locke's thighs and slides him off her lap. She wants to carry him cradled close to her, but she's not strong enough.

Is Dad coming? Locke's eyes fly open and there is almost nothing of his green irises left, only wide, black pupils. Are we there now?

She wraps one arm around his back and takes her suitcase with the other. Almost, sweetheart. We're almost there. Just a little more walking now.

The glass door opens as they approach and they stumble down the corridor. The next door swishes open before she has a chance to stop as well, and Shante wonders if it's a person or a machine who is guiding her out of this city to die.

There are no guards in the dark room, only a square of light that Shante limps towards. She is sweating, maybe this is the beginning of her fever. The light outside is tinged with grey, reflecting off the dirty wall. They walk in its shadow for a while, the warehouses looming and blocking out the sun. Before she has time to think about it, they are walking in bright sunlight again, the warehouses behind her. She blinks, looking around at the sparkling emerald canopy.

The trees greet her with waving branches and the song of their rustling leaves. A bird chirrups away as if it doesn't know she's bringing them death. The forest seems more pleased to see her than the endless road. She leaves the suitcase on the road and steers Locke off the concrete and into the soft mulch of the leaf carpet beneath the trees. She sits in between the exposed roots of a tree with smooth, grey bark and pulls Locke to sit down between her legs.

I feel tired, Mum. Locke drops his head back onto her shoulder. But I don't want to miss Dad.

That's alright my love, you go to sleep. I'll look out for Dad. She wraps her arms around him and shuts her eyes. She can feel his heart thumping against her own ribs. She counts the heartbeats, the way she counted the pulses on the screen five years ago with the cold jelly smeared across her pelvis.

One day, no one knows when, the water will come. It will come for Charlie first, sweeping centuries of silt up the estuary in one long wave that will drown everything she ever knew. The skyscrapers will stand with muddy water making skirts around their knees and needles of spires and network masts will break the skin of the sea like remnants of ghostly bridges.

Somewhere among all that junk will be Charlie's bloated body, floating with the scum of the tide. The thought doesn't upset her; he wants to die like that. It's the only way he can be close to her mother. He took her into the river, and in the end the river will take him back to her.

And then the water will rise and rise and turn north like a magnet, gulping up patches of green land wherever it can. The earth will swell like a sponge as the water drowns everything in its path that can't swim, consuming everything until the earth is only water and air, with everything that used to be land crumbling in the darkness beneath.

It begins with the drums. As soon as she hears the first thumping beat, Shaye's feet itch to follow them and move into the forest. All around her people are standing, adjusting their cloaks and furs, pulling at their children's hands and moving off towards the stones.

The woman kneeling next to her is spinning, and without a word or a look, she gathers up her thread, tucks her spindle into her skirt and walks away from the great fire. Gai Gai stands, adjusts Nata in her pouch. Shaye pauses for a second. She does not want to go to the sacred circle. The squat stones beyond the trees are emitting a powerful sense of dread, so strong it is almost a foul smell. She gets to her feet slowly. Gai Gai waits, shifting from foot to foot with one hand fondling Nata's bare toes.

Ludi slips his hand into hers and trots next to her, trying to match her steps. He seems to know what the drums mean. Shaye has never taught him anything about the ceremony but that mimicked heartbeat seems to call to him, like it does to everyone else.

The forest becomes thick with people called by the drums. All day there has been an atmosphere of lethargy. The rain has become a shower again and people have been crowded around the great fire, tipping handfuls of nuts into their mouths just to have something to do. They have been waiting for the drums, not daring to start any task in case they hear them. Now they have begun, and there is a relief that the waiting is over which some mistake for joy at the ceremony itself.

Shaye walks with everyone else, mindlessly. She walks as if her spirit is completely lost to her, and she doesn't know when it will come back.

The force of the stones in the sacred oak grove compels her to walk towards it, but there is something malignant about its power that repulses her, makes her feel nauseous. She walks through the forest listening to the drums getting louder, dreading the moment when the oaks thin and she'll see the stones. Her hand is slack in Ludi's; it is he who is tightening his fingers around her knuckles to keep her near him. She tries to remind herself that she has a child, to look after her child. She looks down at him, rubs the pad of her thumb over his knuckles.

She passes the initiates leaning against the trees, their arms wrapped around huge birch baskets filled with spirit flesh mushrooms. She reaches in for a handful, passes one to Ludi. He gags on its bitterness, screws up his face but keeps chewing. Shaye eats the rest, and as she swallows their tough meat she is flooded with the memories of Marl's taste yesterday, and the feeling of his hot mouth on hers.

It is not yet twilight, but the gloom in the forest is heavy. The clouds cover the canopy so thickly there will be no sun for the ceremony, and although the moon will be full tonight, they will not be able to see its cool light in the sky.

She sees glimpses of the stones between the thick trunks of the oaks, waiting for her. The fire in the very centre of their circle glows orange. As she walks and chews on more of the mushrooms, the grey pillars loom larger and larger in front of her. The drums are so loud they make her head throb, she is already feeling the spirit flesh's woozy effect. Her vision is expanding, she begins to feel as though she can see behind her. The colours of the trees are sharpening, and now she can pinpoint the difference between the light green of the leaves on a younger oak and the darker green of those leaves from an older one. She can see each acorn on each tree if she wants to, they glint at her, call to her to admire them, and her gaze flits between each of them until she tears it away and focuses on the ground. She keeps eating the mushrooms, her jaw working until it aches.

She arrives in the clearing and joins the flow of people moving around the stones. Only the drumming initiates are allowed inside the line of stones and only they can cross the line between the spirit world and the earth. At first Shaye shuffles around the outside of the crowd, close enough to the oaks to brush her fingers along their damp bark, turning her face away from the fire. But as more and more people arrive and join in the walking, she becomes squashed against other bodies, her nose filled with the scent of the caves. There are strangers all around her, she has lost sight of Gai Gai and the rest of her kin. She is pushed further and further towards the inside of the circle, to pace nearer the pillars of stone.

No one knows how they got there. Not even the initiates. There are lots of stories about their birth, but no one knows the true one and the initiates never say. Some say the great spirit birthed them in the beginning of time, one for every moon, and then they were carved by the spirits of all things as they passed by. Others say they are tears of the moon, dropped to the earth when she cried each time she became full. Still others say the stones were washed up in the forest by a huge wave in a storm, and a team of bears, wolves and stags joined together to raise them to stand proudly.

They stand about as high as Shaye, and twice a man's shoulder width. They are arranged in a perfect ring so that if you were to stand in the centre, where the fire pit is built, you could see them all the same distance away from you. They are the same colour as the wet sand when the tide leaves it bare, and darker now the constant rain has been falling on them, soaking them right through to the earth. Each of them is covered in carvings made by the ancestors, pictures of the sacred animals of the world. Owls with their wings extended in flight; boars with their tusks raised to the sky. Deer with their hind legs extended as they flee a hunter; wolves with teeth bared; snakes curving around their eggs, forked tongues flickering. Tiny fragments of grey lichen grow along the lines, making the stones glow in the firelight. She knows that some of the initiates come here each full moon and scrape off just enough of the lichen so that the carvings are still visible. They say the great spirit does not want these representations of her world obscured, it would dishonour her.

Shaye cannot look too hard at the pictures on the stones, for she is afraid they will come alive and join in with the dancing. She keeps her eyes averted and quickens the pace of her steps along with the drumbeat. She is dancing now, not just taking shuffling steps in time to the beat. Now she clutches at Ludi's hand so she doesn't lose him too.

She glances at the sacred, forbidden space inside the stones to see the initiates pounding their fists on the drums, their short braids bouncing with the effort of it. They make a protective ring around the fire and its red glow makes their tattoos dance over their skin. She looks hard among the tattooed torsos for any plain ones, those of the chosen ones. She can't see them yet. She wonders if they are still in the little dwelling hidden by the oaks, or if they are sitting somewhere inside the stones where she cannot see them. She whispers Marl's name, and the feeling of the word on her lips makes her sob. She says it again, and then again, because no one can hear her over the drums and the spirit flesh frenzy is beginning to catch now, like the glowing ember of a fire as it touches a sliver of kindling.

They will all dance for hours, stamping and pounding a circle around these stones like the sun circles the sky, lending the ceremony all the power of their feet on the earth and their voices screaming in praise. That is how the ceremony always begins. Shaye hears the voices of her kin start to moan in praise of the spirits, a cacophony of sacred names, each group singing about a different tree, fish or spring. She does not sing. Not yet.

She looks inside the stones again and she sees the high initiate, standing apart from the drummers and laden with strings of shells draped around his neck, the symbol of his authority. He starts to move in a circle around his drummers, inside the power of the stones. He moves in the opposite direction to the mass of people on the outside of the stones, and when he starts to shout the sacred names, there is a sigh from the crowd as if they have been itching to hear him all this time.

He shouts the names of the great spirit, the sky and the ocean, and the dancers around the stones shout them back. He calls them again, his kin chant them back at him. Shaye shuts her eyes, briefly, and when she opens them again the world is different. The sky is glistening like a frog bounded from a spring. It looks sly, as though it wants to pull her by the hair and whisper something in her ear. Now the madness of the spirit flesh is upon her, and she surrenders to it. She screams the names of the great spirit after the high initiate, her voice howling above the others, and there are whoops of approval from the dancers around her. Ludi's hand slips from hers. She turns to catch him but he has already been swept behind her.

She dances and dances, the drumbeat commanding her feet to move, until she forgets to look out for the chosen ones appearing in the middle of the stones, until she looks up from her feet – or maybe down from the sky, she doesn't know anymore – and she sees Marl. Her feet don't miss a step, they are obeying the drums without telling her about it now, but she fixes her eyes on him. Look at me, she begs him, look at me. But he is focused on the initiate who is anointing him, dipping a finger in a thick snake carcass and dragging a bloodied thumb all over his face. Shaye thinks of that time when he left for the hunt, and it was she who made him sacred for the spirits.

The drumming slows and with it the dancing, but the rhythm becomes louder, deeper. Now each thump on the skins is a heartbeat, making the sacred oaks shudder with each boom. The people keep moving around the stones, but Shaye sees that people are parting to make way for someone walking among them, carving a path in the opposite direction to the dancers. She sees Duana the blind with her face daubed with snake blood. Shaye wonders if that is what the great spirit looks like as she comes to collect a soul from its grave.

Duana the blind is choosing the bearer of the knife. Of the knives. She has one hand on the shoulder of the initiate in front of her and her other hand is groping into the crowd. The dancers shrink from her touch the way they'd shrink from a yew branch, but it is no use, for although that woman has seen neither the sun nor the moon, she can see the light that animates a person and when she points her finger at someone in the crowd of dancers, more initiates appear as if from nowhere to haul them into the centre of the stones.

Shaye is not counting the knife-bearers chosen, and she does not watch Duana the blind as she moves among them. There is hatred blooming in her guts for this woman who can make a man dead with one gesture of her claw. Hatred like a vine of ivy rising up her gorge and choking her as it spills from her mouth.

She feels herself borne through the crowd with her feet barely skimming the ground before she notices the hands that clamp onto her shoulders. A pair of initiates, one on either side of her. Their clammy skin is pressed to hers, the hard contours of their shoulders squeezing her ribs from either side, and she squirms with revulsion at their tattoos touching her skin, as though the ink might leak off with all this rain and seep into her. She shouts out, shudders, tries to throw herself out of their grasp, but the initiates ignore her and the sacred chanting of the dancing people around her swallows up her noise to make it less than a whimper. The stones loom higher in front of her and she realises she is being taken within them. She gives one last kick, her foot catching on nothing more than a tuft of grass, and then she is taken across the line between the earth and the spirit world. She is trapped inside the pillars of stone.

The heat of the fire makes sweat bubble on her upper lip and the noise of the drums is almost unbearable now she is so close. She wants to put her hands over her ears, gain some privacy inside her mind again, but she can only watch in a trance as the initiates' inked arms rise and fall in perfect harmony, over and over again. She hears the thump of the drumbeat in her belly only a moment after she sees their fists pound the skins, and as she stares and stares the moment between the thump she sees and the thump she feels grows longer and longer until she feels she could lean into that empty space the way she might be able to lean into the blackness between two stars, and the longer she watches and listens the more she yearns to. She becomes convinced that if only the sight and the sound of the drumbeat would separate for long enough, she could leap into it and tumble into the centre of the earth, down to the place where the great spirit lives, and beg her to give Marl and his blood back.

But the drums stop, leaving a thud in the disturbed air behind them and a roar in her ears like listening to the sea song of a shell. The fire smells sweet, there are bunches of musty mugwort burning along with the wood. She turns to face the dancers on the outside of the stones but she cannot see any faces. They are all standing still now, singing the song of the ancestors. Their voices are muted, as though the stones are a barrier the song cannot fully cross. Shaye moves her lips with the words of the song but she makes no noise.

She hears a crunch on the leaf litter behind her and turns quickly – there they are, the bodies for the great spirit. They are bald headed now, their shorn hair lying somewhere within the stones, and their naked bodies are covered in snake blood. Marl stands between the young boy, who trembles with the cold air, and the elder woman, who stands with her eyes shut and her mouth moving fervently with the song of the ancestors. His eyes are sweeping across the still crowd outside the stones, his head craned forward to concentrate. She watches him. She wonders which of his kin he is looking for, who he is thinking of in these last moments of his life. He turns slowly, then sees her, standing in the middle of the stones, just as he is. His eyes lock with hers, and his whole face softens. A surprising joy bursts in her belly. She didn't know that she could feel joy now, the spirit flesh has sucked every feeling out of her but pain, ecstasy and the shocking place inside where you cannot tell which is which. But here it is, joy sneaking through the unreal world the spirit flesh creates, joy to know that he loves her, that he looked for her among everyone else, that he cares that she is here.

His eyes travel down to her hand and he sighs. His eyes shut briefly, as though he has seen something beautiful that he cannot quite believe. She follows his gaze to look down as well.

There is an antler knife in her hand. She doesn't know where it came from, or how it came to be there. Her fingers are wrapped tightly around it and she tries to let it go, but her hands will not obey her. It is smooth and cool, as long as the distance between her elbow and the tip of her middle finger, and curves slightly at the base where she holds it.

Then the drums begin again, slow and steady, a single beat in which there is no gap between the sight and the sound of it, and she knows what must happen now.

The song of the ancestors continues as the initiates take the naked, blood-smeared bodies one by one and lead each of them to a pillar. Shaye watches an initiate kneel so Marl can step onto his thigh and hoist himself on top. He lies on his back atop it, his legs dangling over a carving of a wolf. He shifts, trying to get comfortable, and Shaye lets out a sob. She imagines the stone, cold and grating on his back.

The crowd sings the names of the great spirit, the sky and the ocean, and begs them all to safeguard those passed on. They beg the great spirit to bring back the land, and the elders wail over the song, as loud as they can so the ancestors hear them from the other world. Shaye watches Marl lying on the stone of the ancestors' moon and she listens to her heart echoing the drumbeat. The antler knife is heavy in her hand. It has been listening to the drums and it is thirsty for blood.

The initiates begin to dance now, their feet pounding the earth in time to the slow drums. They dance inside the stones between the drummers and the bodies, singing the names of the great spirit, their voices weaving around the song of the crowd to make a symphony. Shaye stands near the silent drummers uselessly; watching them, watching Marl. The rain makes her cold but she cannot shiver because she feels that she has become one of the stones, and must stand as still as they are, rooted to the earth, watching silently as all other things move and grow.

Only the hands of an initiate can move her, and she finds her feet skimming over the ground as before. She doesn't kick this time. She knows which stone they will take her to. She wonders if they planned this, if there is a song or story lore about the power in a woman spilling the blood of her lover in the name of the great spirit. She sees the other women approaching the pillars where the bodies lie, one woman for each stone. Their antler knives are clutched in their hands, their eyes as wide as the moon she knows is shining, somewhere above the thick cloud.

Marl turns his head to look down at her as the initiates retreat back to the centre of the circle, near the drums and the mugwort fire. He reaches out a hand to hers, and she steps closer to take it and entwine her fingers in his. She looks into his eyes, and she sees that he is at peace. He is going to the other world now. It is she who has to stay behind under this grey sky and live without him.

The singing stops abruptly. It is the spirit flesh that told them to stop, Shaye thinks. The spirit flesh which is like a child arranging twigs and leaves around an ant colony and directing the shuffling lines of insects in whichever way it wants. The drumbeat stops too, and the silence yawns in her ears.

She knows what she has to do. She has witnessed this moment every frost time of her life. She has chewed on the dried mushrooms, she has danced around the stones and she has sung the songs of the ancestors with everyone else, then watched as the blood ran into the earth. But this time it is entirely new and fearful, and the antler knife trembles in her hand.

She shakes her head. No, she breathes. No, Marl, I can't.

Come on, Shaye, Marl whispers, as Cherl did to her when he was teaching her to swim in the low river. You can, I know you can.

No no no. She is not sure if she is making sounds or if Marl is inside her head, hearing her thoughts, coaxing her to do her duty. Please, no, I can't, please don't make me.

Marl grips her hand and pulls her closer. Now her face is next to his, her belly and breasts pressed against the cold stone of the pillar. She tries to shrink from him, she does not want her skin to touch the carvings, but he holds her wrist tightly.

You know what you have to do, Shaye, he whispers. Come on.

He reaches his other hand across his body and grabs her shoulder. His fingers work their way down her arm until he reaches the hand that holds the knife and pulls it towards him.

She struggles, tries to pull away from him, but his grip is too solid. She brings her other hand to the knife to lever herself away but it just gives him greater purchase on her. Even though he is lying down and the rest of his body is soft, he is still the stronger.

He guides her hands towards his neck until the point of the antler knife is touching him. Shaye knows that everyone is watching, that there are no more drums or songs to cover up her tearing sobs, only the breath of the wind through the oak trees.

The drums begin again, a slow, uncomfortable thump.

Boom.

This is the right thing, Shaye, he whispers. He smiles and turns his whole face to look at her better. His neck wrinkles slightly around the tip of the knife. Please.

Boom.

With his hands clasped around hers, she presses the knife into his neck. His skin lets it sink in, even when blood blooms around the tip and begins to drip down his neck. She sobs.

Boom.

He was not lying when he told her that he wanted to die. His body seems to welcome, even crave, this cruel point. She watches the blood thicken around his shoulders, and she is reminded of that day so many springtimes ago, when she lay beneath him under a beech tree and it was he who drew blood from her willing body instead.

Boom.

She cannot take her hands away from his, he holds her too tightly. His blood begins to spurt quicker from his neck, bubbling from the gash she's made there. Now it flows down her hands in crimson streams, and it smells like the hunt.

Boom.

Blood bubbles out of his mouth with a gurgle and traces down his neck. It pools in the shallow crease behind her elbow. His hands slacken, his shoulders slump and she wrenches her hands away from his, leaving the antler knife sticking grotesquely out of his neck. She staggers away from the stone, her feet stumbling over the uneven ground.

Boom.

She steps back to the stone, she cannot be too far away from him. His blood is dripping down the stones now, running along the channels made by the carvings like tiny rivers running into the sea. She holds his face in her hands, pressing herself against the stone whose surface is faintly heated by his warm blood. She feels its dampness on her breasts and belly. His eyes flutter, his lips move. She thinks he is trying to speak, but the words are choking in the blood. She thinks he can still see her, but he is looking past her, as though the great spirit is standing just behind her shoulder, waiting patiently for him to come. He is on the threshold, now.

Boom.

The crowd starts singing again, chanting the names of the great spirit, the sky and the sea, imploring them to bring back the land. Shaye runs her thumb over his cheek, leaves a bloody smear there. Her own face is wet, either with tears or blood, she is not certain. She does not sing the sacred shortest-day song. She moves her lips in a nonsensical mumble, the way she used to speak to Ludi when he was freshly born and suckling. Marl's skin has become pale, it is turning the colour of the stones before her eyes, and Shaye imagines staying here with her hands on his face for long enough to watch the rest of this death and more; to see his body bloat and then begin to leak and then watch the worms come and do their work.

The song continues, the crowd singing louder than ever, but the loudest sound for Shaye is the dripping of Marl's blood along the carvings of the pillar. When she is sure he has gone, when his eyes have become dead pools of stagnant water, when the warmth in his face has seeped out into the cold air, she takes her hands away from him. She doesn't look around at the other stones, the other women bearing antler knives, or the other blood trickling down the pillars of the other moons; she just stares at him. The world is now a world without him in it, even if it is a world where the river will be healthy again. She sinks onto the ground and leans against the base of the stone, facing towards the silent drummers. There is nothing at the top of this pillar now. Marl has truly left her.

There is something restless about her kindred and their singing, like a wolf pack that has scented a kill. They are no longer still, they are jostling each other to come to the front of the crowd and see the blood pooling at the base of the stones for themselves.

There is a bloodlust in them all that won't fade until the power of the spirit flesh they've eaten begins to subside. For some of them, the taste of the dried mushroom will fade by the time the sky is fully dark, and they will creep off into the forest to lie beneath the oaks, their eyes heavy and their legs tingling with exhaustion. But for others the tinge of madness in their minds will linger until the first rays of dawn illuminate the sky.

She slumps sideways and lies on her back. The earth is cold. It has absorbed all the warmth of Marl's blood and taken it deep into its belly, leaving nothing for her. Now it is fully dark, and she watches the high branches shadowed against the light cloud, eerily lit from behind by the full ancestors' moon. The top of the pillar with Marl's body is a dark patch in the sky, but she does not look at it. There is nothing for her there, now. The drums are pounding again, but they feel far away. Their sound drifts over her head, soaring way up into the sky. She is safe down here, where it is quiet and damp, the mud and what is left of Marl seeping into her skirt and staining it. She wonders where Ludi is. Somewhere out there in that stamping, heaving crowd is her son, and she tries to summon his face to hers, to remember him as she shuts her eyes, but she can only see Marl's. Her skin is fizzing. It makes her want to wriggle out of it like a snake and leave her old self behind at the foot of this stone. She wants to leave this place, just like Marl has left his body for the great spirit to eat it and be, finally, sated.

> • <

It is the rain that wakes her up, dripping into her nostrils and making her snort to clear them. The morning light is feeble, illuminating the dark shapes of the stones, still bearing the draped bodies of the chosen ones. The stones are bloodstained, the lichen nestled in the carvings soaked with blood. The fire in the very centre of the stones is smoking lazily, drums lying abandoned just outside the pit.

Shaye feels distant, as though she is watching herself from far away. She gets to her feet. Marl's dried blood flakes and crumbles from her arms as she moves, but she doesn't brush it off. It is the last part of him that she can have for herself.

There is an eerie quiet among the oaks. There are a few people still sleeping, lying in heaps under furs and skins, but no initiates, and no faces she recognises. Some of the heaps are beginning to stir. She takes a few steps so that she is outside the power of the stones, but it does not make her feel better. She does not look at the body atop the stone. She wants to find Ludi, but her legs are moving as if she is dreaming. The wind is low, and the trees are almost silent. Perhaps they are grieving for him too, Shaye thinks.

She concentrates on putting one foot in front of the other as she moves out of the grove and into the forest of sacred oaks. Everything is too quiet, as if there is something very important happening elsewhere that she doesn't know about. Her ears are thick and fuzzy from the drums, but still, she cannot hear a single living thing. The gulls are silent. The blackbirds and the robins are hushed. There is only the distant breath of the sea, beyond the cliffs.

She wants to sing, to beat back the silence with her own aliveness. She promised Marl that she would sing his burial rites, even if she can't have his body to dig a grave for. She opens her mouth, whispers the first words of the burial song, but her voice is swallowed up by the darkness between the old trees. She stops walking. The trees want to tell her something. She listens for a moment, her toes scraping a root, but she hears no secrets, no wisdom, no comfort for what she has lost.

She keeps walking, mumbling the burial song. Tears prickle behind her eyes because she is not singing loud and strong enough, Marl deserves better. She brushes them away impatiently. She had thought she had run out of tears by now, but here they are. She starts to sing again, forcing her voice to be louder, cutting into the silence as she walks.

Nobody is at the great fire pit by the entrance to the caves, and there are no rustlings within of people moving. Shaye frowns, places a finger to the fire stones and finds them cold. Of course. Everyone awake is down at the beach. They have gone to see the great spirit answer their prayers and draw back the water, and Shaye turns to follow the downward slope of the cliff towards the beach.

Still, the silence. Where are all the gulls? Why do the robins not sing? What are the squirrels eating, if they're not darting up and down the branches of the oaks nibbling on acorns? As the trees thin and she walks on the grassy cliff top, she sees the beach full of people below. All of them staring out to the water, still as the stones back in the grove, only the faint wind tugging at their skirts and wraps.

The sand is soft on the soles of her feet. She walks among the people watching the water, looking into the faces of those she passes to try to find Gai Gai, or Sala, or Brig. When she passes a little boy with Ludi's dark hair she bends down to look at him, to check. A pressure is building in her chest at the thought of him being far away. Give me back my son, great spirit, she thinks, her feet hastening on the sand but tripping over the tiny dunes. At least give me that much.

No one pays her any attention, even though she is covered in blood and moving fretfully while all else is so still, as though an enchantment keeps them standing on the sand and watching. As she moves and examines the different faces, she hears snatches of songs. Some are intoning the names of the great spirit, some are singing songs of thanks, some are optimistically singing of springtime. She looks towards the water too, every so often throwing a glance to the horizon when she turns that way, just to see what the water is doing.

And then, a gasp. So loud she whirls around to face the sea. The spell is broken, murmurs ripple through the gathered forest of people, swelling to a rumble as they point at the sea, batting at each other, saying, Look, just there, can you see it, what do you think it is? Shaye stops, wanders through the people until she has a clear view, just a few steps from the waterline.

There is something rising on the horizon. The water is drawing up into the sky as though pulled by some spirit, and it is coming closer and closer. Shaye leans forward, squints. Some around her are doing the same, their faces incredulous, but others are backing away, shaking their heads, falling back onto the sand then standing up again.

The water is coming quickly, running at them like a herd of deer. Now she can see the froth of the waves, now the water is higher than the cliffs, now it has obscured the sun, and the clouds. The horizon is rising to swallow them all, and she sees that nothing will escape its jaws.

Fear soaks her from the outside in. Shrieks and moans of pure terror erupt all around her, and then there is a flurry of sand as everybody scrambles back up the beach towards the forest where they might be safe, but she cannot move. An elbow flails and digs her in the ribs, but she does not follow its owner and run away. She stands and watches the water approach.

There are no stories about this, she has never heard of anything like this monstrous invasion of the sea happening before, and she realises that when the water hits her she will die. She thinks briefly of Ludi, hoping that he will not suffer, that he will pass quickly to the other side. A sound halfway between a laugh and a sob tears from her mouth. It is a sound of madness but there is nothing left to remain sane for now.

She sees it was all for nothing; leaving the plenty-time place, their ceremony, Marl's death, all the grave warnings the initiates gave about not singing the songs and doing the rituals. The great spirit will do what she wants with us, Shaye thinks, as the screams pierce her ears. We are nothing at all to the earth, the sea or the sky, we do not matter. And as the wall of water smacks into her body so hard it breaks all her bones and turns her insides to mulch, she thinks about how useless it was to think it could be changed, when this is what the earth had planned all along. How her home will now lie at the bottom of the sea, the way that perhaps someone else's home has lain at the bottom of the sea she has looked out upon all her life.

And then there is Marl, and her mother, and Ludi too, floating in the water, mysteriously illuminated from behind as though standing before the sun, holding out their hands for her to join them.

Dark River

ACKNOWLEDGEMENTS

My heartfelt thanks and appreciation are due to the following people:

George Sandison, for holding space for this book and so many others.

Dan Coxon, for his sensitive editing and always believing in the work.

Anne, my first reader in every sense.

Dave, for feeding us all.

Irene and Roy, for decades of love and care.

Djamel Eddine, for the trickster tales.

Caroline, Mieke and Roisin, for never doubting.

Dreda, Fiona and Otis, for moving with me from dance to words.

Lorna, Liane and Julie, for their careful and close reading of this novel in its early stages.

And a thousand times Ed, who is heart and hearth and home.

THE ARRIVAL OF MISSIVES

BY ALIYA WHITELEY

☆ 2016 JOHN W. CAMPBELL AWARD FINALIST
☆ 2017 BFS AWARDS FINALIST
☆ 2016 BSFA AWARDS FNIALIST
☆ 2016 JAMES TIPTREE JR. AWARD LONGLIST
☆ 2017 SABOTEUR AWARDS SHORTLIST

From Aliya Whiteley, author of the critically-acclaimed *The Beauty*, comes a genre-defying story of fate, free-will and the choices we make in life.

In the aftermath of the Great War, Shirley Fearn dreams of challenging the conventions of rural England, where life is as predictable as the changing of the seasons.

The scarred veteran Mr. Tiller, left disfigured by an impossible accident on the battlefields of France, brings with him a message: part prophecy, part warning. Will it prevent her mastering her own destiny?

Get a free extract
www.unsungstories.co.uk/trymissives

OR SCAN THE QR CODE

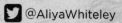 @AliyaWhiteley

PSEUDOTOOTH

BY VERITY HOLLOWAY

Aisling Selkirk is a young woman beset by unexplained blackouts, pseudo-seizures that have baffled both the doctors and her family. Sent to recuperate in the Suffolk countryside with ageing relatives, she seeks solace in the work of William Blake and writing her journal, filling its pages with her visions of Feodor, a fiery East Londoner haunted by his family's history back in Russia.

But her blackouts persist as she discovers a Tudor priest hole and papers from its disturbed former inhabitant Soon after, she meets the enigmatic Chase, and is drawn to an unfamiliar town where the rule of Our Friend is absolute and those deemed unfit and undesirable disappear into The Quiet...

Blurring the lines between dream, fiction and reality, Pseudotooth boldly tackles issues of trauma, social difference and our conflicting desires for purity and acceptance, asking questions about those who society shuns, and why.

Get a free extract
www.unsungstories.co.uk/trypseudotooth

OR SCAN THE QR CODE

 @Verity_Holloway